Fractured & Renewed

Natalie Cammaratta

Cover Design: Emily Chubet

Cover Formatting: Rachel Pearcy

2nd Edition 2023

https://www.nataliecammarattabooks.com

All good things come to an end.

For my readers who have been on this ride with me
and look forward to new stories to come.

Playlist

Enemy – Imagine Dragons, JID, & League of Legends
Everyone Cries – Echosmith
The World We Made – Ruelle
Burn Out – Imagine Dragons
The Fear Of Letting Go – Ruelle
Fall for Anything – The Script
Feel Something – Jaymes Young
Coldest Winter – Pentatonix
Not Today – Imagine Dragons
Over My Head – Echosmith
evermore – Taylor Swift feat. Bon Iver
Freeze You Out – Marina Kaye
ivy – Taylor Swift
Iris – Tommee Profitt & Ruelle
Speechless – Rachel Platten
Power Over Me – Dermot Kennedy
Hollow – Tori Kelly
Run Run Rebel – Hidden Citizens feat. ESSA
Fractured – J. France
My Blood – Ellie Goulding
Outnumbered – Dermot Kennedy

Shivers – Ed Sheeran
Unsteady – X Ambassadors
GHOST TOWN – Benson Boone
Arcade – Duncan Laurence feat. FLETCHER
Control – Loveless
Fallout – UNSECRET & Neoni
Lose You Now – Lindsey Stirling & Mako
Bad Liar – Imagine Dragons
Hardest Thing – Sasha Alex Sloan
Somebody to Love – OneRepublic
I Know You – Craig David feat. Bastille
Brave – Zayde Wølf
Fall Into Me – Forest Blakk
United – Hidden Citizens feat. Rånya
Game Of Survival – Ruelle
Heroes Fall – Hidden Citizens feat. ESSA
In the End – Tommee Profitt, Fleurie, & Jung Youth
Bleeding Out – Imagine Dragons
The Other Side – Ruelle
Walk Through the Fire – Zayde Wølf & Ruelle
Truth to Power – OneRepublic
Safe & Sound – Taylor Swift, Joy Williams, & John Paul White
I Love You – RIOPY

Listen On:

FRACTURED & RENEWED

Cast of Characters

Serenity Ward
Kaycian celebrity; member of the Establishment

Bram Eros
Marshal from Lawson

Adwin Lebeau
Visual Arts graduate; member of the Establishment

Jase Delgado (deceased)
Health graduate

Vogue Taylor
Technology student; member of the Establishment

Frey Dempsey
Technology graduate

Krisalyn Laska
Health graduate

Dixon Blythe
Technology student

Carista Campbell
Eros family friend

Reid Campbell

Marshal from Lawson; Carista Campbell's twin

Travick Campbell

Marshal from Lawson; Carista Campbell's older brother

Kolina Eros (deceased)

Leader of uprising; Bram Eros' mother

Aren Eros

Bram Eros' younger brother

Emrys Eros (deceased)

Marshal; Bram Eros' youngest brother

Minea "Clover" Agnar

Tree-walker; pilot; niece of Montican Director

Ismene Agnar

Director of Montica

Casimir Agnar

Lieutenant Governor of Kaycie; Adwin Lebeau's grandfather;

Ismene Agnar's father

Rocco Agnar

Casimir Agnar's son; Clover Agnar's father

Nemora Agnar

Ismene Agnar's daughter

Priam Agnar

Ismene Agnar's son

Misty

Tree-walker

Grace Ward

Actress; Serenity Ward's mother; member of the Establishment

Anton Ward

Director of Cultural Affairs; Serenity Ward's father;

member of the Establishment

Adelle Nemes

Vogue Taylor's grandmother; member of the Establishment

Emmaline Lebeau

Adwin Lebeau's mother; Casimir Agnar's illegitimate daughter

Parisa Otto

Fashion student

Lanelle Kemp

Health graduate; member of the Establishment

Rollin Karan

Leadership student; member of the Establishment

Sophos Verity

Director of Education and Placement; member of the Establishment

Knox

Tree-walker; Misty's brother

Aspen

Tree-walker

Willow

Tree-walker

Juniper

Tree-walker

Cole Markey

Mayor of Eudora

Aster Rigby

Mayor of Gardner

Tori Foster (deceased)

Security training captain

Snowflake

Serenity Ward's dog

Chapter One
ADWIN

Light flashes, bright as the sun, then gone. That's all there is to see, and that's all it takes. There wasn't much left of Gladstone anyway; Kaycie's uprising destroyed it. The rebels relocated survivors while the Establishment dealt with a bigger threat—the people I'm sitting with now.

"The explosion is indicative of accumulator detonation." Nemora looks like an item has been ticked off a to-do list. No relief. No contentment. I've come to expect my cousin to lack emotion. A trait inherited from her mother.

"Now we can move forward." Ismene closes the holo and with it, this chapter of the ordeal—ever the stoic director, concerned only with logistics.

"How did you know it was there?" My gaze slides across the nearly empty boardroom. The view from the side usually reserved for Rocco and Clover is... unsettling. And Priam should be at Nemora's side. Now there are only three of us.

The family is supposed to rule Montica as a unit of five. I'm nowhere near enough to replace even one of them, much less my two cousins who sit in prison because of my betrayal.

Not because of me. They made their choices. I only shed light on them.

Nemora folds her hands on the table across from me. It's hard to believe she's the same person I saw take down her gargantuan brother in hand-to-hand combat this morning. It's hard to believe this is still the same day. Today has lasted far longer than any day should. "Our agents acquired the intel when they stormed Kaycie's Establishment Center."

Right before they destroyed it.

Images of my city—my home—crumbling and burning wrap my throat in a vise. Instead of doing anything about it, I sit here with the people who ordered the attack. Does this prove my loyalty to them, or make me look like a selfish coward focused on saving my own skin?

The theory is Serenity's band of troublemakers had the accumulator. The power source was supposed to be in the heart of Kaycie with them. Much to my aunt's dismay, it was removed. The obliteration we just witnessed should have happened in the center of my densely populated city.

Were Serenity and the others in Gladstone with it? I don't ask. It shouldn't look as if I care about them. I'm not entirely sure if I do anyway. There are so many other issues.

"Rocco went to find it," Ismene adds. "That proved fruitless. Better to destroy it than to leave it out of our reach."

"I'm glad we can move on, now," I say. "I need to go to Kaycie."

"We must plan your arrival and the announcement of your new position carefully." For someone who was nearly on the wrong end of a coup, Ismene is quick to plan her own. To insert me as the leader of the country is an obvious ploy to control it herself through me, but I'll keep my back straight and chin up like I believe I've come out on top. "The timing has been made even better for you," she says. "The uprising struck again, and our intelligence says no one is in power now. The country is ripe for you to step in."

My chin pulls back. "What happened to the Establishment?"

"The rebels revived the marshals."

I gape at Ismene. "I didn't think that was possible." Marshals are wiped out as thoroughly as Gladstone just was. They're only a shell of muscle.

Nemora arches an eyebrow and shakes her head. "Of course it's *possible*. I wouldn't have thought it would be possible for anyone *there*, but Kaycie is full of surprises."

"I need a plane." I must be precise. Any misstep and she'll realize I know where all the power lies—with her. This is an easy and non-negotiable issue to test my pull on.

She doesn't ask, so I don't say it. I need to secure my family—none of whom Ismene prefers to acknowledge. Grandfather's betrayal of his wife still looms over the rulers of Montica. When he chose to forsake the Director and raise a daughter with another woman, the shockwaves spread wide and fast. The mistress was executed, and he was exiled to Kaycie with his illegitimate daughter. My mother never did forgive him for tearing her from her home, and Ismene acts as if the betrayal was directed at her rather than her mother.

Never one to drag a meeting out, Ismene stands. "You'll have a team for protection. When would you like to leave?"

I look out the plane's window at a smoldering Kaycie. Its shine is dulled by dust and ash. A land of milk and honey turned wasteland. Debris litters the once pristine streets. A monorail line is collapsed.

Buildings have been reduced to rubble. And this was Montica *not* attacking.

I'm in over my head.

Water no longer surrounds the city—connecting the islands was the first ridiculous thing the uprising did. As we descend, the sensation of drowning overtakes me anyway.

Bury it. This is no time to show weakness.

Nemora and I step off the plane. She resembles her mother as she scrutinizes our surroundings—as if this place is undeserving of her presence. We are truly on the same page for the first time. I don't want her to be here either.

The nightmarish walk through the city is made more surreal by the Montican guards surrounding us. People wander wide-eyed as the sun sets on the darkest day Kaycie has ever known. Some make sheepish attempts at cleaning up. Healthcare workers bustle people around, however, there are no marshals in sight. Perhaps they simply abandoned the city and went home. Not that there were many here anymore.

"I think you can lower your weapons," I say.

The guards glare at me, then look at my cousin. Nemora nods, and they holster their guns. Well, in case I wasn't already aware who is in charge here.

I step forward out of our ring of guards to lead the way. The building comes into view, familiar even without its reflective sheen. There's no damage. I saw that in the holo, but my chest loosens to see it in person.

Please be here. With communication systems down, I'll have no way of finding her if she isn't.

We circle around to the emergency exit. Sixteen years I lived in this building, and I might be able to count the times I used the stairs on one hand.

Inside, the building is jarringly unchanged. The world outside is unrecognizable, but the stairs are only dusty from disuse under my racing feet.

"Mother?" I pound on the door from the stairwell. "Are you there?" A guard steps up behind me as if to knock it down. "There's quite enough damage already. Give me a minute."

He backs away. The look in his eyes evinces his distaste of taking orders from me.

"Mother!"

She opens the door and falls into my arms in a teary embrace.

"It's okay." I rub her back and repeat the sentiment—for her or myself, I don't know. When she's calmed enough, we walk into the apartment. She drifts to the wall of windows and stares at the destruction as my Montican escort files in.

"Mother, sit down." I guide her to turn around, and she shudders when she sees the other people with us. She's more than twice Nemora's age, still she cowers away from her. "Please." I walk her to the sofa and sit next to her. "The city is fine now. Everything will be up and running again soon, and this building will be a priority."

"Montica would be safer." Nemora's words startle me. Her expression is all business, like this is a perfectly reasonable suggestion. "You should come back with us."

My eyes must double in size. I didn't think Ismene approved of my mother coming to Montica. Mother sinks into herself, picking at the edges of her nail polish. "I... No. I can't..." Her chest heaves rapidly.

I fix Nemora with a hard glare for throwing that at my mother and stand to retrieve anxiety pills. When I turn the pantry sink on, I realize

I'm lucky it works. Not much else in this apartment will. Should I push for Mother to go to Montica? Can I trust Nemora and Ismene to be near her? I return to her, and she takes the water and two pills I offer. Her shoulders tremble as she lets out a long, shaky breath. Is it enough relief for her to agree to be left with these Monticans?

"Nemora, there's someone else I need to find." I lower my voice. "Would you stay with her?"

"You can't go by yourself."

"You saw what it's like out there. I'll be fine."

"Take a guard." Her voice carries authority as naturally as Kaycian girls carry shopping bags. Nothing she says is a suggestion—it is law—befitting the next Director of Montica.

"It's my girlfriend, and I'd like some *privacy,*" I say under my breath. This could backfire. I don't know what Nemora's feelings on this will be, but what other excuse can I muster?

Her jaw tightens before she nods. "Take a guard for the walk there. He can wait outside the building."

That would be exceedingly awkward if my plans included what I've implied. It'll have to be enough to get away from Nemora for a little while. I can figure out the next step away from her scrutiny.

Chapter Two

BRAM

Dry. Brittle. Dead.

These are the only things I can be. This is all that's left for me. Until the Campbells come.

Carista is flanked by her brothers when they enter the hotel room. I rise from my place on the edge of the bed. All three of them are back together. I'll never get that now. I guess I'm a monster for feeling bitter about their reunion. Jealousy is a bitch.

It should have been scary to wake up in an unfamiliar place, but it's way down on my list of problems. A shiny line of glue has sealed the gashes across my knuckles. Of course. The hospital here is Kaycian run, and the important thing is to keep things neat and tidy. I wouldn't mind punching a wall again to reopen the wounds. Maybe this time I would feel it. How much of my own blood could I see spilled to wipe out the vision of my brother's?

"Carista." My voice sounds like dry bark being pulled off a tree. "Why was Emrys here?" His name is a thousand needles scraping my throat. I couldn't imagine anything worse than discovering my youngest brother was a marshal all those months ago. It was basically a death notice. Then there was hope he'd come back—like Travick and

Reid are. And he did. He came back long enough to make his death complete.

My fist clenches tight enough to crack open my injured knuckles again.

"We don't know how…" Travick and Reid visibly tense as Carista speaks. Their bodies lean toward me slightly.

"What is this?" I say. "I'm not a situation you need to handle."

"We know you aren't." Travick relaxes his stance. "There's no good way to say or hear this."

I look back and forth between the three of them. Each one looks grimmer than the next.

It's Reid who finds his voice. "Agnar was either able to hear what Emrys heard or set an order in his head to look out for… certain information. When Cary told your family about Agnar's connection to Montica, Emrys attacked."

Heat blooms in my chest. The desiccated remains of me crackle.

Carista's eyes flutter, and some tears escape down her cheeks. "He… he killed your mom."

Three mouths move, yet I hear nothing. The crackle explodes into an inferno. The roar of the fire within me drowns out all sound. Flames lick through me, consuming everything that's ever been remotely soft or alive. What's left is forged into a blade.

My mother is dead.

My mother is dead.

My mother, who started all of this, who saved countless people.

She couldn't save her son. And she couldn't save herself.

I don't burst into the physical show of rage they expect. The destruction takes place where they can't see it. So when I slowly, calmly step between them to go to the door, their confusion is palpable.

Carista grabs my arm. "Bram, we have to tell Aren about Emrys. Let's go home."

"I will go to Lawson,"—I refuse to call it home when half my family is dead—"after I kill Agnar."

"Not today, you're not." Travick squares his shoulders toward me, ready to stop me physically if he has to.

"After he—"

"Oh, he'll die." Travick's expression is hard as stone. "I will happily hold him down while you cut off his damn head if that's what you want to do. Not today, though."

"We're in enough trouble with Montica," Carista says. "We can't risk that right now."

My chest heaves with hurried breaths. Sweat beads on the back of my neck.

She takes my hand, running her thumb over the cracked seal on my knuckles. "Let's wait until we figure out how to keep us all safe. Then he's all yours."

I always thought Aren and I were the same. Most of the time I wasn't thrilled to admit I was as headstrong as my younger brother. Proof of how different we are doesn't make me feel any better, though. He really breaks down when he finds out about Emrys. He collapses in on himself as ragged sobs tear through him. I stiffen and look on in disbelief. Not surprised that he feels this way, but that he shows it like this. Maybe my years as a marshal did more damage than I realized. Maybe it broke me—took away my ability to feel anything.

Not a single tear has even threatened to fall from my eyes. Flames inside me have dried my tear ducts. I don't know what's holding me together anymore. I should be a pile of ashes.

No, I shouldn't be surprised by Aren's reaction. I should be upset by my own. I can't mourn myself any more than I can mourn Mom and Emrys, though. Even without the drug they managed to destroy my humanity.

There's no antidote for me, so if I'm going to be a weapon, I will sharpen my edge until it's time to slice through the person who did this.

Chapter Three
ADWIN

The shawl wrapped around Parisa is usually arranged to be glamorous, but curled up on her sofa with her knees up to her chin, she's a far cry from the fashionista I've always known. "Casimir Agnar is from that country?"

"Yes."

"Then why did they attack us?"

A sigh escapes me. "That wasn't their intent. The rebels who stirred up Kaycie had stolen something from Montica, and things got out of hand when they came to retrieve it." If I say it enough times, maybe I'll start to think it's a valid excuse.

She hugs her legs tighter.

"They're going to help us," I assure her. "It'll be all right."

Parisa speechless is a new experience. She fiddles with her fingernails, bounces her knees—everything except look at me or speak to me.

My fingers drum the armrest of the chair I'm perched on. "Pari, I need to find Liam."

She nods absently.

"Will you come? I have a guard with me. We can say we're going to find your family, or—"

"What?" Her eyebrows furrow.

"I can't have the Monticans knowing why I need to see him."

"Are you kidding? You expect me to continue covering for you?" Her volume increases, then she turns toward the window and her expression melts. "What's the point?"

Her phrase would be the same argument Grandfather would use. *What's the point* of being with a man? Certainly not to make an heir to carry on our twisted legacy. Power moves are the only ones that matter. He wouldn't know anything about matters of the heart.

"Hopefully it won't matter soon, but for now..."

"No. I don't want to go out there, and I'm not going to pretend we're anything."

Anything. We've never been romantically involved, despite the rumors we spread. Her friendship has been everything to me, though. Parisa has been my only friend. She's the only person who knew these secrets. Of course, I had to hide plenty of other ones. Still, she's all I have... here. Clover knew the other half of me.

Guilt tightens my chest. *One thing at a time.*

"Okay. I understand." I wouldn't want to be my friend either. Look what I do to them. I push myself up to my feet. "You'll be fine here. Do you need anything?"

"No." She speaks to the general direction of the window—unable or unwilling to look at me anymore.

"I'm sorry for all of this. I know it's scary."

"No, Adwin." Now her red rimmed eyes meet mine. "Finding out there were other islands besides Kaycie was scary. The ocean disappearing and making us not islands anymore was scary. This... I don't know what this is." She presses her hand to her chest and lies down. "Just go."

Kaycians aren't cut out to deal with anything this serious. The uprising was easy enough to ignore—it took place elsewhere—but now they've been hosts to the worst part of the conflict. They need to be protected.

Getting to Liam won't be as simple as Parisa's *just go,* statement suggests. Despite myself, the thought of how much easier this would be at Breck Fortress crosses my mind. Off the balcony. Into the trees. But these windows don't open, there aren't any trees big enough, and tree-walking brings back thoughts of Clover.

The stairs lead to the guard, so I continue down to the basement. Everything to make life in these homes as easy and carefree as possible lives down here. It didn't help anyone today, though. Past it all is the loading dock and my way out.

My distance from the guard grows as I disappear into the night. Has it ever been so dark here? The smoke and dust hanging in the air are more eerie now. At least without watchful Montican eyes on me I don't have to worry about hiding my fury at what they've done. A beautiful, defenseless city of civilians who didn't even know Montica existed, much less the power they could wield. And now I'll be convincing everyone it's the uprising's fault, and Montica will be our great savior. A change of dealers, but the game remains the same. And the deck is always stacked.

Liam isn't at his apartment, so I try his parents'. When I turn the corner toward the building, the damage to the highest floors steals my attention.

Oh no.

I hurry over through paramedics and patients. He couldn't have been— *There!* My lungs deflate when I see him. *He's all right.* Or is he? He stands over a gurney covered in a white sheet. His teeth clamp down on his pillowy bottom lip. Shiny emerald hair is disheveled and matted unlike his usual sleek style. I've seen his hair disheveled before, but he always looked much happier in those times.

"Liam."

He looks up and meets my gaze. His face crumples, and I rush to wrap him in my arms. My face drops to his shoulder, and mine dampens with his tears.

"My parents," he whispers between choked sobs.

"I'm so sorry." I squeeze him tighter. Hopefully he's as comforted as I am by our bodies pressed together.

His chest heaves against mine until he pulls back and drops his chin.

"Let's go somewhere we can talk."

"I can't leave them." He sniffles, and the urge to hold him threatens to tear me in half. But the friendly level of consoling has already been reached. "Can't we talk here? No place is *good* right now."

"This is worse than most." I glance at the sheet covering his parents' forms. "And some privacy would be helpful."

"What does it matter, Adwin?" He waves an arm to gesture to the surrounding devastation. "How can secrets matter anymore?"

"It's not just that. There are things I want to tell you—"

"It's not *just* that, but it's still that, too. Right?"

"Liam, I can't—"

"Don't bother. You disappear for *months*, and finally show up when I really need you, but you still can't..." He turns away from me.

"Obviously, there are bigger issues at hand." I step as close as I dare. He smells like smoke, and even though I'd rather him smell of citrus and sandalwood as he should, I want to bury my face in his neck. "I'm trying to keep you informed, which is more than most will get."

"Why? I'm no different than anyone else."

"You are to me." My words are clipped in a hushed tone.

"No I'm not." He turns back to face me. The arms which have held me as I've fallen asleep cross his chest. "I shouldn't be having this conversation yet, Adwin, but after all this... Life isn't a party anymore.

Things were already scary, and now… Now, I won't waste energy on someone who can't even acknowledge me."

This is so much bigger than when I had to maintain the appearance of being with Serenity. If he'd listen, let me tell him, he'd understand. I know he would. "Please, let me explain."

"There is not a damn thing to explain if you can't so much as kiss me when I'm dealing with the loss of my parents."

He speaks quietly, but my eyes still dart around. When they land back on him, a frown is plastered on his face.

"Exactly. Secrecy is all that matters to you." He shakes his head. "Goodbye, Adwin."

The city around me blurs as I make my way back to my mother's apartment. *It's fine.* It's not as if I was *in love* with him. I shouldn't have gone to him. That was foolish. It's not like I could have told him anything. Of course, I had to make sure he was all right, but we'd never be anything serious enough to warrant sharing confidential information.

Emptiness hollows out my chest. *He couldn't handle any of this anyway.* That's not the important part. It's true, though. My Kaycian lover isn't any better than the rest of them.

I shake out my jaw when I notice it's clenched.

This is for the best. He is a hindrance I can't afford. Other people need me, whether they like it or not, and they take priority.

Thank goodness Grandfather isn't here to have witnessed my surge of emotion upon finding Liam. Where is he, though? He should have been the first person I sought out. How am I to survive this position I've been thrust into without him?

"Where is your guard?" Nemora asks when I enter Mother's home.

"I'm not sure. And I thought they were supposed to be efficient." They are, in fact, and I wouldn't be so bold if the rest of them were present. I continue past her and replace the smug attitude for an affectionate one. "Mother, how are you doing?"

She's melted into the couch, combing through her hair with her fingers in an endless loop. "I'm fine. It's fine here." Her gaze climbs to Nemora. "I will not go back *there.*"

Yes, I've certainly maximized the list of people I can take care of.

Whether or not Mother goes to Montica won't be decided without someone else. I turn back to my cousin. "Do you have any idea where Grandfather is? Despite your feelings, I hope you know we need him."

"You're right. We need to collect him."

Oh. I expected a fight. When did Nemora inch away from her mother's hatred for our grandfather?

"We believe he's at Leavenworth," she continues. "Along with the rest of the upended Establishment."

"What about the marshals?"

"They're dissipating for the most part." She takes the pad from her arm and taps around on it. "It's a good place to bring in some of our forces, though—just in case. No civilians to scare off."

So the invasion begins.

Chapter Four
SERENITY

It's insulting they think I don't hear them. A broken heart doesn't block out the senses, though I wish it could. I wish I was sleeping instead of pretending to. The paralyzing ache in my chest keeps me curled up in bed as much as my desire to avoid talking to them, but my ears work just fine. Their whispers hide nothing.

"We should move her to a new room," my mother says. "Being here will only make it worse."

Right. A change of scenery will fix everything. Plop me into a new place and maybe I won't remember it... Won't remember him...

The silver forget-me-nots weigh heavily on my neck. A gift from Jase. A token to commemorate our relationship before I took the shot to erase it from my memories. Now they're back to torture me. *Remember all the happiness you'll never have again?*

"Are we sure there aren't survivors?" This might be the most amenable conversation my grandfather and mother have had in years. Sad what it takes to bring some people together.

My mother's silence is damning. Not that I'd allowed myself to hope. I've already fallen into this darkness. Already broken beyond recognition. Why let hope raise me up only to fall again and break anything that might be left?

"I hate to leave her."

Please do. Please, please leave.

"Grace, we've left the note. She'll find you when she's up and ready." Grandpa's voice is gentle. That's the voice I usually get. Mamá not so much.

My mother makes an airy, exasperated sound.

"You're one of the only ones they'll listen to. You need to get back to work." Grandpa's dedication to leading Kaycie is convenient. They should go fix whatever can be fixed. There's plenty to keep them busy and away from me. Damage to assess. People to account for.

Telling people their loved ones have died.

At the sound of the door closing, I open my eyes. Sunlight pouring through the window is contrary to every fiber of my consciousness. At least this plain room isn't painful bathed in daylight. There aren't memories to be triggered when it looks like this. Only in the dark of night—when my subconscious took over—would I wind up wrapped in his arms here. Only asleep did I accept my proper place in the world. I never even told him I knew it. I never told him I loved him, and now I never will.

What a waste.

"I take it you were eavesdropping, too?"

I jolt up to attention. "Frey! God, I didn't know you were here." I bury my face in my hands as I catch my breath. "What are you doing?"

He moves from the armchair in the corner to sit on the side of the bed. His face is free of the dust, ash, and blood that mars his clothing. His dark blond hair is mussed in a way that isn't intentional, but he's still the most beautiful boy I've ever seen. "You weren't opposed to me being here when you came up, so I stayed."

If he hadn't followed me and gotten a key to my room, I'd have collapsed in the hallway. I suppose he put me into bed after my sobbing gave way to unconsciousness. I don't feel rested. It would be terrifying to think I could be numb enough not to notice that, except nothing can truly scare me if all the worst things possible have already happened.

I glance at the chair and back to Frey. "Did you sleep there?"

"Yes." His voice offers a shrug even though he remains still. The first time Frey 'saved' me was from flirting with Adwin at a club. He doesn't seem to think sitting silently with me through an entire night of mourning is any more significant.

I hug my arms around myself, gripping the filthy sweater I wore through the battle zone yesterday. "I don't want to talk about it."

"Good." He runs his hand over his forehead and presses his fingertips to his temple. "Neither do I."

Chapter Five

ADWIN

When I arrived in Leavenworth at the beginning of the uprising, I was nobody—only in the Establishment because of my grandfather, but too new and young to matter much. Plus, since most of the Establishment never trusted him, I was at a disadvantage with them.

Will they relish being right about him? It won't matter. He'll maintain his power.

The sun rises on a new day and a new era. I come back in an elevated position, though the Establishment doesn't know it yet.

Two Montican crafts land ahead of us to secure the area—sleeker and sharper than Kaycian hoverPlanes. When we exit our own, we're met with stony expressions. Most of these people were marshals this time yesterday. Two familiar faces catch my eye, and I approach them.

Grace Ward's gaze holds mine as she waits for me to reach her. "I see you're finally showing which side you're truly on." She inclines her chin toward the Montican vessels and guards behind me.

"Kaycie is my home." Now the balancing act. Show I care about Kaycie without condemning Montica. Be as neutral and likable as a person can be when everyone hates me. "You must know I don't wish any harm to it."

Adelle crosses her arms. "We can't be confident in any beliefs we might have held about your family." She's been laying the groundwork for this since before I was born, and it appears she plans to continue. Vogue obviously got her stubbornness from her grandmother.

"Perfect." I hold her eye contact, schooling my expression to be warm and open in the face of her hostility. "Give up your notion that we're the enemy."

"You arrived with those who laid waste to our city." Grace says this like it's a grand joke. Like she sees straight through me.

"Whoever stole their property is responsible for that," I bite out through clenched teeth. It's true in part, and I can't blame Montica out loud.

"What do you think happens now?" Adelle asks, eyes narrowed.

"Now, you set aside your pride and let Montica help us." I don't know if they think I'm an idiot or a traitor, but it doesn't matter at the moment.

Grace looks at me incredulously. "Why would they help us?"

Because they want to buy our regard. "Montica wants cooperative neighbors. They've never been hostile before—"

"Unless you include keeping our country flooded," Adelle deadpans.

"I do not." Breath control does little to calm my speeding heart. That's the point. They'll keep poking at me to make me snap at them. I won't give them the satisfaction. "That wasn't hostile, and you know all about keeping the masses uninformed. Montica will be content to maintain amicable relations with us if we have leaders they trust."

"Let me guess," Grace says, still acting pert despite being one of the most cunning members of the Establishment. "Casimir?"

I lift my chin. "Me."

If she had looked at me with disdain, I could have handled that. But her gaze drips with pity. Little does she know, I feel it all enough without her. My heart speeds further as I build the courage to say the words I've had to protect at all costs. "The Director of Montica is family. She's my aunt—Casimir's daughter."

Both women are practiced enough at hiding their emotions. I don't expect gasps and dropped jaws, but I also don't expect them to boldly lie to me.

"Yes, we've heard," Adelle says.

I narrow my eyes. "Nonsense."

"We found out yesterday." Grace has the audacity to sound bored. "Casimir has killed for the information leak already." She's worn this saccharine smile in movies. "It's making him even more popular."

My jaw tightens. "Where is my grandfather?"

"In prison along with most of the Establishment." Adelle is as austere as Grace is flippant.

"But not you," I say.

"We helped them get the marshals back," Adelle says.

"Congratulations on picking the winning side." Temporary though it may be.

Grace's eyes narrow. Apparently she's the only one allowed to throw sass into the conversation. "Says the boy who stands on the side with the most muscle."

"Glad you have the sense to recognize it." Can I get my footing in this, please? "You know Kaycie, or the Union, or whatever you want to call it, cannot stand against Montica. They didn't wish to destroy the city. They will aid in rebuilding and help us get back to a peaceful state."

The look of pity again. They think I'm in over my head, and I know I am! I won't be doing this alone, though. It'll work out. There's no other choice.

"I'll be taking my grandfather. You don't have the resources to refuse me."

Adelle's face betrays nothing. "He has crimes to account for."

"Would it make you feel better to know that's his situation in Montica as well?" I offer a small smile. I don't know how much they know about his relations with our Montican family. It might appease them to know he isn't loved there either.

"Take him." Grace leans in and whispers to me, all pretense of gaiety vanquished. "Consequences will catch up with him, just as the truth finally did."

"First things first." Grandfather takes a seat on the plane. "Emmaline is not staying in Kaycie." Imprisonment hasn't rattled him in the slightest. He didn't expect to be there long, apparently. I thought he'd be more bothered by the exposure of a secret he spent decades keeping.

Well, that exposure *did* get a sharp response. At first glimpse of the leak, those unfortunate enough to hear it were sentenced to death. Only two died. Now, it doesn't matter as the information is so widely known. We still don't know how everyone found out.

"She doesn't want to go," I say. "Even Nemora told her to come to Montica. She refuses."

His gaze rests on his estranged granddaughter, and one salt and pepper eyebrow raises ever so slightly. "How ever would someone not feel welcome and comfortable around you?"

"Yes, I got all the best traits from you," she sneers.

"How *did* you end up on this outing?" He turns toward me and continues without giving her a chance to answer. "I thought you were closer to Clover and Priam."

"I was…" *Until I betrayed them.*

"They aren't available," Nemora says, "for the foreseeable future. Clover took to some conspiracy theories after Adwin's accident, and he was instrumental in uncovering their plot to displace my mother."

The words she says so casually send a torrent of anxiety-inducing memories through me. Clover and I stuck high in the trees without technology to keep us from falling, my fall, Clover's disappearance after—apparently—Nemora drugged me to get information. I may not have agreed with Clover, but I didn't want her and Priam to be locked away beneath the fortress. It became inevitable when his plans turned to killing his mother, though. And I was the one who told Nemora where they were.

Grandfather rubs his thin lips together as he considers this. "It seems Montica has been as busy as Kaycie. Still, it'll be more secure for Emmaline. She needn't stay at the fortress. She can return home."

Nemora and I begin to protest. I snap my mouth shut and defer to her.

"My mother won't be pleased by that."

He waves his hand dismissively. "Your mother isn't pleased by anything." He looks at me. "What's your objection?"

"Mother doesn't speak to you. How will you convince her of anything?"

His steely glare holds me until he deigns to reply. "Do not underestimate me, Adwin."

⎯⎯⎯⎯§⎯⎯⎯⎯

Further proof that my grandfather is infinitely beyond me in all things—my mother has returned to Montica. Breck Fortress and its inhabitants were frightening, but she agreed when presented with the opportunity to return to her childhood home. Her comfort level with Montica's flying cars reminds me this was how she grew up. The avillipse lands in the sprawling yard surrounding a stone and wood home. It's secluded here, walled in by forest. Perfect for hiding one's second family, I suppose.

Did Clover know about this place? It would be perfect for her. She'd already have routed the way to the treetops in the time I've stood here. The smell of pine would be pleasantly familiar if it didn't remind me so much of her. The thick, gnarled trees are the ones she'd be interested in for climbing, and there are plenty.

Mother's eyes brighten as she steps slowly toward the house. Her head swivels as if she's rushing to get in every detail as quickly as possible. She clasps her hands together to still their trembling. When her gaze lands on me, she looks so wistfully content I think she might cry. "I never thought I'd see this place again. I never thought I'd see *you* here."

"I'm glad I finally get to see it." I offer her my arm. "Will you show me the house?"

"Oh, the house is just a building. There are more important parts." She leads me around the side instead. A cocoon-like swing hangs from a tree. Mother speeds up as she approaches it. When she curls into it, she looks younger. "When you were a baby and you'd fuss, I'd picture this spot. I knew if I could curl up and rock you here, you'd have calmed right down. That robotic swing with its twenty-something modes was absurd. You'd have liked this more."

A dull weight settles in my chest. I wish I had grown up with this version of my mother. The upbringing I never experienced blurs across my mind in watercolor strokes.

"I can't believe it's all still here. Just like we left it." She sighs. "I thought Ismene or her mother would have burned it down. I don't suppose I'll be able to stay after Kaycie is settled." A tear rolls down her cheek.

"I don't see why not." Not that Ismene would let her stay, only that Ismene can't possibly remain in power—for anyone's sake. If Clover steps in, she'd certainly allow it. The number of things I must do to make that happen is daunting. I've barely begun, and I'm exhausted already.

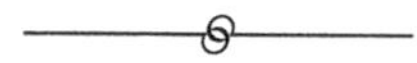

It's a strange feeling to leave my mother in a secluded house in the forest, all by herself. Not that she minds. I wish I could hide away in that retreat, as well.

Nemora remains silent as she flies us back to Breck Fortress. When it looms ahead, my stomach turns to lead. Not for the fortress itself, but what lies beneath it.

I can't ask about Clover and Priam—I don't want anyone to suspect I'll try to help them—but as we approach, sweat beads at the back of my neck. The tunnel into the mountain offers enough darkness to conceal a deep breath as I steel myself. When it opens to the hangar, I'm as impassive as I should be.

Clover only ever passed through here as required. A cavernous open space, but underground made it unbearable. She's even farther down than this now. Confined to a smaller space than she's ever been forced to deal with.

I shake the idea off as we take the lift up to the fortress.

Grandfather sits in the boardroom with his son and other daughter. Ismene radiates tension when he's around. Rocco mostly looks pensive. He's more uncomfortable with Clover and Priam's imprisonment. Granted, it's his daughter who will have the hardest time with it. Nemora's and my arrival is scarcely noted. She sits next to Rocco, perhaps having depleted her capacity to be near our grandfather.

"Adwin needs to be seen bringing aid for the city," Grandfather says as if I'm not taking the seat next to him. "But he needs to do something for the towns. They'll be the most difficult to pacify."

Ismene steeples her hands. "Being Montican can help his image. Kaycie started the marshal program."

"Yes. Perhaps he can take credit for reversing it." He taps his thumb on the table. "Say the attack on the city was part of an attempt to free them."

Ismene nods.

Neither is pleased to work together, but they seem to have found common ground with scheming.

"The towns will see you as their savior," Grandfather says. "They'll kneel before you like a deity."

It's nothing more than a solution to a problem. He doesn't care about gaining me glory. There's no excitement. Still, Nemora's features tighten as if she's restraining an eye roll.

Clover wouldn't approve either. When she took me to the old church turned museum, she told me people should be able to believe in something. The tree spirit painting wasn't what she had in mind. It just happened to be her favorite. Trees would no doubt be a preferred deity over *me*, though.

The plan should work for most towns. However, the town which birthed the uprising is a different story. After discussing the matter with the family, then renegotiating the strategy with Grandfather on the way, I step out of a hoverPlane into Lawson. I must do this alone if there's any hope of an amicable meeting. My grandfather is likely less popular here than amongst the Establishment.

Town hall is one of the nicer buildings here and it'll still need a renovation. I climb the steps where Kolina Eros celebrated her victory over the marshals who held this island. She would be the one to negotiate with now if she were still alive.

It's nothing new for me to walk into a place like I own it, even when surrounded by enemies. The guards who give me this authority would kill me without thought the moment the order came in. I can allow none of it to affect me.

Inside a small holding room is Sophos. He seems to have aged years since I last saw him. There isn't any color in his tired face or eyes as I sit across from him. My presence doesn't seem to matter to him. No anger or hate or anything.

"Would you like a cup of coffee?" I offer.

"No." His red-rimmed eyes remain fixed on the table between us.

"It shouldn't surprise you my grandfather expects me to utilize a drug to ensure I get the whole truth from you."

Now his eyes meet mine—deep pits of scorn. "I'm all too aware that he will sink to any method to secure his interests."

Grandfather had a commChip put into Kolina's son—a marshal—to have an ear in the Eros household. They stumbled upon our greatest secret and had to be eliminated. Of course, that secret doesn't matter anymore. Hence I can at least stop the downward progression of our relations here, even if there isn't any hope of improving them.

"I'm sorry you were caught in the crossfire. You've been through too much already, and I don't want to compound it. I hope we can speak freely, now."

His glare flows past me like a breeze. I have greater problems than Sophos Verity hating me.

"We know your *group* here was at least aware of the extirpation antidote if not involved. There are options of course. We could relieve everyone involved of all memories of the uprising, send you to Leavenworth, *or* we can agree to keep this quiet. You don't want your daughter to lose her home along with everything else. Anyone you tell would be subjected to the same memory loss. So, can we do this peaceably? Can I trust you to be done with conflict for all our sakes?"

Grandfather doesn't like this option. There are so few people whose interests may align with mine that I can't burn any more bridges. If I wind up needing some people from the uprising, this is an olive branch I can offer without drawing suspicion.

Sophos agrees to my terms.

As I suspected. He's too broken to be a problem. Hopefully the rest of this disbanded rebellion is only broken enough to be cooperative, not so broken as to be useless. "Thank you. I hope your misfortunes are behind you."

With the last remaining loose ends tied up as best they can be, my focus turns to my new role. The Agnar family hasn't ruled Montica for generations by luck or chance. Grandfather and Ismene know how to manage people.

Over the course of the next few weeks, the city is cleaned up and repairs begin faster than anyone would have thought possible. Kaycie kisses the hand which helps it, even if it was the hand which hurt it. The towns are awed by Montica's might. And they can't prove it *wasn't* Montica who gave them back the marshals. There isn't much motivation to resist the narrative when we bring repairs, infrastructure, and technology they've lacked for so long.

The memorial service was moving and beautiful, with me at the head of it. I'm now the face of the city. My previous anonymity has proven useful. I'm new. A fresh start.

I'm the one who will heal the country.

Chapter Six

BRAM

Wake up. From a dark, dreamless sleep. Stare at the ceiling until 04:30.

Run. Until my legs and lungs are on fire. Then five more miles.

Work out. Think of the ways each muscle in my body could be used to kill Agnar.

Shooting practice. Consider every location someone could be shot without dying quickly.

Cold shower. Vaguely remember what it was like to feel things.

Fall into dark unconsciousness.

Repeat. Day after day. Week after week.

Chapter Seven

ADWIN

"They hate us." I glance out the window as we fly to Leavenworth. The frosty expanse below won't be nearly as cold as the deposed Establishment members. They may have disagreed on most issues, but there is one topic they can unite over: Agnars are abhorrent. "How are we ever going to get them to cooperate when they despise us?"

Grandfather sips his tea with a calm that unnerves me. "It doesn't matter if they hate us. People will work with anyone who can be of use to them."

"And when they think our usefulness has run out?"

"They will turn against us." It doesn't seem to worry him.

I turn to the window and stare at the passing landscape with unfocused eyes. Kaycie created the Establishment to spread the pressure, the responsibility, and make it less lonely at the top. Except it's impossible to get people to agree on anything. Safety in numbers falls apart when those numbers make the group crumble from the inside. Better to go at it alone. No one can betray you that way. It's a theory Ismene forced onto the personal lives of her family, as well.

I can't disagree with her in that regard. My friendship with Parisa served no purpose, and Clover's nearly got me killed. Liam was a liability. I'm safer with no friends, no lover. But there are certain things

I can't achieve alone, so I do need allies. Even ones who are bound to turn against me. Grandfather is unconcerned by the prospect of betrayal. He's certain he'll always have the upper hand and can withstand whatever is thrown at him. I can accept it, because the desire to remove me is precisely what I need in an ally.

We land in Leavenworth and Grandfather leaves me with only, "Hold your position," before splitting away.

There was no opportunity to inquire about how he could possibly convince the Wards and Adelle Nemes to be cooperative. We have an unspoken agreement to limit what we say when all our words are undoubtably reported to Ismene. He only has to convince people to go along with the new status quo. The 'whom' of our endeavors might be equally challenging, but my 'what' is more complicated. Enough so that I can't even tell *him* what I'm doing.

But as I enter my office, I find another obstacle before that dreaded task.

"Our great leader, descended from on high." Lanelle Kemp is propped on my desk. Her beauty always looked like a weapon, but it would appear she's honed that. Everything about her is calculated—rose gold hair pulled back to be business-like, but loose pieces framing her face to soften it, a conservative neckline to offset the shortness of the skirt which teases a scandalous view. "Sorry to intrude, but since I seem to keep missing you, I thought I'd force the issue this time."

"I've been busy, as you might imagine." I pass her and take my seat. The *governor's* seat in this office I've acquired. I haven't spent much time here, preferring the city of hopeful people to this base of hostiles.

Lanelle twists to face me—every angle of her body meant to tempt. Little does she know... "Adwin, none of us are in a position to begrudge you and Casimir your secrets or power moves. All those self-righteous braggarts forget it's what we've always done our-selves." She places her hands on the desk and leans in, bringing her face so close the spicy notes of her perfume wash over me. "I don't even blame you for keeping us cooped up here. Many would love to snatch the power back from you, but I'm flexible. I'm happy to be part of this in a different way now. Besides, you're still one of us. You need help from Kaycians, not just Monticans. Let me help you."

"You say you've made power moves as if it's past tense. Here you are, still making them."

The smile which plays over her lips gives her a deviously cheerful appearance. "You know what I am, both because you've seen me at work and because we are the same."

My jaw clenches. Unfortunately, there's no argument to disprove her statement.

"I'm not horrified by the things your family has done." She examines her perfect fingernails. "We've all done terrible things and we've always had our reasons. Speaking of which, how did Agnar manage his issue in Lawson?" She speaks of it as if it's something to be proud of.

I rub my chip absentmindedly. "He planted a Montican comm-Chip in the marshal. It gave him a line of communication to hear what was going on and direct action." I'm protected against extir-pation, so it can't be used against me the same way, but the idea twists my stomach.

Lanelle's brows furrow slightly. "Do you have one?"

"Yes."

She reaches up and brushes her fingertips behind my ear. "Fasci-nating." Her attention shifts from my ear to my eyes. How many times has she successfully seduced people with this penetrating gaze?

"Careful, Lanelle. I might think you're offering more than assistance running the country."

"I'm available for *anything* you might need help with." My attempt to embarrass her backfires spectacularly. "You're the most powerful man in the country, now. Don't you want to see people kneel before you? I'm happy to oblige."

"Wouldn't that hurt Rollin's feelings?" I don't know if she's still sleeping with him, but with limited options it's a safe enough bet.

She shrugs it off. "There aren't feelings to hurt. People like us don't have the luxury of such attachments. We do what makes sense, and when business and pleasure mix, all the better."

"Well, that's not the kind of assistance I need right now, but you could do me a little favor on your way out."

She straightens without looking offended by the rejection. Easy enough when there wasn't any real desire on her end either. "Certainly."

"Find Vogue Taylor and send her here, please."

At that her jaw tightens. "Of course." She stands and her hips swing with each stride to the door. Without turning to face me, she adds, "At least I know you really don't want what I offered."

Vogue glares at me when I approach her in the hotel lobby. She should be pleased I acquiesced to her demands. She refused to come to me, so here I am. The first of many careful moves I'm sure I'll be making to gain her favor.

"Do you think I'll bow to you now, oh great leader?" A member of her crew sits next to her—Dixon I believe. As the story goes, he was the one close to figuring out the accumulator. It would be impressive if it hadn't summoned a rain of fire on Kaycie.

"Are you so opposed to the rebuilding?" I sit across from her, already tired of measuring my every move. "I don't see what I've done to earn such hatred from you."

Her green eyes narrow. "Shall we start with your treatment of Serenity, or how you took credit for Krisalyn's work?"

My gaze drops to my feet. Someday I'd like to explain to Serenity. I think she'd understand. On the other topic... "Does it matter who brought the marshals back? I thought you just wanted to help people."

"It matters"—she sneers—"if you use it to trick them into following you."

"You keep my secret, and I'll keep yours." They may not have gotten credit for the good, but they also weren't blamed for the bad. I kept them from being ostracized by Kaycie for drawing the attack *and* kept Montica from punishing them. By now she should be thanking me. I counted on having that appreciation before asking her for anything.

"Why bother?" She twirls a long platinum strand of hair around her finger. "You have no love for us, and we have no leverage." Not anymore.

"Why *did* you take the accumulator to Gladstone?"

Dixon joins our conversation. "Obviously it was dangerous. We couldn't risk another incident like what happened in the city."

"Well, I'm glad you got out before they blew it up."

Vogue rests her neck on her hand, looking at me suspiciously. "Why do you care?"

"I'm not a monster. I don't want you dead."

She holds eye contact with me. "You don't care about those who are."

Serenity's boyfriend. I didn't want him dead either, but what am I supposed to do about it?

"Can I see Serenity yet?" Grandfather wouldn't approve of me asking—I can do as I please—but I can't completely burn the bridge with Vogue. There's already next to nothing left of it, and she's probably the most useful person in Kaycie.

"No." Her expression is icy. Why do I keep thinking I'll be able to get somewhere with her?

"Vogue." Dixon rakes his fingers through his hair. "Maybe it would snap her out of this."

Her head whips toward him so fast, I'm surprised her neck isn't hurt. "No. If it was remotely acceptable to shock her out of it, then we'd—" She buries her face in her hands and groans.

Dixon shakes his head and turns to me. "She won't speak to us, so it's not like she'll talk to you anyway."

I sigh with resignation. The extended dose of amnesia left Serenity fragile, then she was front and center for the destruction in Kaycie that claimed her boyfriend. I can't begin to imagine the state she's in. Now I'm stuck dealing with the more difficult of the pair. "Vogue, you know I didn't cause Jase's or anyone else's death. I'm sorry for it, but there's nothing I can do. You don't strike me as someone to wallow in the past." This is precarious. I can't tell her anything of importance until I trust her not to sell me out, but I have to give her something substantial to earn her trust. "I thought you'd want to move forward. I do, but I can't do it without you."

"What could you possibly need me for? You're on top of the world, Adwin."

From someone else that phrase might be congratulatory. From Vogue it's an accusation.

I lean closer and keep my voice low. "I'm from Kaycie. Do you think I'm pleased by what happened there?"

"I think you were with the people giving the orders and you didn't *stop* it." Her ferocity makes her a youthful mirror of her grandmother.

"You think Ismene keeps me in the loop? I was in Montica, but I wasn't with them when it happened. I found out afterward." I could have been there, but I was too drained by my betrayal of Clover and Priam. Even if I had stayed, they wouldn't have listened to me. I'm sure of it. Nothing would be different, so there's no use wondering or blaming myself. "Montica is our best option for getting things settled and rebuilt, but I don't want them to have a hand in our affairs."

"Of course not. You'd want to run everything by yourself. You don't need the name to be an Agnar." Vogue's cruel beauty is somehow different from Lanelle's. Different weapons, different ways to cut.

"That's not what this is."

"What is it then?"

Dixon rolls his eyes. "It sounds like a trap."

They think I'm trying to trap them, but really I'd be giving them an easy way to trap me. She'd enjoy handing me over to Ismene—would rejoice in my downfall.

"Fine, Vogue. I'll make the first peace-offering. You're all free to leave Leavenworth. Go between the towns and the city. Whatever you want."

"How very generous of you."

I press on, ignoring her sarcasm. "You can't take credit for the marshals. They'll hear. And before you go trying to push out Montica's rule, remember that we need them to rebuild Kaycie. And you must realize you'll have better luck with someone helping from the other side."

She smirks. "You love to be needed."

How the hell would I know what it's like to be needed? I'm the one here needing you. "When you're ready to get back into the rebellion game, let me know." I stand and walk away.

Of course, Vogue is impossible to work with. But at least I knew where she was. My next option will be considerably more difficult to find.

Chapter Eight

SERENITY

Wake up in a panic after watching the EC explode. Again.

Shower. Wash off the sweat from the fever dreams. The hot water warms my skin, but the piercing, bone deep cold remains. My veins have frozen over—ice splinters and cracks with each movement. The water's spray reminds me of the plaza fountain.

Cry.

Eat. Whatever happens to show up for me. Nothing has any taste.

Wish to be alone. The faces that come to check on me change, but they're all the same. Eyes full of sadness and worry. Questions ranging from vague surface inquiries, to probing inquisitions. I answer none of them.

Walk. If I don't get out of my room, they'll really try to fix me. The cold doesn't bother me. The trees are bare and dead looking, but they'll come back. I'm not sure I can say the same for myself. Snowflake trails behind me without a leash. She's not as happy as she used to be either. Does she miss him, or is it my state dragging down her mood? Maybe it would be kinder to give her to someone else.

Sleep. This should be the easy part. It doesn't require movement. It takes place in the only position I want to let my body be in. Until...

Sleep ends abruptly. This time a different nightmare jolts me awake. My throat tightens at the thought of swallowing the amnesia shot. That day shouldn't even rank in the worst of my life anymore, but I keep coming back to it.

That night, I cried because I thought I was losing Jase. Little did I know what *really* losing him would feel like. But we were willing to sacrifice our memories to keep everyone safe. At least, that's what I thought at the time.

Sadness is painful, but at least it seems fitting. Everyone is sad. Sad makes sense. I should be sad. But the sadness is fading, and somehow it's even worse now. The feelings moving in to replace it make me wonder if my heart wasn't just broken—maybe it was reshaped, too.

In all the years of putting on a perfect smile, even when I was hiding the uprising, never did I so thoroughly wish to hide my feelings as I do now.

How broken am I?

Chapter Nine
ADWIN

"How was the city?" Mother sips tea, gaze fixed on her fireplace. She's been more relaxed, but my comings and goings put her on edge.

Whiskey warms my throat on its way down. "Reconstruction is going well. Will you want to visit sometime?"

"Probably not."

"Are you lonely here?" I'm not around enough, and the family isn't welcome, especially her father. Not that I know where he is in the world most days.

"No." She offers me a sad smile now. "Being in a city full of people, alone with all I knew, the world I loved stolen from me—that was lonely. To be here, even alone, is freeing. It's nostalgic, too. I didn't know I was a secret at the time, but it kept me isolated. Now, I'm used to being alone. I like it."

"If you say so." I finish my whiskey and force myself up off the armchair. I don't want to go, but I have to. Motivation is hard to come by in my mother's house. It's so lovely, and she's happier than I've ever seen her. It's tempting to think everything could continue like this. But our situation is far from secure. And Clover...

"I wish you didn't have to go to the fortress." Mother stares into the fire, unable to watch me leave. "Be careful around them."

"I always am." As I slide my feet into boots, I wonder if it might be easier on her if she knew I wasn't going to the fortress. Not that I'm going anywhere safer, and I like to keep her cushioned by plausible deniability. They think I'm here, and she thinks I'm there.

If anyone discovers neither is true, I want to be the only one it comes back to.

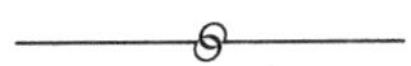

Avillipses don't make me sick anymore. Too many rides to count and learning to fly one cured me of that. The queasiness this time could have any number of causes.

The memory of what happened last time I was out here.

The danger of being out here alone.

The impossibility of what I'm trying to do.

The consequences if my family in the fortress finds out.

This is a terrible idea, but it's all I've got. I'm as sure as I can be that I can't be tracked. Even if Vogue couldn't have helped me with my endgame, she'd have been incredibly valuable in this now. But I go at it alone. Hopefully that'll change soon.

I land and go the rest of the way on foot. The location of the now-demolished treehouse is hard to find when the world is covered in snow and ice. This is the winter Clover wants? Even with the Monti-can tech, getting around in it is miserable. My legs sink knee-deep into the snow with every step. My face is freezing.

Charred ruins in the trees mark where Clover and her tree-walkers plotted to take Ismene out of power. I wonder how successful they'd have been if I hadn't ruined their plans?

"Misty!"

If Clover's lookout still haunts this area, she'll already have eyes on me. A chill runs down my neck, but the feeling of being watched is probably imagined. Clover told Misty to disappear, but how far would she go? Could she survive outside in this weather? I have no clues on how to find her. All I know is she used to be here.

"Misty, I'd like to speak to you. I didn't tell the agents anyone had gotten away that night. You know that." Not that I could see her then, but I'm sure she saw it all. "I'm here alone. I won't turn you in. I want to help Clover and the others."

Talking out loud in the middle of nowhere by myself is absolutely ridiculous.

Misty was the only one who escaped. My two cousins and the other four accomplices have been locked away in the bowels of the mountain since that night.

"Please give me some idea of what I can do to earn your trust. I need your help to free your friends."

A rustling catches my attention, and I spin around in time to see a fox tail disappear into a log.

Of course, it wouldn't be that easy.

"Think about it, Misty. I'll be back."

I'll keep coming back here, even if it means risking my position and life.

Chapter Ten

SERENITY

A dizzying carousel of babysitters rotate through my days—my parents, my friends. I love them, but they don't understand that every question chips away at me. Maybe eventually they'd get through the ice this way, but I'd be dead by then. Crushed into pieces too small to put back together. And the pieces would still be frozen.

Frey is the only one I can stand. He's the only one who doesn't try to make me talk. Silence between us is as comfortable as we can be in these circumstances. I've never been so grateful for emotional unavailability.

One person remains conspicuously absent.

As Frey and I sit on the floor, quietly playing a card game, I do something I haven't done in a while—start a conversation.

"Has anyone spoken to Bram?"

His mouth falls open. My question has surprised us both. "No. We haven't."

"I'm glad he's home. He needed time with his family." Maybe someday I'll be functional enough to meet Emrys. At least some good came of that horrible day in October. How long ago was that? I glance through the window at the gray day. Timekeeping hasn't been a priority.

Frey doesn't respond, and I look up to see him frowning at me. "What is it?" I ask.

He presses his lips together before answering. "Bram's reunion with them was probably pretty difficult."

My heart is racing by the time the story is done. Snowflake looks at me warily as I pace the room. She hasn't seen me this active in a long time. It's no comparison to my reeling mind.

I stop and turn to Frey. "Can you drive?"

"Yes?"

"Great. Drive me to Lawson?"

A small grin appears on his face. "Sure. When are we leaving?"

"Now."

Maybe they put some kind of tracker on me to alert them of my movements, because Vogue, Dixon, and Krisalyn cut us off in the lobby.

Vogue smiles tentatively. "It's so good to see you up and about."

"It'll be a bit until you see it again. I'm leaving."

Her eyes widen. "What?"

I cross my arms with a huff. "What's today's date?"

The three of them share confused looks. "January 20th," Krisalyn says.

Oh God, have I been a recluse that long? "It's been almost *three months* since Bram's mother and brother *died*, and no one thought I should be told?"

Dixon gapes at me before finding words. "Serenity, you had a lot to deal with..."

"You told me about Adwin's crap, and Gladstone, and— Don't look at me like that. Yes, I *heard* you. I just don't care. What kind of heartless shrew must Bram think I am that I haven't reached out?"

"No, he knows you're—"

"I don't want to hear it." Whatever Vogue thinks I am is probably better than how I feel, but I don't want to know anyway. "I'm going to Lawson."

"Your parents are away," she says. "Wait until they get back."

Do the circles under my eyes lessen the impact of the skeptical look I'm giving her? "I don't care. I'm going."

Krisalyn takes my hand. "I think it's a good idea. Being here isn't helping." I squeeze her hand, but Krisalyn is the person I have the hardest time facing. Our sorrow is too similar. Jase was her best friend, and our shared loss makes me recoil from her. I hate myself for that.

Vogue wraps her arms around me, and it quickly turns into a group hug with Dixon and Krisalyn too. "We love you," Vogue mutters. "I'm sorry we didn't tell you. We just don't know how to help you."

When we all release each other, I sniffle. "Stop trying. There's no helping and that's okay."

Vogue's frown could break hearts. It would break mine if my heart wasn't already pulverized. "You know that goes against all my prob-lem-solving instincts."

I sniffle and attempt a smile. "I know."

Frey and I go out into the cold afternoon. "Thank God for the weather. That was too warm and fuzzy for my taste."

Chapter Eleven

Routine keeps me moving. It's horrible to compare, but I can't help thinking this must be like extirpation. Marshals may have been more aware of their surroundings, though. All I see is the punching bag. Everything around me is veiled in smoke. Acrid and blurry. Only a little different than the fog Serenity described her amnesia as.

"Bram."

I freeze. The voice catches me off guard. I haven't been rattled since... *then*, but now...

I turn around and wonder if I've lost my mind. This can't be real. Serenity can't be standing here in front of me. But if I were dreaming, I doubt she'd look so pale. She wouldn't look sallow and beaten, in a security-issued jumpsuit with her hair tied back in a simple pony-tail. Still, seeing her stirs something in me. Something I thought had burned away. The phrase 'a sight for sore eyes,' doesn't quite cover it.

"I'm so sorry I didn't come sooner." Her voice is so much smaller than it was. "They didn't tell me. I just found out today."

Found out what?

Oh.

Only Serenity would feel guilty about not being here for me when she's been in her own hell. It douses my anger like a bucket of ice water.

"You had your own problems to face. I knew about yours and I wasn't there for you. It should be me apologizing."

She steps toward me slowly. "No, you were there when it mattered."

The memory of her sobbing against me tightens my chest into a knot. How did I bury that in my own suffering? Had I forgotten about her?

She lays her hand on my arm. Does it look smaller because it's been so long? Or has my self-imposed training schedule reshaped me that much? "Your hand is freezing."

She pulls it back. "Sorry. What's your current stance on hugging?"

"I'll accept one from you, but I probably smell terrible right now."

Her eyes brighten a shade, and she wraps her arms around me. Holding her again feels familiar in a physical sense, but something about it is foreign, too. To say it's a feeling of hope or joy would be an overstatement. It pulls in that direction though, away from despair and wrath, if only a little.

Back at the house, I shower and dress. Serenity doesn't comment on my commandeering of the former Kaycian outpost. The house two doors from the one I grew up in is where her friends stayed after we broke the world. Now I'm here hiding from my broken family. I come out to find her cradling a cup of coffee.

I sit across the table from her. "I thought you preferred tea."

"Coffee is a necessary evil." Sadness swirls around her like a storm.

"I've been worried about you," I say, "but figured I wouldn't be very consoling like this."

She inhales the steam from her cup deeply. "I had plenty of people worrying over me and trying to console me. I'm not particularly interested in that."

"Yeah. People mean well, but..."

"Their questions gut me every time."

Leaving Serenity alone with her well-meaning friends feels a lot like abandoning her now. There wasn't a conscious decision to leave her with people who would be capable of taking care of her. I was too lost to think of it. How could I subject her to being around me though? Maybe it wouldn't have been so bad. "I know. I won't ask you questions if you don't ask me."

"Thanks," she says into her coffee. "So you're under assault too?"

"Not much anymore. They might have given up on me. You know I can do a solid job of shutting people out."

"That I do. Why haven't you sent me away yet?"

I said shutting people *out, not you.* "You're different. You're the only person who knew me during most of the insanity. It's probably unlucky for you to be the person I trust. I'm not the most pleasant company."

Her lips turn up almost imperceptibly at the corners. "I'm honored." She says it without any irony or sarcasm. It must not be obvious how much of a mess I am if she actually thinks it's a good thing.

"How long will you stay?" I ask.

"I don't know. I basically barricaded myself in my room for the last three months, and now that I'm out, I can't imagine going back. I don't really want to be in Leavenworth at all. And the city is out of the question." She shakes her head. "God, I sound like a lost puppy. Don't judge me."

"I'd never." She cocks an eyebrow at me. "Anymore," I amend. "And you're not lost. You can stay here if you want."

She presses her lips together. "Thank you." Another word hangs there.

"But?"

"But I think everyone would lose it if I don't go back."

"Don't worry about them. You need to take care of yourself."

"I'm not sure I know what that means anymore."

Who would have thought I'd end up having so much in common with Serenity Ward?

Serenity and Frey took back the Kaycian outpost, so I slept in my old bed last night. I'd rather burn this house down than be in the place Mom died. Before the sun rises, I go for a run. The frosty air stings my lungs, but I savor the pain. The cold seems to actually dig into me today. I can't pretend the change is from the weather. It's her.

It's not the same as it was before. My brain didn't fall apart when we talked yesterday and late into the night. I was just grateful to have her. Being friends with her without conflicting emotions is the best option I can hope for. Neither of us can deal with anything more. It's for the best my feelings were extinguished along with everything else that wasn't anger.

After my run, I shower, change, and head over to see Serenity and Frey. They're both on the couch, coffee in hand, when I come in.

"Good morning," she says. "Frey is abandoning us."

"Why is that?"

He rolls his eyes. "Carista is putting me to work. We're assembling the team and going back to Kaycie to test a theory." He spent last night with Cary and Reid while Serenity and I caught up. I didn't realize she was recruiting him for something.

I look at Serenity, and my eyebrows pull together. "Aren't you on that team?"

"I've retired from my life of espionage. There really isn't anything for me to do anyway."

She used to get so frustrated about not being useful. As much as I understand her reasoning for withdrawing, it's sad to see.

"You can call us if you want to come back," he tells her. "Or find someone here to chauffeur you."

"I'll figure something out when I'm ready."

"All right." He squeezes her hand, then gets up to take his mug to the kitchen.

She glances up at me. "Only the two of us for breakfast then?"

"Yeah. And if you're staying a while, you'll need some stuff, right?"

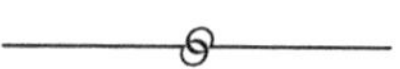

"A year ago, if I had told you you'd be going shopping with me now, what would you have said?" There's almost a smile in her voice.

I glance at Serenity from the side of my eye as we walk into town. "I'd have said you couldn't possibly need more clothes. More importantly, how have we known each other for over a year?"

"In some ways it feels a lot longer."

That's true enough. A lifetime's worth of shit happened in the last year. When we first met, I was pigheaded enough to be aggravated by her presence. Now she's the only person who *doesn't* make me want to punch things. And to my surprise, shopping with her isn't so bad since she's getting normal looking clothes. Far from the glamorous dresses she used to wear, jeans and sweaters are a welcomed change. She wears one such outfit out of the store, pulling her hands up into the gray sleeves. I carry a full bag of the rest.

I almost ask why she didn't go more colorful. Does she think colors would be too happy for her? I wonder if she realizes how nice the sweater looks, matching her eyes like that.

"I'm sorry I didn't think this through," she says as we walk to my neighborhood. "All I could think about when I left Leavenworth was seeing you, and I didn't consider staying, and I've never thought about money—"

"It's okay." Once it would have pissed me off that she's never had to think about money. She had enough credit—Kaycie's version of money—to get whatever she wanted, and people gave her even more so she could be a walking advertisement for them.

"I assume my parents have town money." She bites her lip and shrugs. "When I see them again, I'll pay you back."

"I'm not worried about it." This is the weird part. I don't have to care. Between the general balancing of the towns with the city, and the *compensation* for my family's contributions, I don't have to worry about money anymore. If only I could tell my twelve-year-old self that achieving this would be worse than anything our normal life ever was.

"Since Frey is gone,"—Serenity snaps me back to the present—"you could come back and stay at the house."

I nod. "Yeah, I might do that."

"What have you been doing with your time?"

"Mostly channeling my rage into workouts."

"Not surprising." I arch an eyebrow her way, and she explains. "Have you looked in a mirror lately?" Her eyes skim over my torso, and heat floods my neck.

"Well,"—my voice cracks a little—"it's a distraction. I tell myself it's for Agnar's sake, but it's not like killing him will be difficult once I'm *allowed* to."

Serenity stops short and looks at me wide-eyed. "You don't know, do you?"

"Know what?"

"Agnar's back in Montica."

"*What?* After everything he did, who the hell would just *give him back*?" The flames kick up in me. The one thing I've wanted this whole time, and we release him!

She runs her fingers across her forehead and sighs. "Is this still our fight, though?"

"Serenity, he..." My throat constricts.

"I know." She lays a hand on my chest and looks deep into my eyes. "If you're still in this, I will be too."

"You don't have to be."

"It's okay. Agnar and his entire family should answer for what they've done to us. Let him be there. That way we can rain hell down and take them all out in one swoop."

Her intensity is chilling. Hearing that from her lips makes me wonder how deep her scars run. It aches, but since everything aches constantly, I can handle it. But can I live with myself for dragging her back into this?

"I don't like hearing you like that," I say. "You were never meant to be a fighter."

Mischief sparkles in her eyes. "I'm not completely useless in a fight... given the right weapon."

Chapter Twelve

SERENITY

My body jerks. I wake panting and sweaty.

I should be used to it by now, but it's awful every *single* time. Though I didn't feel it then, when I rub my hands together now, I'd swear I can feel the glass shards slice my skin. The thunder of explosions, the rain of debris—so different from the storm Jase and I ran through on that first night together. I wrap the thick blanket tighter around me, but still I shiver. This house is cozy, but my ghosts have followed me.

The running list of all the ways it could have been different runs through my mind. If I hadn't been so furious with Jase about the amnesia shot, he would have been with us and gotten out. If I hadn't gone to Lawson, maybe we'd have figured things out sooner. If I hadn't gone running into the EC the night of the uprising, I'd never have taken the amnesia shot. If I hadn't seen Adwin that night by the train station, I wouldn't have kissed Jase. We wouldn't have been together and wouldn't *that* have solved a whole gambit of problems. Because it's utter nonsense, the idea that it's better to have loved and lost.

Though it packs on more guilt... I wish we had never been together. There is one other 'what if' buzzing in the back of my mind—lurking, waiting for me to give it a chance even if it'll darken my soul beyond repair. I don't let that idea form into words. I can't.

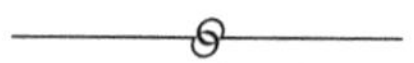

When Bram comes out of his room in the morning, he stops short and cocks his head. "Do you always wake up so early?"

I tap my fingers on my coffee mug. "It's a fairly new habit. And I couldn't risk you leaving without me."

"You're sure about this?" His tone is *just* patronizing enough to be motivational.

"Yes. I need to get moving again. I had done a good job of that during my first stint in Leavenworth last year. It's a shame I let that go."

Rather than making excuses for me, Bram says, "I *have* to see you with a sword."

I stand and put the coffee cup in the sink. "You'll have to take my word on it." Since sword fighting isn't remotely practical in real life situations, the marshal training gyms don't have them. "Let's go."

My lungs and legs scream at me. I've never been a runner. How do people even get to the point of enjoying this? Jase did. The thought pushes me forward. This burning in my lungs is such a different kind of pain, I embrace it. To be free of pain is unrealistic but changing it a little is a reprieve.

When we come to a stop, I lean onto my knees panting.

"You okay?" Bram asks.

I can only nod as cold air scrapes through my chest.

"I'm impressed you kept up."

I straighten and put my hands on my hips. "I assume you slowed down for me."

He shrugs and leads me into the marshal training gym. "At this point, slowing down a little is probably a good thing."

In the gym, I do a thorough stretch of my neglected limbs while Bram continues with his routine. He was right, slowing down would definitely do him good. No wonder he's packed on so much muscle. It's been a while since he's acted like a machine. This exertion of near-superhuman strength is a regression that breaks my heart. I didn't think there was enough left *to* break. This does it.

It's as if all the time he spent with me, he was restrained, waiting to set his rage free. Not that it's ever gone. When we talk, I can see it in his eyes and taught jaw. Sparks that I'm afraid to ignite. There are worse ways to channel it than this, but no amount of strength is going to bring back the people he's lost. Nothing I can do will either.

On our way back to the house, I ask, "Same time tomorrow?"

"You'll need to rest," Bram says. "Your legs will be too sore tomorrow."

"Oh, do you stop to heal before pushing forward?"

He narrows his dark eyes. "Are we still talking about muscles?"

"Of course. I wouldn't ask about anything else. We have a deal." No matter that I'm clearly testing the boundaries of said deal and using wordplay to do so. "But if your schedule doesn't include breaks, neither will mine."

He'll see what I'm doing plainly enough, but if it works...

"Fine," he says, "I'll take a break."

"A suggestion is not a question and hence not included in our deal, right?"

"Technically."

"I think you should get out of Lawson for a while. I didn't realize how suffocated I was by Leavenworth until I left."

"I've thought about that. It seemed like a dangerous idea to go be alone, though." He's bordering on self-destruction even with family around, so that makes sense.

"Bring Libby," I say. "She'd keep you busy."

He puffs out a breath. "I can't handle her by myself for an extended period of time."

"I can come if you want. I have nowhere to be." Not that I have any more experience with toddlers than he does.

"Sophos could probably use a break," he admits.

It has to be hard to jump into being a parent and so quickly and be forced to do it alone. Sophos looks like a shell of himself. This new responsibility while grieving Kolina has taken its toll.

"Well, the world is our oyster," I say. "Where do you want to go?"

Chapter Thirteen

ADWIN

"Is there anything you've asked for that you haven't gotten?" Patience is more difficult to come by when I'm at the Breck. Issues in Kaycian towns seem petty when this place pulls bigger issues to the forefront of my mind. My heel bounces under the desk.

"No." The voice in my comm lacks patience as well. I should have ignored the call.

"Then I don't see the problem." I drop my head into my hands and rub my temples.

"The problem"—Aster Rigby sounds like she's speaking to a child which doesn't help—*"is that we need to be involved."*

As Mayor of Gardner through the uprising, she should know that being in charge is more trouble than it's worth. But even as I take care of everything she brings up, she's not satisfied. These calls are inching toward the boundary of my tolerance. I can only play nice for so long.

"Aster, you can ask anyone in the city—getting what you need quickly and easily is something you'll get used to, and dare I say, enjoy."

"If you think we'll—"

"Someone's come in. I've got to go." I end the call before she can protest.

Nemora tilts her head from the doorway of my office. "You didn't have to do that on my account."

"You did me a favor." It's still difficult to think of her as an ally. Mostly because she won't be for long.

"How are things in the flatlands?" Is this her attempt at friendliness? Rather than making me comfortable, it sets me on edge.

I eye her warily. "Fine?"

She goes on, ignoring the question in my voice. "And your mother?"

"Why do you ask?"

Nemora sits, failing again at making this look like a casual conversation, because a relaxed Nemora is suspicious. "Don't you find it strange she never comes into Nyberg or to the fortress?"

"No. She's had a lifetime to develop her fear of this place. Being home is more than she ever thought to hope for. I don't think she wants to risk rocking the boat."

"I didn't think Kaycians knew that idiom."

"I'm only half Kaycian. And I've holidayed with Grandfather at the dam." Being out there was the only opportunity for water sports. The damned rebels would probably complain about watercraft being kept from them even though they've been rendered useless by their own doing.

"It's a shame we're letting old conflicts keep us separated. Our family is already so splintered."

Is she trying to bait me into asking about Clover and Priam? She can't actually be suggesting we reunite our *family.*' It's outlandish she'd even include my mother in the term. "I don't suppose Ismene agrees with your idyllic sentiments."

Nemora sighs. "She needs to move on. She'll never stop punishing our entire family for Casimir's actions unless she can come to terms with the past."

Is she serious? "My mother wouldn't dare come here. Ismene would have to invite her personally." Which will never happen, and good thing since even then she wouldn't want to.

"Maybe someday." Nemora rises and glides to the door. "I'd love to get our mothers in the same room."

I look around my empty office, having no idea what happened. My mission to keep Ismene and my mother apart—as assigned to me by Grandfather—feels even more important.

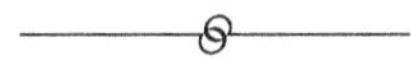

Finding the former site of the tree-walkers' headquarters is easier this time. The anxiety over it remains the same. Absurdity has perhaps increased. Last time provided no evidence this was where I should be, however I'm repeating the process.

"I'm back, Misty."

Back and still talking out loud to someone who isn't here—like a lunatic.

"I brought you a little something from Kaycie. These are my favorite chocolates. The green speckled one is filled with rosemary infused caramel. It's divine." I set the box on a large rock and pace around, waiting... for what? She's not going to come out because of a stupid box of chocolates.

I look up and around at the trees. She could be close by, and I'd never know. I hang my head and my shoulders slump. At least without her here, I can drop the confident posture. It's just as likely she's long gone. What options are left to me if I can't find the only ally I might have in this damned country?

These trees nearly killed me once, but I braved them again only to set off a battle in their branches. I reach up and wrap my hand around a branch, the connection between the glove and the tree pulls like a magnet. I add the other hand and walk my feet up the trunk, the pull and release of the boots is still familiar even after all this time. Seated on the branch, I close my eyes and drop my chin to my chest.

What do I think I'm doing? I'm not Clover. I don't play in trees or try to change the trajectory of nations. I'm out of my depth. None of this is my nature. My genes are made to hold power, not destroy it. But what has this Agnar blood gotten anyone? A trail of broken family members, and countries which may be better off without us. It's safer to keep it all going, though.

I rub my eyes before I open them. Still no sight or sound from Misty.

But the chocolates are gone.

Chapter Fourteen
SERENITY

Eudora's wide-open spaces are so different from the city towers, I could almost forget about my ghosts. The first time I met the mayor, Cole Markey, I was a half-broken, confused representative of the Establishment. Now I'm a completely broken mess, colder than this winter, though the weather is turning. He looks back and forth between Bram and me with restrained curiosity as we check out the house he's letting us stay in.

"Thank you for this." I run my hand over the brick mantle of the fireplace. This house is so cute.

"Don't mention it. There's plenty of firewood, and the kitchen is stocked." He points to the bigger house up the road. "My sister lives next door if you need anything."

Bram shakes his hand. "We appreciate it."

"Your family sacrificed a lot. It's the least we can do."

Bram tenses, and I slide next to him to run my hand across his shoulder blades. "Everyone did," I say to Cole.

He nods and takes his leave. Libby comes bounding in from the hall and drags me in the direction of the two bedrooms. She and I agree we'll share the one with the bigger bed. When we come back out to

Bram in the living room, Libby says she's hungry and the flaw in this plan becomes obvious.

I look at Bram. "You know how to cook, right?"

Last year in Lawson, Kolina let me shadow her in the kitchen a little. Unfortunately, those skills didn't stick. I press my lips into a thin smile. There's no need to mention anything from that time and risk upsetting Bram. It was a nice time. It was when I was most content in the brief period between regaining my memories and the city burning. Much like now, Bram helped me escape my problems. Looking back, I didn't even know what sadness was. As it turns out, being angry at someone who's alive isn't so terrible. It's much worse when they're gone.

We have pasta for dinner, after I nearly blow up the house. Why is it even possible for the stove to have the gas run without lighting? Seventeen years has not prepared me for much, but I do manage to wash the dishes. Bram is quiet, except when Libby demands his attention, then he lights up. This was a good idea.

The evening wanes, and a greater calm than I've known in some time settles over me. Libby's eyelids droop halfway into a movie. Bram takes her sleeping form to bed before the princess saves her sister. By the time I join her, I'm relaxed enough to be convinced I'll sleep soundly.

Until I wake up with a jolt in the middle of the night. Libby stirs, and my panic shifts to guilt. I don't want to wake her. Sleeping next to her was probably a bad idea. The charm of all this made me forget how sporadic my sleep has become. I slowly get out of bed, tiptoe to the living room, and wrap myself in a throw blanket on the sofa. *Ugh. Three in the morning.* Through the window, sparkling flurries of snowflakes make their way to the ground. Without thinking, I get up and go out the door.

My bare feet crunch into the thin layer of snow. I hold my hand out to let the snowflakes land and melt on my skin. I wouldn't have been surprised if I wasn't warm enough to melt them. The door opens behind me. I turn and gasp. Bram's large frame fills the doorway. "You scared me!"

"You scared me. What the hell am I supposed to think when I hear the door in the middle of the night?"

"Did I wake you? I'm sorry."

"No, I wasn't really..." His frustration dissolves. Gently he asks, "What are you doing out here?"

"Just watching the snow."

He steps to the side and holds the door open for me so I can walk back inside. We sit together on the sofa, and Bram envelops my hands in his. "You're freezing."

"I'm always cold."

"Why are you awake?" He tries to rub warmth into my hands.

"I woke up and didn't want to disturb Libby. It probably wasn't the best idea for me to share a bed with her."

His warm eyes invite me to expand on the issue, but he doesn't ask. "You can go to my bed if you want. You should sleep."

"So should you."

"Well, that's probably not going to happen."

"Me neither." I lean against him, and he wraps his arm around my shoulders. We are quite the pair of messes, aren't we?

Cole's sister stops by to invite us over for dinner. It's certainly a safer option than me cooking. It's also considerably more delicious. The roast she makes is *incredible,* and being surrounded by a big noisy family is a nice change of pace. As it turns out, people are okay to be around if they aren't concerned about my problems. Three little girls and a boy run around with Libby, earning regular rebukes from Faye. They laugh and argue amongst themselves without worry.

I keep an eye on Bram, not sure if this is too much for him. He's quiet, but that's nothing new.

"I have a couple of casseroles for you to take," Faye says after dinner. "Of course, it wouldn't occur to Cole that two young people from the city wouldn't know how to cook."

Bram bristles. "I'm not *from* Kaycie."

A giggle bubbles in my chest. Such a foreign feeling. "Bram would never want to be mistaken for one of us *dreadful* Kaycians."

Faye grins and sweeps her curtain of black hair behind her shoulder. "You were there long enough, honey. Anyway, you'll be able to pop the casseroles in the oven and have yourselves a proper dinner."

The casseroles come back with us, in addition to a sled Libby managed to finagle from our too-generous neighbor. "Miss Faye says if it keeps snowing tonight, the hill will be ready tomorrow!"

"That'll be fun," Bram says as we trudge back to our house. The whole place looks so beautiful with a blanket of snow on it. My own icy heart has been lifeless, but out here, the cold is magical.

Inside, I get Libby ready for bed while Bram gets a fire going. When I come back to the living room, we've both changed into sweats, and there is a pillow on the sofa. "What are you doing?" I ask.

"You don't want to sleep with Libby, so you take the other bedroom. I'll sleep here."

"Don't be ridiculous, you don't even fit here." I sprawl across the sofa to make the point more true. "It's mine."

"I'm not letting you sleep out here."

"I'd like to see you stop me." Obviously he could physically move me, but he can't keep me anywhere.

"Fine." He lifts the pillow along with my head to sit and places the pillow on his lap. "I'll just wait until you fall asleep, then move you to the bed."

"I'd wake up."

"No you wouldn't. I carried you sleeping for two blocks through Kaycie once." He tenses and his eyes lock on mine, wordlessly checking to see if I'm okay. I'm glad he isn't being so careful with every word, even if he's looking at me like he just said something horrible. A lot about that situation was, but in this context, it was kind of funny.

"I was not *asleep*. I was unconscious from a bad mix of alcohol and pharmaceuticals." I grin up at him, and he relaxes. The curve of my mouth is unfamiliar, but to put Bram at ease, I'll try to relax out of my frigid impenetrability.

"What you're saying is it'll take a while for you to fall asleep since you're sober?"

"Oh, I'm not falling asleep if you're going to move me to *your* bed." No harm in staying like this, though, lying on his lap.

"I'm staying here until you do."

"Then we are now in a contest to see who stays awake the longest."

Amusement lights his eyes to temper the mild annoyance of his head shake. "That's an incredibly stupid thing for us to do."

"It sure is."

But stupidity does not stop us.

Chapter Fifteen

BRAM

The sound of a door opening wakes me. Libby comes into the living room and cocks her head to the side. "Why did you sleep on the couch?"

I stretch and find sore spots in countless places. "Because Serenity is stubborn."

Serenity puffs out a breath, eyes still closed, her head on the pillow in my lap. "You're one to talk. You're only jealous because I won." The sleepy rasp of her voice threatens to stir something in me, but it can't.

"I don't think anyone won." Although if she can still turn her head without wincing, she might have.

"You wanted to move me to the bed. You did not. I won." She sits up and stretches down to her toes. "I bet the soreness from sleeping like that is making your loss feel a whole lot worse."

"At least you're humble."

She stands up and ruffles Libby's wild hair. "What do you want for breakfast, little miss?"

While Serenity gets Libby cereal, I twist my back with a decisive groan. *So stupid.*

"You better pull it together," Serenity calls from the kitchen. "You know what all that snow means, don't you?"

"Sledding!" Libby cheers.

"Sledding!" Serenity agrees.

These two might be harder on my body than the obsessive workout routine.

Therapy animals are common in the city, but I never would have realized a toddler can serve the same purpose. Libby is a little ray of sunshine and a welcome diversion. She certainly keeps us busy enough.

Serenity zips up Libby's coat and smooths it down. Tears glisten in her eyes. Libby goes running outside while Serenity stands to put on her own coat.

"Are you sure you want to go?"

She gives me a soft shove on the shoulder. "Would you let me stay here and mope alone?"

"Since when do I *let* you do anything?"

"Good answer."

It's a quiet walk through the sparkling snow. Serenity falls into a reflective state but perks up when Libby demands her attention, then back again. Is Libby helping, or is this sweeping the problems under the rug?

The three of us make it to the hill Faye directed us to last night. We send Libby down on the sled first. She giggles and screams the whole way down. And then doesn't bring the sled back with her. Rookie mistake on our part.

I go down to retrieve it and sled down with her to avoid this issue. When she insists on me pulling her *up* the hill on the sled, the regret about my sleeping position flares. Next time, Serenity goes down with Libby, and I'm not sure who has more fun. They climb the hill, hand-in-hand, smiling and flushed.

"Sure, for Serenity you walk."

Libby sticks her tongue out at me. I'm officially outnumbered by strong-willed females.

The rest of the morning is spent with all combinations of the three of us sledding. When Serenity goes alone, I push her hard enough to almost send her into the trees beyond the hill. She tries to return the favor but ends up falling flat in the snow from the effort. Snowballs are thrown. Fun is had. And Libby falls asleep in my arms on the walk back.

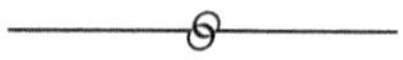

My little sister takes up such a small part of the big bed, which makes the fact that Serenity and I both slept on a couch extra ridiculous. I close her door softly and find Serenity on the couch with her fingers pressed to her temples. I sit next to her, and she looks up, searching my face with a sad curiosity.

"That was fun," I say, though my tone isn't convincing.

"It was," she says with equal lack of emotion. She leans her forehead onto her hands and lets out a slow breath. "Does it make you feel guilty? Well... I'm not supposed to ask you that. It's really my way of confessing that *I* feel guilty. For any happy moments. It feels like..."

"A betrayal?"

She nods. "Like I'm forgetting. How can I possibly smile when..." She sucks in a ragged breath and grips the floral necklace at her throat.

I wrap my arm around her shoulders. "I know."

She curls into me, burying her face in my neck. I hug her tight against me. "The miserable times are expected," I say. "When any small happiness also leads to misery it's a different beast."

"When do you think..." She sniffles. "When do you think we'll allow ourselves to be happy again?"

I lean my chin onto her head and sigh. "How about this? *I* give you permission to be happy."

"I don't even know what happiness could look like now."

I do. It looks a lot like this. This... without her pain and tears, would be more joy than I would have ever hoped for. Having her around makes me feel like *maybe* some of the hell we've gone through is worth it, because it was through this that I know her. Turns out the losses which burned me out didn't consume my feelings for her. This affection has always been an anchor. It used to drag me down—drown me, but now it's all that keeps me steady. I cling to it because there's nothing left without it. Still, holding her when she cries drags knives through me. I wish I could fix this for her. But there's no fixing it. All either of us can do is wade through, picking up the pieces as we go.

Serenity sits up and wipes the tears from her face. "I give you permission to be happy, too."

Chapter Sixteen

SERENITY

It wasn't so long ago that I was determined to not show any emotion in front of Bram. I hated the idea of him judging me or thinking me weak. Then he told me I was strong, and he hasn't retracted the statement even after seeing me breakdown so many times. Being stuck together used to feel like a curse—for both of us no doubt—but I'm so lucky to have him. The others would try to tell me it'll all be okay, and it's *not* okay. Bram doesn't sugarcoat it.

Instead, he lets me move on from this little breakdown without acting like I might crack again at any moment. The rest of the day feels normal enough—for Eudora. Of course, it's a new reality compared to life in Kaycie, but new gives me room to breathe. Libby wakes up and doesn't even give us time to remember our sorrows. Entertaining her is a full-time job.

Place in oven is the kind of cooking I am actually capable of, and after dinner, Libby goes to bed.

When Bram comes out of her room, I'm stretched on the couch with a book. He lifts my feet to sit under them. "Can we not have a repeat of last night? I'll concede to your win, but I can't spend a night like that again."

"You certainly shouldn't," I say. "Go to bed."

"I won't be able to sleep knowing you're on the couch."

"You did last night." I'm not sure how bad a time he's had with sleep, but we both slept through the night. A miracle for me.

His eyebrows pull together, but he doesn't say anything. I can't tell if he's okay or at the precipice of depression. Not when all he seems to do is search me for how I'm doing. We may have agreed not to push each other, but his concern for me is painted on his face. As if he doesn't have enough of his own problems to sort through.

"Lying on the sofa won't be much better for you," I say. "And I can't go to sleep knowing you're crunched up out here either."

He hesitates, jaw clenched against whatever he's thinking. Are we not at the point of saying what's our minds yet? Then I realize why he's staying tight-lipped. The solution to this problem makes my chest tighten... but we did already spend a night together. And when has Bram ever asked me for anything? Nothing is ever for his comfort or well-being unless I force the matter.

I give him an out. If he feels uncomfortable saying it, then I will. "We could both sleep in the bedroom." Oh, saying it out loud makes it very different. Damn him for making me be the one to do it.

"That sounds like a reasonable truce." His nonchalance dissipates the tension. Until we fall into the same contest as last night. Who can hold out the longest?

The words in front of me blur as I think of all the scenarios. Which will be the most uncomfortable? Me already being in the bed and him coming in, or the other way around. If he goes to bed first, I might stay here, which would be mean. Not an intentional deception, just me being an awkward coward. So *again*, I bite the bullet and make the first move.

The book snaps shut—a little too loudly—and I stand. "Okay, good night." Maybe this is better. Maybe I'll be asleep before he comes in and avoid the strangeness of the situation altogether.

No I won't.

Curled up with my back to the door, I know that's not going to happen. My fingers tap randomly, not a tune, just agitation. I start to wonder if he'll do what I had thought of and stay out there. I'm about to go drag him in here when the door opens. The bed shifts as he gets in.

Once all is still again, he whispers, "Good night, Serenity."

As it turns out, this isn't the strange part at all. The anticipation was awful, but this is tranquil. Sleep pulls me in easily.

———— ❦ ————

I get outside and turn back toward the building. There's nothing else anywhere. I'm alone in the world watching the EC explode for the hundredth time. Resigned to this misery I've endured so many times, I simply wait for it to be over. I wait to wake up panicked and shivering.

To my horror, the dream doesn't end. Have I numbed to the point of needing longer nightmares?

A wall of dust and debris rushes toward me. This time, I'm not alone. Someone steps in front of me, blocking the cloud of ash. Bram. *The image of us standing there together with his shoulders hunched over me swirls and changes to him holding me as I sobbed in the tunnel, then in Eudora.* In the space between awake and asleep, I shift and vaguely realize he's holding me now, but... I stay asleep.

———— ❦ ————

Is this what waking up used to feel like? It's hard to imagine I ever just woke up—discontinued sleeping and transitioned smoothly into a day. Not to mention this is the second day in a row. For a moment I wonder if I didn't have the nightmare, but then I remember... I did, only it changed. Bram was there. And Bram is here. His hand, a warm weight on my waist. Perhaps it's his warmth that's slowly melting the ice rooted in me. This slow thawing is so much more comfortable than carving at it with deliberate 'help.'

When I get ready for the day, I grab my necklace by force of habit. The cold metal in my hand is heavier than the sum of its parts. It probably hasn't been helpful. It's not like I could forget even if I wanted to. I put it away instead.

For the rest of the week, sleeping next to Bram is perfectly comfortable and normal.

Chapter Seventeen

How has it already been three months since Kaycie was under fire? Three months since I last saw Clover. Three months since I found myself gripped in Ismene's clutches. Years of playing a part, only to switch it for another. I used to act like I was no one of consequence even though I thought otherwise. Now I know my own insignificance but portray confidence.

Familiarity in the Breck's halls doesn't bring comfort with it. The people who work here hate me. A lifetime in Kaycie taught me to recognize that. The shimmer of the city doesn't blind *everyone* to the duplicity of tight smiles and keen glares. It's been three months since I spoke to the only people left in Kaycie who I had ever bothered to care about. They want nothing more to do with me, and I can't blame them. We live in entirely different worlds. People like me make theirs possible. Good for them.

Voices are muffled from the other side of the door, but for anything to come through means the occupants are shouting. Maybe this meeting can wait. I slide away, but the door opens, and I freeze.

Rocco holds the doorknob, facing into the office. "Be careful what you dig up. There are secrets you'd be happy to leave buried." He turns and startles upon seeing me. His eyes widen momentarily then narrow.

He's avoided me since I got Clover arrested. "Adwin." He dips his chin in greeting, his pressed lips nearly hidden in his brown beard, then he leaves.

I peek into the still open door. "I can come back if you—"

"No, come in." Nemora's eyes dart back and forth under closed lids as I enter. She opens them and gestures to a chair.

I sit and say nothing. I'm in no position to ask her what that was about.

"Priam may be a traitor, but I almost miss him." I can practically see the gears whirring in her mind. Genius-level intelligence must be exhausting. I can't imagine how much runs through her thoughts at any given time. Is it lonely?

"That's reasonable," I say. "He's your brother."

She shrugs. "When he has practical goals, he does manage to be useful."

"I know I'm not comparable, or I'd offer to make myself useful."

Her lips purse as if she's considering it, but then she lets out a breath and relaxes—as much as Nemora is capable. "No need. You have plenty on your plate. How are things in Kaycie? My mother has too much going on right now with the Collective, but I'm here for anything you need."

"Oh? What's going on with the Collective?" The organization to preserve international peace and security has long shunned Kaycie. I forget Montica is still included in it.

"Questions about our goings on with Kaycie. It's fine." She waves a dismissive hand. "How are things in your towns?"

Our meeting concludes without noteworthy discussion. Afterward, we take the lift up to our suites. When we reach our floor, I gesture to let Nemora out first, but she declines. "I need to go get something from Mother's suite."

"Good night then." My feet carry me to my Breck home, but my mind wonders if Nemora is looking for the secrets Rocco recommended leaving buried.

———⊗———

"I brought you chocolates again. This time you're going to need to talk to me." My third weekly visit only feels slightly less ridiculous than the first two. I hold onto my offering so she can't take it while I'm not looking. "I can get you whatever you need, but I don't know what that is unless you tell me."

Without a breeze, the forest is eerily quiet. Does Misty have trouble moving around without the cover of rustling branches? Clover said she was like a ghost out here, and I can't help but feel she's haunting these woods. Her stealthy snatching of the last gift without my notice proves that much. Did she watch as her friends fought, lost, and were taken into custody? I'm surprised she hasn't sought her revenge on me. I've gift wrapped myself for her. Does she think I'll keep coming? Perhaps this her game. It's more fun to drag it out, raising my discomfort and paranoia with every eerie visit.

My boots crunch into snow and ice as I pace around. Then my hands and face smash into the frozen mix. I groan through clenched teeth, cheek freezing while I muster the energy to get up. I twist to a sitting position and search for what I tripped on. There's nothing around me at all.

Not even the chocolates.

"Really, Misty?"

I drop my chin and press my fingers to my temples. A slip of paper floats down and lands before me. In vain, I look around. Of course there's no sign of her. This is a start, though.

Chapter Eighteen

BRAM

After breakfast, Libby runs off to get ready. She's excited to go home—young enough not to feel the memories there. I can't decide if it's lucky or terrible that she won't remember.

Serenity lingers at the table, biting her lip. Did we make this weird? I should have let her sleep on the damn couch like she wanted. I'd have stayed up all night feeling bad about it, but that would be better than making her uncomfortable. I hold my tongue, waiting for her to be ready to say whatever it is she needs to.

"So,"—she drags the word out—"I spoke to Cole and Faye yesterday. They said I could stay here."

Stay. By herself? I can't imagine what my face looks like as I realize she wants me to leave her here. It must be something though, because she hastily adds, "I just can't go back to Leavenworth or Kaycie, and I like the space and fresh air here. I think it's good for me."

"Um, yeah, you should do whatever is best for you, but..." *But I can't even think of leaving you.* "Do you think it's a good idea to be alone?" How do I say that without sounding like I think she can't take care of herself? Especially since it's really me being selfish. Our week together has been such a breath of fresh air. Not because of the literal fresh air, but because of her. Would my lungs even function without her?

"I know how to make coffee, and toast, and sandwiches. I'll survive." She shrugs, hugging her tea to herself.

My heart rate increases, and I try to swallow my panic. "Do you want me to stay with you?"

I want to stuff the words back in my mouth the second they're out. What the hell is wrong with me? All this is going to do is make things more difficult for both of us. I don't want to put her in a position to feel bad about sending me off, and I refuse to cling to her in order to save myself. I brace for the inevitable rejection.

She puts the cup down. "Well,"—*Here it comes.*—"I would love that, but I didn't want to ask." She buries her face in her hands. My heart stops. "I came here because I was worried about *you*, but somehow it shifted to me needing you to feel okay, and I didn't mean for that to happen, and I feel like I'm using you—"

At the sound of my nearly hysterical laugh, she looks up. Shit, what do I say? I can't say what I'm really thinking—*Feel free to use me, I'm a horrible person who is soaking it up like a sponge.*

"Don't feel guilty about me helping you." *I'm amazed I can do it.* "You're helping me at the same time."

"Am I?" She looks up, her face washed with concern. "I feel like a burden."

I lean back against the counter and cross my arms. "You're way too small to be a significant burden."

She releases a breathy laugh. Simultaneously, joy and guilt rush through me. Seeing her mood shift in even the slightest positive direction is a relief, but am I reveling in being the cause?

"Are you sure you'd want to spend more time here?" she asks. "They're going to put me to work. I don't know if you're cut out for farm life."

"I can't possibly be less suited to farm life than you are."

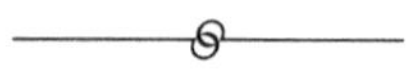

Serenity rides with me back to Lawson to take Libby home. My body tenses by degrees as we get closer. Years spent wanting to go home, but now it's the last place on Earth I want to be. I can't believe I had stayed there so long. Could it have only been ten days ago that Serenity appeared and shook things up for me? Living in a cycle of rage and fire feels like it was a long time ago.

Libby squeals as she runs to hug Sophos. He still looks like hell, but his eyes brighten for her, and his smile is warm. Serenity sits with them in the living room while I go find Aren. He was surprisingly understanding about me leaving. We really haven't fought since... everything.

According to his message, he's at the house our Kaycian friends had lived in—where I've lived to avoid our childhood home. I go down the street, and walk in to find him with Carista, Reid, Travick, and oddly, Frey.

"What are you doing here?"

"Nice to see you, too," Frey says with a grin.

Travick eyes me tentatively. "How are you doing?"

"Getting there." I almost roll my eyes. Serenity doesn't ask such pointless questions. "What are you all doing here?"

Reid bounces his heel. "We always have to watch our steps. It feels like there are eyes and ears everywhere now."

We were left with our knowledge of what happened with Montica and how the marshals were brought back. It's lucky, but also unsettling. Agnar stops at nothing to keep information contained. "What's going on?"

Frey crosses his ankle over his knee. "We took the accumulator to the city to see if we could do anything with it without summoning an armada—"

"What?" My head spins. "I thought it was destroyed."

"No," he says. "Montica thinks it was destroyed when they flattened Gladstone. I don't know where they got that idea from, or why they think it was successful, but anyway—"

"*Anyway*, you just thought you'd try for a repeat of the deadliest day in Kaycian history? How can you be *so* arrogant— Well of course you can, it's you. But this—"

"It wasn't my idea." Frey's gaze slides to Cary.

She twists the ends of her ponytail. "It's probably the only thing we've got to even the playing field against Montica."

"There's no evening the playing field." I lean on the wall and drop my head back against it. "We aren't even playing the same game. We don't know the rules—Montica writes them."

"They're turning all the towns into little Kaycies," Aren says. "Give people what they need, keep them in the dark. Don't ask questions. Don't be involved."

For a second that doesn't sound like such a bad thing. I hate myself for the thought.

Travick crosses his arms. "We didn't wake up to submit to someone else."

They shouldn't have to. After having no control over anything for so long, how could any of them live with this now?

"So, are you ready to get back to work?" Aren was the one who broke down, so how am I the weak one who can't deal with every-thing?

My jaw clenches as I figure out how to say this. "I'm not staying here. I'm going back to Eudora."

"Why?"

"I don't want to be here." *Please don't ask if Serenity will be there...*

"Is *she* going too?" Time hasn't tempered Aren's aversion toward Serenity.

It's bad enough I know the real reason without him pointing it out. "Yes."

Aren rolls his eyes. "Is she not good enough to satisfy after a whole week, or so good you can't stop?"

"Is she *what?*"

"Aren!" Cary's jaw drops. "What the hell is wrong with you?"

"What? Are we supposed to pretend he *didn't* go spend a week screwing that—"

A punch to the jaw sends Aren and his chair tumbling. Everyone else is on their feet, shouting and pulling me away from my brother, but my focus is on his narrowed eyes.

"You're welcome for stopping you before you made that even worse for yourself." My fist shakes at my side.

He gets to his feet. His face is already beginning to swell. "I didn't complain when you wanted to go. If a tumble with your girl would shake off your— How is that a bad thing to say?" My glare cut him off this time.

"Why the hell do you assume anything happened between Serenity and me?"

He looks around the room for assistance. Did they all think that's what was going on?

"I mean..." Cary grimaces and mumbles incoherently.

"*What*, Car?"

"When you found out Emrys was a marshal you had a one-night stand, so..."

"We brought *Libby* with us!"

"She sleeps like ten hours a night," Aren says.

"Well, if you all thought Serenity was going to be the magic bandage to fix me, I'm surprised you didn't get her here sooner."

"Her overbearing friends wouldn't let us!" Aren gestures toward Frey.

"That wasn't me," Frey says with a cool shake of his head.

How many people discussed this possibility? I swallow as my toes curl up in my shoes.

"You're all assholes. Serenity is the only one who gets it. *That's* why I'm leaving." I slam the door on the way out.

How stupid was I to think Aren was sympathetic for letting me have this time? He doesn't understand shit! He thought I was just going to go sleep with Serenity—who's as damaged as I am—and be back to normal? I'm better than I was, and technically we *slept* together, but they all thought *that*? Really?

I storm home getting angrier with each step. A switch flips when I open the door to my house, and Serenity smiles at me from the couch. My skin prickles. *Idiots.* Do I feel awkward because of what they assumed we'd done, or because I'm thinking about that possibility? Those thoughts used to be there, but after everything, they're gone. They need to be gone.

"Ready to go?" she asks.

"Yeah."

She says goodbye to Sophos and Libby, then Libby gives me a big hug. "Thanks for taking me on a trip."

"Anytime, munchkin."

"I'll miss you." Her sweet voice calms my nerves. But she's not coming with us this time. I doubt the effect will last once we're gone.

"I'll miss you, too."

Serenity and I walk out, and my fury burns at Aren and the others for making this uncomfortable. She was the only person who could make me feel at all normal, and they ruined it. Yes, I needed her, but not like *that*. The whole thing keeps me silent as we get back in the car.

"Are you sure you want to go?" Her eyebrows are pulled together, and I wonder if she's more worried about whether I'm okay right now or the idea of me not going with her. Both options soothe my buzzing nerves.

"Absolutely."

Chapter Nineteen
SERENITY

Bram's white-knuckle grip on the steering wheel keeps me quiet. Obviously, I don't ask. I just lay my hand on the center console. Eventually he wraps his own around it. *I'm here.* He knows it, and I hope it helps.

Back in Eudora, we have a quiet but uncomfortable evening. Even with a movie on, not asking Bram what's bothering him becomes difficult. If he wanted to tell me, he would. There's always diverting his attention, though.

"I'm not sure if there's been a night where I haven't watched the EC crumble in my sleep."

His expression drops, and guilt twists through me. Am I just making him brush off his own grief in favor of mine? But then he says, "I don't dream at all."

"That might be better," I say. It worked. My problems give him a segue to talk about his.

"Maybe. But who doesn't dream *at all* for months? It makes me wonder if I'm really alive."

"Dreaming can't be what makes a person alive or not. I was having nightmares when I was quite lifeless in Leavenworth."

"I'm sorry I wasn't there for you, but I'm glad I didn't see you like that. Is that terrible?"

"No. I'm glad you didn't see it, too. And there's nothing to be sorry for. You're here now, and I don't think I was ready to do any of the work to get better."

"Are you, now?"

"I guess so. Even the nightmares are changing."

The question remains unspoken—only glinting in his eyes.

"You've been showing up in them," I say.

"In your nightmares? That doesn't sound good."

I pat his knee. "It is good. I used to wake up right after the building collapsed. Now I get to the parts where you were there for me."

Bram drapes his arm over my shoulders. "I'll be whatever you need."

I tuck into him. "I know." I do know he means it, however unfair it might be. "I will for you too."

He rubs my arm, and it occurs to me I don't know what I could be besides a distraction. Maybe that's enough, though.

When I get up to go to bed, I almost go back to the room I shared with Bram while Libby was here. The bed I'm *supposed* to be in feels too big and empty now.

Chapter Twenty

BRAM

Put to work indeed. Our first morning back, Serenity learns the basics of chicken care. If anyone could see it, this would be the most talked about topic in Kaycie. No one would believe it.

I'm assigned to fence repair duty. Having something to do centers me. It's nice to have a task, and work with my hands. It's still physical but not as strenuous as what I've been doing. More importantly, it's different. And this place is different. A place Emrys and Mom had never been. The guilt for not thinking about them can be better than the pain of remembering. We were so close to being back together and being a family again. Emrys couldn't even try. He didn't give us a chance to support him. And who could blame him? I would have been useless. I don't know how to deal with this shit. I've done nothing to help Aren, so I guess I'd have abandoned Emrys too. At least Carista is there. *She's the one who's been there for my family, after all.*

My absence used to be against my will. Now I'm out of excuses.

The hammer goes right through the wood when I swing it to knock a nail in. *Shit.*

Jobs like this keep rolling in. It's a way to pass the time faster. Serenity and I run every morning before working on the farm. There's something I never thought would apply to us. It goes unspoken, but we both know her insistence on keeping up with me is to keep me from overdoing it. I try not to feel guilty for that. It helps that her learning to throw a punch is kind of hilarious. She's determined, though. I guess it's good for her to do something physical too. That thought threatens to pull my mind to a direction it cannot go. A direction I'm still pissed at Aren for sending me to.

"Keep your core tight." I press my hands against her lower back and stomach, feeling her abs flex. Part of me would like to linger there. I shake off that feeling and put my palms out to her again. Her fist connects with my open hand. "Oh, come on. I barely felt that."

She groans. "Well, I don't actually *want* to hit you."

"What if I call you a puppy again?"

She jabs me with a little more force.

"That's better."

Her grin quells the fire still smoldering under everything. Or changes it to something different. I'm still burning, but this is a sweeter agony.

Chapter Twenty-One
ADWIN

The painting of the gnarled tree god comes to mind. *I just don't see why people shouldn't be free to believe whatever they wish.* Clover meant it as a generalization. She wouldn't worship trees that way. Who would have thought my actions would come to look like I've taken up that ancient superstition? It makes about as much sense as me coming out to the forest with fresh bread and mint leaves for a phantom girl I haven't even seen.

"As you requested." I place the items on the same rock as that first box of chocolates. "You don't need to snatch them and run, though." I'd like to think she won't be able to catch me off guard twice. Obviously untrue.

I sit on the ground next to the things she asked for so I might catch her this time. Or maybe it's to have a shorter distance to fall. Probably a bit of both. I stare at my gloved hands, unmoving, willing myself to hear every sound. She can't be completely silent. There must be some sign of her I've been missing.

No matter how hard I try, all I hear is the rustling of branches. Snow sliding off one and plopping onto the ground. A bird in the distance. Priam knew which bird call was out of place. They all sound the same to me.

Movement pulls my attention to my side, and a blur zips over the rock. Before I can fully turn my head, an impact at the side of my mouth sends me sprawling into the snow. I press my fingers to my lips, and they come away bloody.

"That's one way to say, *thank you!*" I push myself back up to see that—of course—the items are gone. Another slip of paper has taken their place.

I've had about enough of this. I pull myself up into a tree, keeping to branches I can reach without jumping. Up one tree, over into another. It's pointless, but so was chasing Clover, and I found her that time. *I also almost died that day.* I push the thought from my mind. I circle the area, winding farther out from the silently agreed upon meeting spot with Misty. Even with the boots and gloves, it isn't long before my arms and legs ache. When I give up, the ground is an impressive distance away.

Memories of my fall turn my knees to water. Reaching for Clover's hand—that moment we both knew I was going down. I should have died. Clover would have been better off if I had. Maybe everyone would be. I press my forehead against the rough tree trunk. Frosty air burns through my nose when I inhale a deep breath. My hands shake against the bark, then the magnetic connection between them and the tree evaporates. Was that thought conscious enough to be a command?

"Reengage gloves." My voice is hollow.

The phantom thought that floated through my mind was illogical. Perhaps dying back then would have helped. Now, what's done is done and I may be the only person who can set any of it right. It's not fair for me to matter now, after everything. But I do. I have to continue on.

Slowly I descend. Shivers rattle my chest despite the warmth provided by the specialized clothing. On the ground, I make one last plea. "Please, Misty. I need to fix my mistakes. It's not like I could capture you even if I wanted to." I sigh and grab the slip of paper she left. "I'll be back next week. I'll keep coming, because you're the only person who might be on my side."

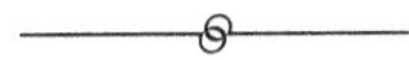

Muffled thuds and grunts reach me as I follow my comm's directions to Nemora. Desperation is muddling my sense. There's no way she would free Clover and Priam. Still, I find myself seeking her out. They all grew up together. Clover is as much a sibling as Priam is to Nemora. She has to have some sympathy for them. Some desire to see them free.

When I round a corner, Nemora comes into view. She twists away from me as her leg slams into a dummy with a force I imagine would knock me unconscious. Stray strands of hair stick to her sweat-dampened face. The same punches and elbow thrusts I saw that night in the woods appear lethal. At the time, I was impressed she was a match for Priam. Now I'm surprised it took her so long to take him down.

The upbringing my cousins had couldn't be more different from mine. Even after Grandfather stepped into my life, he never displayed any interest in physical strength. I'd assumed he raised Ismene and Rocco the same way. I was quite wrong.

Or things took a drastic change after he was exiled.

Nemora huffs out a breath and turns to face me. There's no doubt in my mind she was aware of my presence the moment I saw her. "How can I help you?" Her breaths are surprisingly steady.

"Why do you do this?" This display sidetracks from my intended purpose. "You're all geniuses. You have plenty of ways to hold onto power without physical brutality."

"That's where Kaycie failed, Adwin. Only being smarter than others is just as bad as *only* being physically stronger. We need to be both. We need to be everything. Your leaders created a strong army and left themselves weak. How did that work out for them?"

"There were extenuating circumstances with that."

"There always are." She stretches her hands and rolls her wrists. "We have to be willing to do anything. But that's only useful if we are capable of doing anything." Her gaze scans over me. "I don't suppose you came here to learn such things."

"No, I..." Willing to do anything included fighting and imprisoning her own family. Why did I think she'd falter on that? "I have plenty to learn from you. This doesn't seem like something I'd be cut out for."

"No, I don't think you are." She swings a small towel onto her shoulder, grabs a bottle, and takes a drink.

I step aside at the doorway and follow her out. "Is your training always this intense, or are you letting off steam from your disagreement with Rocco?" It doesn't matter how I ask. Nemora will only tell me if it benefits her.

"This is a difficult time for everyone—domestic and international challenges barraging us alongside family matters. He's stirring things to draw the attention away from Clover. It's unlike him." She shrugs. "Difficult times do strange things to people."

We get into a lift, and I press the button for our floor. "What's so unlike him?" I ask.

"Lying in general. Especially for the purpose of slandering our family."

"Oh. Yes, I thought everything was family first."

"It is."

"Well, I'm sorry you have to deal with that." The door slides open, and I gesture for her to exit ahead of me.

Her lips press together in something that could be interpreted as a slight smile. "The family was glued back together. That usually means we're stronger than we'd ever have been otherwise, but cracks still live underneath the smooth exterior."

If my grandfather cracked the family, I'm trying to smash it to pieces that can never be put back together. Perhaps with this book from the Breck library.

I wish Misty would speak to me, rather than leaving notes after sneak attacks. This last one gives me hope that we're making progress. I read the book she requested twice already. Being a figurehead with no real power affords me as much free time as I want. In fact, I'm certain people are more annoyed when I actively participate. Just the boy in the way while the adults are trying to get things done.

"Hello, Misty. You're welcome to this book without a physical assault." I sit it on a low branch and back away to give her a clearer path to her latest demand. "See?"

"Did you read it?"

The breathy voice sends me spinning and searching for the source, regardless of how idiotic I look. She spoke to me! From wherever she's hiding, she spoke. "Yes, I did. Do you think you'll find something in this history of the mountain and fortress to help us release your friends?"

"What did you find?" Her voice comes from a different direction. I whip my head around to find her standing on a branch, leaning casually against the trunk of the tree she's perched in. Her thin, petite frame contrasts with the way her light eyes pierce me. She looks formidable despite her size. Even from a distance the look sends a chill down my spine.

"There were tunnels under the mountain," I say. "Unfortunately, they were sealed off."

Misty shrugs, her expression cool and unchanging.

"Do you need the book?" It's still sitting where I left it.

"No, I just wanted you to read it."

"Why?"

"You said you wanted my help."

"Help me then."

"I did."

"That"—I point at the book—"does not help. Even if the tunnels are accessible, I can't get Clover and the others out of the prison."

"And you think I can?" Before I can reply, she flips off the branch and drops lightly onto her feet. Her short coiling hair bounces with her landing. Clover said *tree-gymnast* didn't have the same ring to it as tree-walker. It's still my preferred title for these springy women. "If I could get them out, it would already be done."

"Maybe together we can figure something out."

She narrows her eyes—hazel I can see now that she's closer. "You don't strike me as the kind of person who would change his mind. Wasn't locking up your cousins all you thought it would be?"

"I had no idea they were planning an assassination, so I didn't think their punishment would be so severe."

"*They* weren't planning that at all." She cocks her head in accusation and judgement.

No, that was only Priam. Clover wouldn't have been willing to kill Ismene. Was it despite Ismene being his mother or because of it that he wanted to take it so far?

"I know. Can we work together then? I can get you into the fortress to—"

"No. I'm not going into the fortress."

I scrub a hand over my face. "Where do you even live? Surely not out here." I gesture to the forest with a wide sweep of my arm.

A smirk pulls at her lips. "I manage."

"You could go to Kaycie while we figure something out."

An arched eyebrow is all I get for the ridiculous offer.

I sigh. "What do you propose then?"

Her slight shoulders rise and fall with a deep breath. "Bring me whatever you can find on the prison. We'll see what we can come up with."

Finally, we're getting somewhere. "Same time next week?"

She nods. "I do so enjoy our weekly meetings."

"This is the first time you've shown up for one, except to strike me."

"That's my favorite part." She winks, jumps to grab hold of a tree branch, and in a blink, she's flipped up and disappears.

Chapter Twenty-Two

BRAM

Days turn to weeks. Our routine becomes comfortable. And un-comfortable as I grapple with my feelings for Serenity. Denial is over. Who was I kidding?

I'm sure she's not ready for anything resembling a romantic relationship, and I can't risk losing her as a friend. I'd much rather have this than nothing.

Except every day she gravitates toward me more. She prefers having my arm around her, always sits on the couch with her head on my shoulder. Every touch makes me want to push things with her.

Serenity pushes things in a direction that should be completely different, but somehow it all comes back to the same thing.

The involuntary jump of her shoulders when the gun fires is as attractive as anything else she does. Five rounds hit the target, even if they aren't quite at the center. She presses her lips together and her eyebrows bunch toward each other. I drop my earmuffs to my neck before removing hers.

"I'm not very good at this." She gazes down range and sighs. No matter how much she's changed, her perfectionism hasn't faltered.

"Stop beating yourself up. You're not bad, only too tense. Relax." I press her shoulders down, and my hands linger momentarily before I pull them away. The urge to touch her gets stronger every day.

"The recoil scares me."

"It's not *that* strong."

"You're not a good judge." She side-eyes my arms, then releases the empty magazine and replaces it with a full one. Those graceful hands pull the slide back, and it should not be a turn on, but I'm mesmerized. She puts her ear protection back on and looks at me expectantly.

What am I supposed to be doing? Oh.

My brain catches up, and I slide my ear protection back on. Something sparkles in her eyes, and she smirks before turning back toward the target. I'm back to that awkward, idiotic state she used to put me in. It kind of sucks, but I was only out of it because I was half-dead inside. This is better, even if it is a mild form of torture.

Serenity rolls her shoulders and neck as we leave. "This is going to hurt tomorrow."

"What is?" I ask.

She laughs. "Everything."

"You should take a break."

"I will when you do." Her gray eyes bore into me. She knows she can wield her own well-being as a tool to make me care about mine without realizing how deep my feelings for her go. No, she's perceptive about a lot of things, but blind to this. If she knew, she'd make her feelings clear one way or the other. She wouldn't leave me in this place where I overthink every touch and interaction. I can't tell her and make her decide, though. She's got too much shit to work through. And being shut down... actually that wouldn't be as bad as her feeling weird around me afterward.

"Let's take a break then," I say. "What do you want to do tomorrow morning?"

"God, I don't know. What is there to do for fun around here?"

"I'm sure you can think of something while you're playing with the chickens."

"Stop mocking my relationship with my flock." Her indignation isn't an act. She's really grown attached to them.

"I bet they're delicious."

"I will end you if you eat one of my chickens." The smile is always worth teasing her for.

"That's why you're learning to fight, isn't it? To protect them."

"If that's what it comes to, I'll do what I must." She thrusts her elbow toward my gut. I catch it and pull her around, spinning her until she stops with her back against me, and my arm across her.

"The chickens are doomed."

She leans into me as she laughs, and I could stay like this forever. Serenity's body pressed against mine, her violet scent firing off too many memories at once. Bad idea. I twirl her back out.

"I know you don't believe me, but I just can't fight *you*."

Because she doesn't want to hurt me. Hilarious since my skills exceed hers by... a lot. She's okay at it, actually. Fencing translated enough of the strategy, and everything she does looks like a dance. Her body moves so fluidly...

Snap out of it.

"Well, I doubt you'll ever have to fight anyone." *Again.* She escaped the EC that last terrible day in Kaycie, but barely. The thought of her being alone and in trouble might be enough to make me drop my vendetta against Agnar.

"Here's hoping." She grins and splits away from me—toward the chickens she's taken such a weird liking to.

I walk into the house, and the sound of a kitchen cabinet closing triggers me to reach for my gun. My steps are silent, but the tense, stealth routine melts away when Cary comes into view.

She glances at my hand poised over the holster and shakes her head. "I thought people were neighborly out here in the country?"

"Not so neighborly to ignore things like breaking and entering."

She smiles and shrugs. "How are you doing?"

"I'm all right. What are you doing here?"

"It's been a long time. I wanted to check on you." She hops up to sit on the counter. "And things were left kind of... shitty last time I saw you."

"Thanks for reminding me. I'd prefer to forget the entire thing." Because the things they assumed about Serenity were bullshit, and also because it made me realize I'd like some of it to be reality.

"I'm sorry." She sighs. "Yes, I thought you'd end up sleeping with her. I don't agree with Aren, though. I never thought she was a stopgap. I know you really like her, and I want to see you happy."

I lean back against the counter and drop my head back to look at the ceiling. Talking about it makes it real, and I can't afford to do that. I push my annoyance down. She means well. "Thanks, Cary."

"Even though we miss you, take as much time as you need."

My gaze comes back down to land on her. "How is everybody?" I need to get the conversation off me.

"Libby is good. Sophos is getting there. Aren is complicated." *That's the nice way to put it.* "Trav is kind of weird. All the marshals are trying to regain a sense of normalcy. Except, no one knows what normal is anymore. Reid is good, though. I think it was a little weird for him to come out here again, but—"

"Reid is here?"

"Yeah." Her eyes widen, and she bites her lip.

"Where is he?"

"Umm, I don't know."

I scratch my forehead. No wonder Vogue and Frey had such an easy time getting information from her. "Cary..."

"He wanted to talk to Serenity."

My jaw clenches. "Why?"

Chapter Twenty-Three

ADWIN

"We could be on a plush leather sofa. By a fire." I place a metal cube on the rock where Misty and I meet. She's nowhere to be seen, as per usual, but I know she can hear me. I drop to a crouch and feel the air breeze over me.

"He can be taught." Misty folds her legs under herself as she sits. Even on speaking terms, she still saw fit to greet me with physical attacks these last few weeks. January hops into her lap and curls into a ball, using its own tail as a pillow.

I've gotten used to strange. A fox that acts like a lap dog. Being on constant alert for an assault *from my ally*. All standard operating procedure now.

"Will you name the next one February when that one dies?" I tip my chin in the fox's direction.

Misty clutches January to her chest and shoots lightning at me from her eyes. "How dare you!"

"Obviously your life expectancy—"

"Probably isn't great thanks to the company I keep. Did you bring it?"

I sigh and open a holo from the cube. "Be my guest."

Misty purses her lips in concentration as she manipulates screen after screen. Our brief greetings and her demands for different files are all she spares for me. Every muscle on her remains tensed when she's with me. Even when I'm not around, I can't imagine she relaxes much. She has to be on her guard at all times. She won't tell me where she lives or anything about the other tree-walkers. She even seemed reluctant to let me know January's name.

The fox looks at me with narrowed eyes—as suspicious of me as his... *owner* is? Do people own foxes?

"Does this help?" Apparently, I've been a miserable failure at getting her what she needs. It's a special kind of misery to be spoken to like an idiot child by a girl who is a child herself.

"Yes and no." She blinks at the screen and turns toward me. "Yes, it's the information I wanted, but it can't really help. Opening the prison cells would be easy enough, but the camera feeds from them can't be cut. Agents would be on them before they're down the hall."

"There has to be some way to manipulate the feed."

"Maybe for one of the three Agnar geniuses." Her lips quirk. "No offense." Not that she likely cares if I'm offended by her reminder that my three cousins are smarter than me. I'd argue nature versus nurture, but what's the point? "It's not like we could paste a picture of them over the camera and move on. There has to be movement, vital signs... It's beyond my capabilities."

"But it could be done."

Her expression sinks into an exasperated look. "If I can't do it, you certainly—"

"Not me. I know, I'm useless. Thank you. But not *everyone* from Kaycie is as inept as I am."

She rubs her forehead. I don't know if she's not saying that Kaycians couldn't possibly be more capable than her because she's trying to be nice or because explaining that to me is beneath her.

"Come with me to Kaycie."

Her chin snaps up, and she looks at me wide-eyed.

"Talk to the people who might be able to do it. Explain it to them to see if they can do anything."

Her fingers weave into January's fur as she contemplates.

"I promise you'll be safe. I'll get you back here as soon as possible."

I wish I had a clue as to what she's thinking about. What she's considering and what I might say to convince her. Finally she makes eye contact with me again. "Fine. Schedule the meeting."

My stomach sinks. Only half this battle is won. Now I need to get Vogue to agree. And that's only to find out *if* this scheme is even possible.

Why can't anything be easy?

Leaves crunch under my feet as I pace my mother's yard. The climate difference within the protection of the dome is staggering. Though, I can't say I agree with Clover's idea that the winter outside is desirable.

What am I nervous for? Misty watched me turn in her brother and friends, and she's willing to work with me. I can get Vogue on my side.

I bounce on my heels while the call goes through. Except it doesn't. She didn't answer. This isn't going to work.

It has to! I call again.

"What do you want?" Her voice comes to me as a hushed reprimand.

"Hello, Vogue. Hope you're doing well."

"Cut the pleasantries, Adwin. What do you want?"

"The same thing I wanted before." Not that I would repeat it over comms.

"Well, what I want is to never have to speak to you again."

I drop my head back, letting the sun warm my face. "After you help me, that'll be just fine."

"In what universe do you think I'd do anything for the person who ruined everything? Our lives are a disaster now, and it's because of you. I realize you've never cared about anyone, but some of us actually value our human connections, and to have them all lost or shredded leaves me in no mood to help you!"

I press fingertips into my temples. She can't expect me to bring back the dead. "Is Serenity still keeping to herself?" It's the only thing that would rattle Vogue like this.

A hiss whispers through. *"She couldn't even stand to stay here. She's been gone for months."*

"What? Why didn't you tell me she was out and about?"

"Because it is none of your damn business!"

"Where is she?"

Chapter Twenty-Four
SERENITY

Sounds like the chickens are in a tizzy. Dorothy is out of the coop, bobbing her head back and forth as she examines me.

"What are you doing?" I pick her up and stroke her bronze and blue feathers. "I don't know how good your hearing is, but Bram was kidding. He's not going to eat you. Don't run away." We get around to the other side, and I jump when I spot an unfamiliar figure. Wait. Maybe not completely unfamiliar. "Reid?"

"Hi." He pushes his chocolate brown hair out of his face. It's getting long. "Sorry to surprise you like that."

"No, it's fine." I put Dorothy away and turn to him. Last time I saw him he was a marshal. By the time he woke up, our mental states had basically switched.

"Even though we've never formally met, I feel like I know you," he says.

I can't exactly reciprocate the sentiment. All I know is that Carista practiced fighting with him when he was a marshal and somehow lived to tell the tale.

"Dixon talks about you a lot," he continues.

"Oh. Do you see him much?" My stomach twists at the thought of the friends I've cut myself off from. I miss them, but it's so hard...

"Yeah." His cheeks flush a little. "A lot actually."

I suck in a quick breath and feel immediately brighter. "That's great!" Now I picture him with Dixon. Reid is cute despite being brawny. He seems shy, which would be adorable alongside Dixon's zealous personality. Awe, I want to dish about this with Dixon.

"It is great," he says, smiling at the ground. "We've all got so much to process, and not doing it alone helps."

"Absolutely."

"It's great Bram has you, now. He was in rough shape."

"I'm glad we have each other, too." The words come out before I think about what I'm saying. They're true, but does he think Bram has me the way he has Dixon? "Wait, you don't—"

"Reid!"

Carista's voice pulls his attention past me. I look over my shoulder in that direction.

"It's time to go," she grumbles. "Hi, Serenity."

"Hi." My thoughts couldn't be further from this interaction. Do they think... Bram and me?

"It was good to see you," Reid says.

I think I nod or mumble some kind of response, but I'm in a fog. It hangs over me the rest of the day. Questions whisper through me. Memories replay in a new filter.

Have we been building a relationship beyond friendship?

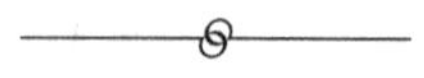

Water pouring on me used to elicit sad memories, but now all it does is soothe sore muscles. The entire rabbit hole I spent the day in was crazy. Bram and I aren't being romantic; we're really good friends.

Good friends who need each other a lot, because we've both been through incredible tragedies. Sure, he's always on my mind. Of course, I gravitate toward him. It's not... No. God, if sledding brings on guilt for having fun, I can only imagine what that would do. Not a problem. We're not going there. This is just another example of people always assuming I'm *with* whatever guy happens to be next to me.

When I come out of the bathroom, Bram looks at me curiously from the living room. "That was a long shower."

"I was hoping the hot water would help my shoulders."

"Did it?"

"Not really." I plop down between his legs on the sofa. "It's your fault. You fix it." I tie my wet hair up in a knot to give him access.

"It's not *my* fault. I told you not to be so tense." His warm hands slide up my shoulders even as he argues with me. "And this was all your idea."

"Don't muddle things with facts when I'm blaming you for my stupidity." His thumbs press up my neck, and a sigh escapes me. "You won't break me," I say.

He increases the pressure on my neck and shoulders, and it's a miracle I remain upright. I could just melt here. Even with the added force, Bram is surprisingly gentle. I've watched his hands lift weights the size of me, come near putting a hole in a punching bag, and shoot guns with terrifying precision. That his hands can also be so tender is amazing. But that's always been Bram, I guess. So much more than he appears.

"Whoever's fault it is," he says, "you're doing awesome. You should be proud of yourself."

"Thanks." I do enjoy the look on his face when I shoot a gun—impressed and surprised. But is it just that, or is there heat in that gaze too? As he rubs circles into my muscles, the way his hands linger on me when we're training flashes through my mind. How much do I like that? *Oh, here I go down the rabbit hole again.*

That's not it, though.

"I don't know how I'd have gotten through all this without you." The thought finds words and slips out.

"Me neither."

I lean back against him, and he wraps his arms around me. This feels good—right. Being close to him is a comfort, but does it also set off butterflies in my stomach?

Okay, it does *now,* but that's because I'm thinking about it. And really, why would he want that? I don't even know why I'm the person to help him deal with all the trauma he's faced. "I haven't done anything for you." Again, his presence weakens the filter between my mind and mouth.

"Are you kidding?" He turns me toward him, sitting me on his lap. "You shook me out of my funk. You got me out of Lawson."

"That was only because you were worried about me."

"So what if it was? Why did you wake up from your trance and leave Leavenworth?"

My gaze falls to my knees. "Because I was worried about you."

"Don't ever feel guilty for anything I do for you, Serenity. I still feel bad that I didn't go to you first." His hand strokes up and down my lower back, and his eyes soften as they look into mine. "I'm sorry you've gone through so much."

Tears sting my eyes. "You've been through more."

"I'm used to losing the good things in my life."

"That's horrible. You shouldn't resign yourself to being unhappy."

His throat bobs. "I'm pretty happy right now."

Oh my gosh, we are more than friends.

How did I not see it before? Hesitant longing radiates from him. The flames in his eyes are not anger. How long has that been the case? Memories flash before me. I try to pinpoint it, but that's not what matters now, is it? He's attracted to me, and I was too lost in my own head to notice.

I told him I'd be whatever he needed me to be. Is this what he needs? Can I give that? I wouldn't have thought myself capable. It's a lot to think about. What I do know is Bram means the world to me. He woke me up and got me nearly back to normal.

"Me too. I'm happier than I thought I could be." That's a fact I wouldn't have questioned this morning, but the reasons behind it are confusing and... exciting now.

I'd feel guilty for even thinking about it, but didn't Bram give me permission to be happy? Will he also be the source of it in a bigger way than I thought? My gaze flicks to his lips, and the need to know spirals through me.

If he kissed me, the floodgates would open, and I'd welcome the rush.

There are only two ways this ends. One risks ruining the most important friendship I currently have, and I'm a coward, so I go with the awkward way. "I'm also more tired than I ever thought I could be." I stand up, feeling like I'm coming up for air. "I'm going to bed. Goodnight."

As I walk away, I swear I hear him release a breath before he speaks. "Can I ask you a question?"

I swallow before turning around. "Do I get to ask one too?"

"Sure."

"Okay, then. What's your question?" Fear courses through me. I might not know how to answer. Is he going to ask me how I feel about him? I don't know exactly.

"When we 'met' at the compact signing, what did you think about me? Before you realized who I was and accused me of kidnapping Vogue."

I relax, but only a little. "That's what you're using your question on?"

He nods. "You were terrified the first time we met. I'm curious how the different circumstance affected it."

That ridiculous event. Me in a ballgown, unaware I had lost months of my memories. Bram had taken me to Union Station before, but I didn't remember. Then I was there, and he showed up to rescue me.

My skin prickles. "I thought you were very attractive."

I turn on my heel and go to my room. Door closed, I roll my shoulders, which are more tense now than they were before the massage.

I watch the door, half expecting the knob to turn or a knock to sound. Not just expecting—wanting. I want Bram to come to my bedroom. *Wow.* These kinds of feelings aren't lost to me after all. How far do they go, though? How far do I want to go? Did I drop that information and walk out as an invitation? *Maybe.* It's true, though. Behind two veils of amnesia, my first feeling when Bram and I met that day was allure.

He doesn't come. Eventually, I shake off the tension and get into bed.

I don't get much sleep. Nightmares aren't the problem anymore. My dreams are quite different now—happy dreams. I still wake up with my heart racing far too early in the morning. I give up, get out of bed, throw on jeans and a T-shirt, and get outside. I need to get my body moving.

Chapter Twenty-Five

BRAM

My no coffee rule might need to be broken today. Between over-analyzing every move Serenity made, freaking out over my actions, worrying about our friendship, guessing about her thoughts, and burying the *painful* want I had last night, I was way too busy to sleep.

I can't believe Cary sicced Reid on Serenity like that. All this time trying to hide my feelings to keep her from being in an uncomfortable position—blown.

"She doesn't recognize when people have genuine romantic feelings for her."

"You came a long way to tell me shit I already know, Cary."

"Vogue thinks it's because everyone has always faked interest in her or were interested in her for the wrong reasons."

"Your new friendship with Vogue isn't surprising, since you've picked up butting into stuff that doesn't concern you."

She rolled her eyes. "I'm just trying to open her eyes to the possibility. It's up to her what she does with that. She has no idea what's going on!"

"Nothing is going on!"

"Are you really okay with that?"

When I come out of my room, Serenity's door is open, but she's not in there. She's not in the house at all.

Shit, last night made it weird. I messed up. Typical. Carista got me wrapped up in my head, and Serenity completely broke my ability to conceal anything. I might as well tattoo my feelings across my forehead. It felt like she wanted it too, at least I think she did. I've seen her soft side. Last night was—different. She looked at me like she was seeing me for the first time. Kind of like when we 'met' for the second time at Union Station, except this time wasn't painful. Was it attraction both times?

God, I wanted to kiss her. She was so close, right there in my arms, it would have been easy to pull her in. I think she felt the same, but I chickened out. Then her answer to that question, walking away without another word. I wanted to follow her. Needed to. I couldn't make my feet carry me there. What would I have even said? Did we need words?

Now she's gone, so it's probably for the best nothing happened. Like an idiot, I've scared her off.

I go searching and find Serenity sitting behind the chicken coop looking up at the clouds, a basket of eggs next to her. I thought she'd be wildly out of place here, but somehow she fits. When she hears my footsteps, she looks up and smiles. "Hi."

Okay, that's a good start. "Hey. Is this patch of dirt taken?"

"Just don't crush my eggs." She moves the basket to her other side so I can sit.

I do—close enough for our arms and legs to touch between us. Because I'm a dumbass and I can't control this anymore. How she feels calm around these damn birds is beyond me. I swear they're growling. "How are the chickens?"

She shakes her head. "Megan and Robin keep pecking at each other. I don't know what to do with them."

Better that she dwells on this than anything else, I guess. "How are you doing?"

She glares at me under raised eyebrows. "We had a deal, and you used up your question."

"That is a perfectly innocent and normal question." But the reminder of her answer to my other question makes my gut tingle.

"I'm fine." She shrugs it off, just as willful as when we first met.

Now it's my turn to glare at her.

"That is a perfectly innocent and normal answer," she says.

I tilt my face toward the sun and close my eyes. "Don't be an egg. That's my thing."

"What?"

"The boiling water." I reach around her—all too aware of how close her warm skin is to my face—to grab an egg. "You were never meant to hole up in a shell."

"It works well enough for you." She nudges my arm with her shoulder. "But I think I'm cracking you."

"Is that so?"

She nods without looking at me.

"And what do you think you'll find inside?" *Remember the idea to deescalate this situation? Nope. Okay.*

She turns to me. Her eyes drag down my body and back up to my eyes. My skin prickles under her gaze. "I don't know," she says.

My heartbeat picks up. How do we keep landing here? Why can't I manage a moment with her without the air buzzing between us? I'm dangerously close to pushing us into a new zone. If that happens, I don't know if we'll be able to get back to our comfort level. I should stop.

"I know what's under your shell." I roll the egg in my hand.

"Do you now?" Her gray eyes are going to burn a hole through me.

"Sure. You're still soft."

Before she can respond, I smash the egg onto her head.

As she takes the world's most dramatic gasp, I burst into a fit of laughter. That ought to be stupid enough to derail this tension train.

"What the hell was that?" she screeches as egg and shell run down her face. She wipes it off and flicks it at me. "You're such an ass!"

I'm laughing too hard to respond. I can't even look at her, so I don't see her grab an egg. I just feel it crush onto my head before she punches my arm.

"I don't know what's worse! Having to wash eggshell out of my hair or wasting the eggs! That is *so rude* to the chickens!"

I swallow back my laughter. "If the chickens see you like this, they'll think it's worth it."

"Oh, really? How do I look?"

My gaze takes a long, slow journey up and down her body, from her boots, to the dirty jeans, the T-shirt that hugs her form, and her face—flushed and alive and smeared with egg. "You look perfect."

The tension train careens into me. Problem *not* solved.

She blinks slowly. "Give me your shirt."

"Excuse me?"

She holds out her hand. I narrow my eyes, then do as she says. I pull my T-shirt over my head and hand it over. She uses it to wipe off her face and scoots closer to wipe egg off me. I inhale deeply, tempted by the scent of her sun-warmed skin. She leans closer, pressing her hand onto my thigh. Her eyes trace down my bare torso. Heat washes over my neck.

"Now you look perfect." Her voice is lower and more sultry than I've ever heard it before. She's too close. Last night's dare returns, glimmering in her eyes. I wasn't sure then. This though...

This is trouble, and I don't even care.

I pull her against me, and her mouth opens for mine when our lips meet. *Holy shit, I'm kissing Serenity.* Her lips are soft, but she kisses me with hunger, like she's been dying to do this. The length of time I've thought about doing this simultaneously feels like forever and a snap. A time when I didn't know how she tasted is already forgotten. Fire burns me up—more consuming than the flames of rage I had been harboring. These lick through me, igniting everywhere our skin connects.

She pulls a hand down my chest and sighs against me. The sound shatters the meager semblance of self-control I still had. I shove the basket away as I lay her down, but it spills, and she hits the ground with a squishy *crunch*.

She tenses and covers another gasp before laughter erupts from her.

Propped over her on my elbows, I drop my face to her shoulder and laugh too. Having her body pressed against mine and shaking as she suppresses giggles instead of sobs is... everything.

"That's awful." Serenity sniffles and wipes her eyes. Seeing her this carefree is worth whatever shift may have just happened between us.

"Normally, I would think it's a very bad sign for you to be laughing when we're in this position."

She smirks at me—the intensity gone, but the spark is still there. "I bet you can make me stop laughing."

A groan rolls through my throat at the invitation, but the comedic relief brought me back to my sense enough to realize this is a terrible idea. Logistically for sure, not to mention what's at stake.

"You don't mean that," I say.

She drags a finger down the side of my neck. "I do though."

Her touch, her words, are everything I've hoped for, but I slam on the brakes. I must be some exceptional kind of stupid. "Maybe some other time." I indulge and brush a kiss on her collar bone before sitting up.

She props herself up on her elbows and looks at me indignantly. "Am I not attractive when there is literally egg on my face? Because I might point out it's your fault."

"You're *very* attractive, *especially* with egg on your face. I ruined my plan with that move."

She sits up and frowns when she glances over her shoulder at the mess behind her. "What plan would that have been?"

"The plan to not act on my desires."

"Why would you do that?" Her gaze holds mine with innocent curiosity. Like it's that easy.

Because I don't know if you've healed enough. Because even this taste of you will leave me hollowed out if I can't keep having it. Because it would be the sweetest torture to get you back on your feet only to watch you walk away, and I'm too selfish.

I don't say any of that—for both our sakes.

"Because if we're going to do this, it's not going to be rushed behind a chicken coop where anyone could walk up and ruin it." I slide my hand up her thigh and let it rest at the curve of her waist. "We'd need to take our time... and enjoy it." Her cheeks flush red, and I want nothing more than to feel every silky inch of her skin, but I pull back. "Only if you're sure."

I stand and offer my hand to help her up. She stands without saying a word.

"I don't want to mess this up," I say.

She blinks a few times, and her demeanor relaxes. "I'm sure you aren't *that* bad at it." She grins and walks off toward the house. Over her shoulder she says, "Lucky for you, I don't have anything to compare it to."

I watch her walk away—her hair and back a mess of crushed eggs. The idea to follow her and help wash it out knots my stomach. Except... *She doesn't have* anything *to compare it to?*

Chapter Twenty-Six
SERENITY

The moment the door closes, I lean back against it. Egg shells and goo squish against me again. Despite the mess, a nervous giggle slips through my lips. My lips which were just on Bram's. I can't believe that just happened. And it was so... good—and fun and hot and right. I feel lighter, though also somewhat unnerved. When is the last time either of us laughed like that?

Behind closed eyes I replay the scene. I wanted more. I still do.

I rub my lips together; the ghost of his kiss lingers on them. If I had known how good it would feel, I would have done that a long time ago. Bram said he was trying not to act on his desires. How long has he been resisting these urges? My heart flutters thinking about it. The only thing more surprising than how my view of Bram may be changed, is my own behavior. Who was that bold, confident woman? I'm tempted to think I was acting, but it wasn't intentional. I got lost in the moment—in Bram—and that's what transpired. I was about ready to broach the subject when he threw the moment away with that ridiculous stunt.

A shudder courses through me. I push off the door and walk to the bathroom. After I turn on the shower and peel off my filthy shirt, I smile at my egg-filled hair in the mirror.

The way his eyes trailed over me when he said I looked perfect makes me squirm just thinking about it. He looked like he was giving up, giving in, so I did too. In the shower, I pull my fingers through my hair, extracting the gritty eggshells tangled through it. Brazen though it was, demanding Bram's shirt was absolutely worth it. He is so gorgeous it would be painful if that body hadn't pressed up against mine. The feel of his hands on me—strong and longing. I want to let those hands explore me.

Clean, dressed, and as anxious as I've ever been in a positive way, I leave the bathroom committed to holding onto my boldness. Bram and I need to let ourselves have what we want. We deserve it. We should figure out what exactly that is… together. But when I find Bram in the living room, all laughter gone from his face, my excitement turns to dread.

"I just got a call," he says. "We need to go to Leavenworth."

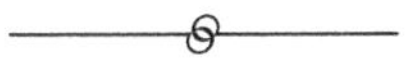

My concern about where Bram and I are symbolically headed is buried deep under distress about where we are literally going. My fingers tap away on my lap, but I scarcely hear the tune. I close my eyes rather than watching as we barrel farther from our hideaway and closer to a place with misery woven into its memory.

Bram's hand wraps around mine. I open my eyes and frown at the worry creasing his face.

"I don't want to be there. This escape has been… great." I drop my gaze, unsure whether he wants this morning's events to be included in that or not. "I'm scared that being back with everyone is going to make it feel like we were just turning a blind eye and abandoning them."

Seeing their faces might serve as a reminder of what a terrible friend I've been, or how fickle my heart is...

Bram squeezes my hand. "They spent months trying to breathe life back into you. They won't be upset about you taking care of yourself."

Looking at our intertwined hands, I can't help but wonder if there is a limit to how much better I should be at this point. What will Krisalyn think? I take my hand back and run my fingers through my hair. "Why does Adwin even want to see me? I have no power."

His palm lingers on my thigh a moment before he moves it to the steering wheel. "I guess you'll be the first to find out."

Leavenworth looms ahead, and my stomach drops. When we're close enough to see Vogue waiting for us, the dread dissipates.

Tears squeeze out of my eyes as we hug. "I'm so happy to see you." She pulls back and holds my shoulders at arm's length. "You look fantastic. Sun-kissed and strong and—" She hugs me again. "It was so hard to stay away, but I'm thrilled you're doing better."

"I'm sorry I stayed away so long." We release each other and walk arm-in-arm into the base. Bram is already ahead of us. It's an effort to keep my attention on Vogue rather than watch him. "I'm surprised you didn't come after me."

"Krisalyn wouldn't let me. Clearly nothing we were doing was helpful."

"That's not your fault. There wasn't anything you could have done. Really."

She restrains herself to a sad smile. Will Vogue be upset that she wasn't the one able to get through to me—my best friend who I've gone through everything with? What will she think of me if I not only moved past my loss, but also my love? Love that was held for her own girlfriend's best friend.

"How is Krisalyn?"

"She's doing well. After all our close calls, I'm a bit of a clingy, needy mess, but she's tolerating me."

I lean into her shoulder. "I for one, would love to see the great Vogue Taylor be a clingy mess. Krisalyn is a miraculous person to bring that out in you. I'm glad you found each other."

"Thanks." She barely whispers it. We're being too careful, trying not to say the wrong thing, or stumble across something that will upset the other. I never thought anything with Vogue could be uncomfortable. I hate this feeling of walking on eggshells.

There are other more pleasant things that can happen on eggshells. My stomach tumbles, and my cheeks warm. Without the extenuating circumstances, Vogue would eat that story up. Part of me wishes we could giggle about it together. The other part enjoys having this secret with Bram. Or I would if I knew where we stood on the matter. There's no time to worry about that now.

Dixon is the first one to me. "My love has returned," he says as he pulls me into a hug. "And hallelujah your hair is getting long again."

"It grew fast just for you."

Krisalyn is more reserved. Has she blamed me for Jase's death as much as I blamed myself? Frey is easier—cool as a cucumber, as per usual. And just like that, we're back together.

"So," I say, "no theories on why Adwin wants to see me?"

Vogue sighs. "I offered to take the meeting, but alas, I have to assume he's afraid to be near me. In which case, he's finally getting smart."

Krisalyn shrugs. "We don't know, but he isn't here yet."

"While you wait," Dixon says, "I have a present for you." He leads me away from the rest of our friends and into the studio where my mother and I fenced during our first stay in Leavenworth. "Ever since

I saw you take down that marshal at the EC, I've been dying to see you with a real sword."

"Technically you took down the marshal. And me in the process." Blacking out in the middle of a fight and waking up to my friends was quite the experience.

"You were holding your own. Anyway, I love that you can handle a sword, but swords aren't exactly convenient to carry around, hence you had to improvise at the EC. Never again! I made this." The item he places in my hand looks like a large silver pen. It's heavier than it appears. Dixon steps back and says, "Point it away from us. Now, do you feel the slightly soft depression?" I nod. "Press it."

I do, and a thin blade shoots forward the familiar thirty-five inches from the grip. "Dixon! How on earth?"

"Do you think you'd understand if I explained it?"

"Nope."

His smile brings me right back to my living room in the city. Simple times hanging out. "Give it a swish, or whatever you do with it."

Again, I do as he says. The shape of the grip will take a little getting used to, but it's balanced beautifully. "I'm guessing this is sharper than the ones I usually play with?"

A devious smile fills his face. He pulls a piece of paper from his pocket and hands it to me. The blade slices through it as easily as the air. "What do you think I'll be doing, Dixon?"

"When have we ever successfully predicted what kind of trouble we're going to get into? I just want you to be prepared for anything." I press the hidden button again, and the blade retracts. "It isn't affected by EMPs, it isn't recognizable to metal detection or anything, and you can carry it in your pocket. Furthermore, it only opens to your fingerprints." He taps the button, and nothing happens.

"Thank you. I appreciate you thinking of me."

"Of course. A long sabbatical can't make me forget you." He winks.

I throw my arms around him for a tight hug. "I missed you."

"I missed you too. Way before you physically left." We release each other and he looks at me warmly. "It's nice to have you *really* back."

I want to ask him about Reid, but what if he asks me about Bram in return? I don't even know where we stand, never mind that I don't know how the group will react.

Dixon leaves me to get used to the feel of my new toy. I put the VR mask on and get to it. The deficiencies for lack of practice are almost made up for by my increased strength. It feels good to have a sword in my hand again. Bram will be thrilled to finally bear witness to this. But it's not Bram's voice that interrupts me.

Chapter Twenty-Seven

ADWIN

Serenity spins, stopping with her back toward me again. Or at least, this should be Serenity. I'm not sure I believe it's her. She looks too strong swinging that sword to be the girl I dated in a previous life. Back when I thought I had problems and secrets, but hardly knew the definition of the words. Convincing Vogue to ask Serenity to meet with me was more drama than I ever had to deal with in Kaycie before all of this.

The VR mask she wears keeps her from seeing me, so I have to announce my presence.

"Hello, Serenity."

She comes to an abrupt stop, tensing from head to toe. Slowly she removes the mask and turns to look at me. I knew she wouldn't be as friendly as she was the last time I saw her now that her memories have returned. This is still more hostility than I expected. It's more than she had toward me before everything went to hell.

"Adwin,"—her voice drips with animosity—"I can't imagine why you'd want to see me. I've never been as interesting as, oh I don't know, Liam."

The hairs on my neck stand on edge. That's the least of what I need to hide right now but trusting Misty's cloak to keep this conversation private still unnerves me. "Oh, you know about that."

"Indeed I do. You told me yourself while you were—I think—drugged and climbing trees."

Damnit, Nemora.

She rests the blade on her shoulder, and my long-held theory that she would be more cooperative than Vogue feels flimsy. "Why were you even dating me?"

"I was encouraged to keep an eye on you. Perhaps unite our families."

An incredulous breath puffs from her lips. "How very Medieval of you."

"Says the woman with a sword."

She tosses the sword lazily, letting it swing in a circle before catching it again. "I think the woman with the sword can say whatever she pleases."

"Fair enough."

"What do you want? I hope you don't expect me to curtsy or something."

"Far from it. I have no interest in ruling Kaycie." Her eye roll isn't surprising. "I want to remove Ismene from power. I believe that would serve both countries well."

"She's your aunt."

"Half."

"What does this have to do with me?"

"It's not only you. Can we sit, please? Maybe get a drink."

"I'm not having a drink with you." She stalks to a bench by the wall and sits.

I follow behind her. "Serenity, listen, my cousin is imprisoned in Montica. I need help freeing her."

Her eyes shift back and forth. "Wouldn't your cousin be Montican royalty?"

"Not what they call themselves, but yes."

"What did she do to land in prison?"

"Kaycie isn't the only place with rebellion issues."

She purses her lips. "A relative of *yours.* A rebel?"

"Hard to believe, I know. But if she gets out, she can relieve Montica of Ismene, then you and all of Kaycie can be free of me."

"You wouldn't give up your own power." She stands and glides away. "I don't know what kind of trap you're setting, but I'm not falling for it. If you want to give Kaycie back, step down."

"I can't while Ismene rules. It's either me or her until she's out of the picture."

"Why should I believe you're on our side?"

"Kaycie is my *home*. Do you think I'm pleased they destroyed so much of it?"

She sneers. "You have no idea how much they destroyed."

"Are you angry? Good. Do something about it!" She wrings her hands, and I continue. "Do you have any idea how miserable it is to act like you're allying with a person you hate?"

"Worse than dating a person you hate?"

"I never hated you."

"You only thought I was an idiot."

God, how long did I speak to her under that damned drug? "I thought you were sweet and lovely, and better than most of Kaycian society, but honestly, you know now that Kaycians are generally..."

"Idiots?"

When did she become *this* difficult? "Will you help me or not? I need Vogue, and you're the only one who can convince her."

"It's not up to me. I can't control her. I'll ask *everyone* to meet with us so we can decide if this is something we can and want to do, together."

"Who is *everyone*? I only need the hackers who took down Leavenworth."

"We are a package deal. We work together, or we don't work at all."

It wasn't so long ago that Serenity and I watched as our elders tore at each other's throats in this meeting room. *Everyone* turns out to be five of the six original Kaycian rebels (all but Jase), the marshal who wasn't really a marshal in service to Sophos, and a couple of other marshals who are, apparently, the brothers of the girl Sophos brought to Montica. She greets me with a sneer as she walks in.

"I'm sorry, I don't believe we had the pleasure of meeting when you came to visit Montica. I'm Adwin." I extend my hand, but hers flies up to slap my face.

"I don't care if you were drugged. You thought the terrible things you said." She sits while Sophos' guard—Brad?—grins at her side.

I could kill *Nemora.* Misty's eyes sparkle as she looks at up at me, but she keeps her expression neutral. I can only guess that everyone's obvious disdain for me makes them more viable allies in her eyes. I'm even less popular here than I was in Montica when I first arrived. "Can we just..."

"Of course," Serenity says. "Adwin is here as a...*friend.*" Her reluctance to say the word is not hidden *at all.* "We may have common goals, and we'll need to decide if we can and want to work with him." She gestures to me and takes a seat.

"Thank you all for meeting with me. This is Misty. She's from Montica and worked with the group who was planning Ismene's takedown. I know you all think I'm the enemy, but that's not the case. I'm stuck with Ismene and Montica, just like the rest of you. This group within Montica is both eager to and capable of taking Ismene down, but I need your help to release them. They've been imprisoned these five months."

Dixon leans into his elbow and cocks his head. "Oh *really?*"

Vogue whips her head in his direction. "Don't start."

Dixon gapes at her. "I missed our chance for a prison break before!"

Serenity stifles a laugh and turns to me. "You want to free people who are trying to take down *your family?*"

"The rebels are my family too."

Vogue picks at her nails lazily. "If they're so capable, how did they get caught." *God, she's a cocky one.*

I take a deep breath. Nothing about this sounds good. "I... turned them in to Ismene's daughter."

"Oh, this just gets better and better," Frey says.

"I didn't realize how corrupt Ismene is. It was before she leveled half of Kaycie. My cousin is the only person who can strip Ismene of her power."

"I thought it was your cousin who arrested the rebels?" Dixon says.

After a breakdown of my family tree and whose side everyone is on, Carista says, "You handed Clover over to them?"

"You know her?" one of her brothers asks her.

"She was the pilot who greeted us when we went to Montica."

"If he betrayed his own cousin..."

I don't even care who said it. "Look, I figured the worst they'd get was house arrest, but things escalated quickly. One of Clover's own team has trusted me enough to work with me to release them." I gesture toward Misty. "Will *you* or won't you? Don't forget, I've kept Ismene away from you all this time."

A room full of people glance at each other silently. Krisalyn Laska speaks for the group. "What would you be asking of us?"

Chapter Twenty-Eight

BRAM

Misty's silence isn't nervousness or shyness. She looks at us like she's determining our worth. The worst part is she's probably the youngest person in the room. Do all Monticans think themselves so far above us?

When she does speak, her voice is somehow airy and firm at the same time. "Adwin believes some of you have the advanced programming and hacking skills needed to orchestrate this break out."

Vogue and Frey's gazes meet in a conspiratorial look. I had almost forgotten how much their combined egos grate on my nerves.

Frey fixes an intent look on Misty which would make most girls blush—her face remains impassive. "We specialize in making trouble. What do you need?"

After a lengthy and technical explanation, Adwin and Misty leave to let us discuss amongst ourselves. The moment they're out of the room, I lean toward Cary. "Thank you for hitting him. If I had done it, it would have been messier."

"He's an asshole." She says it too loudly and gets a variety of grins and smirks from around the room.

"Yes, we know he's an asshole," Frey says, "but do we believe him?"

Most eyes go to Serenity. She knew him best. She crosses her arms and shrugs. "In my experience, he didn't actively lie or trick me. He just omitted information."

A lot of information.

"Even if everything he said is true,"—Krisalyn looks wide-eyed at Vogue—"we cannot send Vogue in alone like he's suggesting."

"Of course not," I say. "She needs protection."

Vogue rolls her eyes. "I'm not helpless."

"I didn't say you were. You're one of the most dangerous people in this room—in most rooms—just not when faced with a physical attack."

She preens, and I remind myself her ego does *not* need any help.

Carista sighs. "Well, if our lovely smooth-faced boys can't go, I guess that means me."

The girls can look Montican. The guys, not so much.

"You're not the only woman here who can fight." Serenity rolls her shoulders back. "I'll go, too."

I rub my forehead. Her friends look at me with wide eyes, waiting for me to argue, but I can't.

Awkward, quiet agreement happens, and Adwin and Misty are invited back in.

Frey crosses his arms. "Look, we can probably do it, but it sounds like we'd be taking big risks and there isn't much in it for us."

Adwin folds his hands together. "I'm not offering you any less than the uprising did. There's nothing left to give besides the hope that things will be better afterward."

That was good enough when someone we trusted asked us, although in hindsight, we shouldn't have trusted Sophos. It's going to have to be enough. Plans are made, and as people start to leave, my cuff vibrates with a message from Vogue. She and I remain seated as the rest of the room clears. Serenity looks at me curiously, then averts her eyes and leaves. It's strange not being alone together. Having other people around changes our dynamic. Does being around everyone make her regret what happened—God, just this morning? How has so much changed in such a short time?

When Vogue and I are alone she says, "Since *when* is Serenity someone we send in as a fighter?"

"Since she spent the last two months training with me."

She presses the heels of her hands over her eyes. "I just got her back. How can you volunteer her for this?"

"I didn't. She wants to do it. I would have fought about it if she couldn't handle it." I mean, I want to.

"She can?" I nod. "You're still worried enough to make sure you're close by."

Having faith in Serenity is not the same as being able to calmly watch her walk into trouble. Of course I have to be close enough to help her if it comes to it. Travick has to go fly the plane anyway. I'll stay on board while the girls go into the fortress. Just in case.

Vogue sighs when I don't bother responding. "I'd like to interrogate you about the months you've been hoarding my best friend, but she'll tell me if she wants to. Despite my discomfort over not knowing everything, whatever happened worked. Thank you."

"I needed her just as much."

Maybe all these catastrophes have chilled Vogue out. Maybe I can ask her for clarification on... "Hey, Serenity told you about the weird call with Adwin last year, right?"

Vogue sighs. "Yes. I'm jealous that Carista was the one to hit him."

"Me too. Anyway, the... embarrassing part." The moment when Adwin said he was glad Serenity was 'clinging to her virginity,' the way she flushed—I was embarrassed for her. But a relief I didn't think

I needed ran through me that he hadn't been with her. "Serenity made a comment that sounded like..."—*Holy shit, how do I even say this?*—"that's still true, which didn't make sense, because... Jase..."

Vogue's eyes light up with mischief. Nope, this hasn't chilled her out. *Shit, shit, shit.* She's going to run wild with this.

"Are you asking me... if Serenity is a virgin?" Her delight in making me uncomfortable is the worst part.

"No." I push away from the table and stand. "I'm not asking you anything. Bye."

"No, no, no. Why do you want to know that?" Covering her mouth with her hands does nothing to hide her giddiness.

"I don't." *Ugh, kill me.* "She's been mourning Jase, and I wondered about how... *close* they were."

"First of all, it's very bold of you to assume I know such intimate details about her. Secondly, of course I know such intimate details about her, but it would break *every rule* to talk about it." She stands and slinks toward the door, fixing me with a hard stare. "Fortunately, I don't have to worry about a conflict of interest here, because nothing *happened* to talk about."

Vogue leaves. Her meaning is clear enough. Serenity did *not* have sex with Jase. I don't miss the warning in her tone: tread carefully.

The day that started with kissing Serenity, ends by being the first time I don't say goodnight to her since we were reunited. Well, last night we were too strung up to say goodnight.

We only have a couple of days to get ready to go to Montica, and Serenity needs to focus. So I don't even look for her, I go straight to my assigned hotel room and drop onto the bed. Thanks to my lack of sleep last night, I fall asleep quickly, but my dreams are so much more realistic now that I know the feel of Serenity's lips.

She's easy enough to find in the morning—already sweating as she lays into a punching bag.

"Good morning."

She whips toward me so fast her ponytail hits her in the face. "Hi." She drops her chin to her chest and stretches her fingers.

"Nervous about Wednesday?"

"Wouldn't it be idiotic not to be?" Of course she should be nervous, but knowing she needs to be on high alert doesn't stop the instinct to calm her.

"Yeah, I guess." I put a water bottle down on a bench slowly to keep my eyes off her longer.

"I'm no idiot. Despite what Adwin may think."

I shake my head and face her again. "I'd like to think I know you better than he does."

Her teeth scrape across her lip as she nods. "You certainly do."

My throat tightens. Before I can make an excuse to leave, she says, "Want to be a moving target for me?"

"Sure."

Is she thinking of this as an outlet for sexual tension like I am? As our bodies move, even though it's against each other, my mind wanders to what else our bodies could do together. Until she connects a punch to my jaw, snapping me out of *that*.

"Oh my God! I'm so sorry!" She brushes her hand over the spot, and our eyes meet in a too-intense stare. Her hand trembles at my face before she draws it back slowly.

"Maybe this isn't the best idea." I don't know how my mouth can be so far removed from what every nerve in my body is aching for.

Serenity steps back and nods.

Shit, we messed it up. I knew it.

"Geez, what time do you start?" Cary says as she walks in with Reid. It's easier to breathe now that we aren't alone. "Don't make me look bad, okay?"

I rip my gaze away from Serenity and shoot Cary a grin. "Don't make it so easy."

She throws a water bottle at my face, but I catch it. Cary turns to Serenity. "I'm dying to see how living on a farm prepared you for this."

"Shall we?" Serenity gestures to the side.

"You better hope she's gentler with you than she is with me." Serenity's cheeks bloom red, and I hurry to add, "She just caught me in the jaw pretty hard."

Okay, I can't talk. I walk out, intent on avoiding Serenity until we go to Montica. Damnit if this girl doesn't make me a blubbering moron.

Chapter Twenty-Nine
ADWIN

Misty, Vogue, and Frey speak in a language which is only scarcely recognizable. Misty appeared suspicious of the Kaycians who threaten to be as smart as Montica's finest, but since they're her only hope, she's relaxed into a begrudging acceptance.

"It's a lot to do on your own." Misty sighs. She has other places to be while Vogue tricks the computers.

Frey rubs his jaw as if that might solve the facial hair issue which keeps him from going to Montica. His gaze meets Vogue's. "You can do it."

She nods. "I can do it." From anyone else the tone might sound confident, but it's not Vogue-level confident.

I'm not sure who is convincing whom, but since they all seem to be getting along—and I am serving absolutely no purpose—I excuse myself.

Outside, the world can't decide what season it wants to be. Unlike Montica where these things are controlled, days are as likely to be warm as they are snowy. I still wouldn't say I completely disagree with Montica's policies, even though I have irrevocably chosen this side. A chill creeps down my neck which has nothing to do with the crisp breeze. There is no clear path, so I navigate murky waters with nothing but hope that I'm heading toward something a little better. But I've never been prone to hoping.

Leavenworth is too quiet with the marshals gone and minimal Montican presence. There's enough surveillance in place that Ismene doesn't need people here to look after things. Everyone understands Montica's power and wouldn't dare to try to leave without permission. For now, keeping them here is the easiest option. The Establishment is universally hated and holds enough knowledge to cause problems for every other side of our conflicts. Knowing the reasons doesn't do anything to lessen my guilt for containing the people whose station was so close to my own.

As I walk into the bar, Rollin's gaze lands on me and leaves no question as to whether he blames me for his current situation. "May I?" I gesture to the seat next to him.

He takes a gulp of his drink. "Not like I could stop you from doing anything."

I exhale slowly as I sit. "I worry for your safety in the city after all that's transpired. You must understand that."

"Of course. We all understand keeping people in a cage to keep them safe." He taps his glass. "It's just different from this side of the bars."

"We were always on both sides," I say. "We grew up having to stay in Kaycie."

"That was a nicer cage."

"The Establishment kept you here before, too," I remind him.

"While we were working things out. Now we're just sitting here, quietly waiting to see what's to become of us. We've lost all the control we once had."

"Worse things have happened to the leaders of fallen empires."

His glare pierces me.

"It wasn't a threat. I'm just saying it could be worse. I'm trying, Rollin. I'm trying to make this as easy as possible for everyone."

"Not for everyone, Adwin. It's easiest if you're lucky enough to be Montican. Then, somehow despite how rigid you and Casimir are, those who took the side of the damned uprising are favored now. Why can the Wards and Nemeses travel freely? They opposed your grandfather. Why don't the Martels have to stay here?"

Because we need them. Grandfather has something going on with the elder Wards and Nemeses. I need the younger ones. There are too many sides now, too many twisted plans and deceptions. But I can't explain any of that. "I understand why you chose the side you were on. It's the side I'd have chosen. But when the house of cards came crashing down that side was down. It's a risk we take when we play these games."

"You say that as if any of us had a choice but to be in the game. We were born into it."

"Yes we were." DNA is a chain we can never break free from. "What has Lanelle been doing?"

He shakes his head. "I don't know. Drowns in research to pass the time. She's become neurotic. I don't see her much."

She's one I don't feel bad about keeping isolated. She was barely stable before all of this. At least she can't get into much trouble here.

Chapter Thirty

SERENITY

There is no one around the Montican plane, as planned. Travick opens the hatch and our team files into the back of the craft in the pre-dawn darkness. Vogue, Krisalyn, Carista, and I look like we have our outfits painted onto us. The green and white patterned Montican uniforms leave little to the imagination. Our varying braided hairstyles are nice, though. Vogue slides to the end of the bench lining one side of the stark compartment, twisting the end of hers where it lays over her shoulder. Travick climbs in after Bram and shuts the hatch. Misty has a different hiding place, apparently. Now we wait.

I haven't seen Bram in nearly forty-eight hours, but I swallow my paranoia and sit next to him. Whatever the reason for his avoidance, my anxiety is rising, and I need him. We sit in silence, all of us. I tap my toes in my boots and lean my face into my hands. *God, this is crazy.* Montica already crushed us at home, and we think we can walk into their nerve center?

Long, firm strokes press up and down my back, and I relax a little. Even if we did muddy our relationship with that kiss, Bram and I will be there for each other when it counts. I still don't like having that hang over us open-ended.

The plane rumbles when the engines start. I reach over without looking and grip Bram's free hand. Then we start moving. I squeeze his hand to keep mine from shaking.

"It's not like you haven't flown before."

I turn, and his small smile reassures me. "I don't remember much from the first time." *I was quite drugged.* I glance at our joined hands, and a torrent of emotions swirl through me. Guilt, anger, uncertainty... hope.

"Bram, I was thinking, if we're going to be in Montica, right under their fortress, we should make a move on Agnar."

"Don't you think it's a little late to form that plan?"

"When else could we have planned it? You've avoided me for the last two days."

He drops his chin and lets out a long breath. "You had more important things to focus on... and I didn't want to make you uncomfortable."

The only thing uncomfortable about being with Bram is stifling the attraction between us. This isn't the time or place for that conversation, though. "I'll never feel uncomfortable around you." I lean my head on his shoulder, and he wraps his arm around me. "Please don't pull away from me."

"I'll be at your side until you tell me to get lost."

The thought is repulsive. How could I *not want* Bram around? "Don't hold your breath. Snowflake is cuddly, but she can't replace you."

He stiffens, and I tip my head up to see his lips sucked in and his eyes closed. I ball my hand into a fist to restrain myself from brushing my finger across his lips. The press of them on mine is seared into my memory, but I need it again. I need to feel his desire, the spark between us. He seems so unsure now, but that doubt melted away when we shattered the wall between us.

Later, I tell myself. We'll figure it out as soon as this is over.

After a while, Travick checks the screen strapped to his arm and informs us we're almost there. The motion of the plane changes, then we come to a stop. Now we wait some more. As nervous as I am about walking into Montica's fortress, the waiting has got to be worse. This is excruciating.

"Two more minutes," Krisalyn says. Vogue clasps her face as they kiss.

Jealousy rips through me. That's how I want to be sent off. *Damnit.* I turn to Bram. "We should have talked about what happened on Sunday."

"We can do that when you get back."

"What if—"

"Don't finish that sentence." He puts a finger on my lips, and my heart races. "This will be quick, and we'll be on our way back before you know it. Okay?"

I try to channel his confidence, but all I can manage is a nod. A pulsing noise shrieks outside the plane.

"Time to go," Carista says.

Bram presses a kiss to my forehead. "Hurry back. You owe me a talk."

I squeeze his hand before turning away. While Travick opens the hatch, I slide my pod into my ear and arrange my hair over it. My hand brushes over the sword and gun at my hip. *This is real. We're really doing this.*

Carista leads Vogue and me through the hangar. The sheer size of this space is mind-boggling. And it's *in* a mountain. People walk with hurried purpose as the alarm wails. We do the same.

The route seemed more straightforward when it was only on the map. In reality, the labyrinth of hallways looks like we'll never find our way out. We weave through and take a staircase down a couple of flights, deeper into the Earth. The alarm isn't as loud down here at least.

We go through the door for the prison's administrative office. The large desk sits empty. Good. Vogue goes straight to the corner and pulls up the rug revealing the door down to the inner workings of the space. She nods and tells me she'll be right back before dropping in.

Carista closes the door and lays the rug back over it. I sit at the desk, tapping the dark wood.

"You should see the top of this place. It's beautiful." Carista bounces back and forth between her feet. "Montica would be a nice place to visit if it stops being enemy territory."

I only nod. I don't want to think about spending time here, I just want to get out. As is the popular opinion around here. Opening the doors for the Montican rebels isn't the difficult part, apparently. It's the making it look like they're still locked up to give them enough time to get away that Vogue and Frey had to get creative for. It's all well beyond what I can comprehend. I glance at the screen on my arm—*five minutes.*

The door we came through swings open, and Carista freezes. So far Adwin's information has been good. Let's see how that holds up. A mountain of a man walks in, not bothering to look at me as he rushes through the room toward the opposite door.

"Can I help you?" I ask.

The door doesn't open. He looks at me for the first time. "Open this door."

"I'm sorry, I—"

"Who are you?"

"I'm new. Genny is training me, and I'm not to let anyone into the prison while she's away."

"Good thing I'm not *anyone*. Open the door."

"I can't do that."

He notices Carista, who is doing her best to be invisible in the corner but failing miserably. "You look familiar."

Her face goes ghostly pale. The phrase *can't lie to save her life* comes to mind and feels all too literal. But how could she look familiar?

"We were about to go get a cup of coffee." I stand and round the desk to keep his focus on me. "The alarm went off, and now Genny hasn't come back." I turn to Carista. "You should really evacuate, too. Go."

Carista turns toward the door slowly, but the man grabs her arm. "No, where do I know you from?"

Her hands ball into fists. *Here we go.* Her knee shoots up to his groin, but the man jumps back in time. He dodges her fist and catches my elbow as I throw it toward his stomach. I fly across the room like I weigh nothing. The desk slides a few feet when I double over into it. Bram and Travick are background noise in my ear pod. I shake off my daze from the impact.

Carista has unleashed a level of skill I didn't see in the last two days of sparring with her. She's incredibly fast and strong... It's not enough. She can't connect with him. She pulls her gun, and it skitters across the floor before she can aim it.

I grab it and get to my feet just as Carista crumples to the floor. The man turns to face me and the gun. I don't think I can actually pull the trigger with a person in front of me. Not that I have the chance. He spins me around him so fast I don't know which way is up. "Would you stay *still!*" My back hits the wall, his arm presses against my throat, and where my left hand is pinned up near my head, a blinding pain burns through me.

The scream that erupts from me is cut off by harder pressure on my neck. From the side of my eye, I see a knife sticking out of my palm, holding me to the wall. My stomach roils. Fire sears through my hand.

"Now, care to tell me what a couple of Kaycians are doing here?"

I shudder, and he pulls his arm away from my neck when my shoulders convulse forward. I don't vomit, but it gives me the space to pull the silver grip from my hip. When I press the button, the blade extends directly through his stomach.

His green eyes widen. I summon every ounce of strength I have to raise the sword, opening up his abdomen. Dark blood pours onto my hand. My knees buckle, and the man stumbles back in shock.

I retract the blade. My body starts to slide down the wall, but the pull in my hand sends a new wave of white-hot pain through me. I scream through gritted teeth. Before I can even attempt to pull the knife out, the door flies open again.

Chapter Thirty-One

BRAM

The second she's gone I regret everything. Supporting the idea of her doing this, staying away from her the last two days, maybe training her at all. I let Serenity walk into enemy territory. I hate this *so much*.

Travick heads toward the cockpit.

Before we follow him, Krisalyn squeezes my hand. "They're going to be okay."

Sure, that's what I said the *last time* I let Serenity run off into enemy hands. Then I didn't see her for two months, and she didn't remember me when I found her again.

We pass through a much more comfortable looking passenger cabin and to the flight deck. Travick sits at the controls.

"Are you sure you're going to be able to fly this thing?" I'm asking this question way too late. It's not that I don't trust him; I just need to occupy my mind with something.

"We'll find out soon enough," he says.

We listen as Carista tells Serenity how beautiful Montica is. Then Serenity is speaking to some man. I stop breathing as Serenity tries to send Carista out. Then the groans and grunts of a struggle begin.

Travick tells Krisalyn to stay put as he rushes to catch up to me. He looks at the map while we sprint through the halls, guns in hand.

Lucky for the people who would be here, the area has cleared out. Through our comms, Vogue says she can't get back to Serenity and Cary. There's a banging noise, and Vogue swearing to herself.

Serenity's scream pushes me faster down the stairs. Its abrupt stop is even more terrifying. The man speaks again, so there's still hope... She has to be alive.

I don't feel my feet hitting the floor as I run. I throw the door open. A sweep of the room, and I've got a man holding his bleeding stomach, Carista on the floor, and Serenity...

Two shots end the suffering of the man faster than I'd prefer to, but there's no time.

I race to Serenity and grab her under her free arm to keep her upright. She drops her head and sobs. "It's going to be okay. I've got you. We're getting out of here."

There's a screech behind me when Vogue enters the room. "Oh my God!" She reaches for the knife but hesitates. "This is probably going to hurt."

I hold Serenity's face. "Look at me." She does—her beautiful gray eyes swimming in tears. "Focus on me, okay? One, two." I nod and Serenity's face twists in agony as Vogue pulls the knife out of the wall and her hand. She collapses forward into my arms, trembling from head to toe.

"We need to go." Travick has Carista slung over his shoulder.

I scoop Serenity into my arms. She presses her injury between her chest and her other—also bloody—hand.

Vogue leads the way. Racing out, I toe the line between holding Serenity securely and crushing her. She doesn't complain. She remains in a tight ball around her hand. *What I would give to be the one in pain instead of her.*

We get back to the hangar without incident, and hurry into the plane's passenger cabin. Krisalyn scrambles to figure out what's going on as Trav lays Carista down on two seats. He disappears into the cockpit.

I sit, holding Serenity on my lap. She buries her face in my shoulder. I hold the back of her head. Breathless and exhausted from terror, I don't say anything. We just sit together in silence as the engines send a vibration through the plane. Vogue sits in the row opposite, staring at Serenity with wide eyes.

"Oh, thank God." Krisalyn sits Carista up. "Here, drink some water."

"What the..." Carista shakes her head, trying to get her bearings as the plane starts to move.

Krisalyn pops over to us. "Let me see it." Gently, she pulls Serenity's hands to herself. She sucks in a breath through her teeth. "We'll get this cleaned up and bandaged. They'll have to stitch it up when we get back to Leavenworth." She brushes her fingers over Serenity's right hand but can't find an injury.

"Not mine," Serenity whispers. "That blood."

"Good." Krisalyn steps away to grab supplies.

I kiss the top of Serenity's head and blink back tears. It took almost losing Serenity to restart my tear ducts. *It was too close.* The thought of letting her out of my sight ever again seems impossible.

Krisalyn comes back and says, "The pain killer might make you a little woozy, but if you really want to rest, I can give you a sedative."

Serenity shakes her head. Krisalyn injects something into her forearm, and soon she's relaxed against me. By the time Krisalyn has cleaned both hands and wrapped the injured one, Serenity's eyelids are drooping, and the ground is far below us.

She tucks her hands back to her chest and curls into me. I stroke her back, and whisper, "Let's go home."

"To Eudora?" Her voice is slow and sleepy.

"If that's where you want home to be, yes."

"Your home."

"You don't want to go to Lawson."

"No, not—" She yawns and doesn't finish the sentence. Her chest rises and falls in slow, even breaths. If I hadn't heard it myself, I wouldn't believe those same lungs had released a heartbreaking scream so recently.

Vogue leans over and taps the screen in front of me to recline my seat. She gives me a small, grateful smile before returning to Krisalyn.

Serenity's weight on me acts like a security blanket. With the relief of having her safe here with me, sleep claims me.

Chapter Thirty-Two

The first time I arrived at the fortress comes to mind. My nerves are more on edge this time. The ability to appear calm and confident doesn't always do the job of quieting the tumult inside. A still sea can have a strong current under the surface.

As I took the lift up out of the hangar, Misty slipped through the shadows, hiding in a different kind of forest. While I crossed the Breck's atrium, Misty laid a trail of devices to instigate our diversion. And as Nemora and I catch up on the week's events, the alarm starts to ring.

She frowns and pulls up a holo. "Smoke in the hospital," she says out loud, though not really to me. This isn't particularly interesting based on her shrug. As expected. She returns to the topic of the Establishment. "Those spoiled has-beens should be grateful they aren't truly imprisoned. It's unbelievable that they have the nerve to complain, as lax as you've been with them."

"They aren't exactly used to a world with consequences."

"Further proof that Casimir was soft out there." A new holo flashes before Nemora. This one holds her attention—her mouth pulls into a tight line. "Now the hangar? Perfect."

"Do you have to deal with that?"

"Not really. They're evacuating everything underground. Everyone knows procedure. It's only a glitch in the day."

"*Everything* underground?" I clear my throat and bite my lip. Not that I need to fake nervousness, only the reason behind it. Concern about retribution from Clover and Priam is the only acceptable feeling I can have about them.

"Not them. The prison is a bunker. It's safe from anything."

"Good."

Good that she assumes I'm afraid of them. Good that she thinks the prison is safe. But Misty is an emergency they didn't plan for.

"*I'm in position,*" Misty says in my head. "*Vogue is about to be.*" Her voice whispering through my mind without seeing her is familiar enough since she can keep herself invisible in person, too.

I need to stay with the family to avoid incrimination. I'll be more useful to everyone if I maintain my position. So I sit quietly while Nemora checks and dismisses notifications as the interruption to the day whirls on. When she takes a call, I fiddle with my cuticles lazily while I send a silent message to Misty. "*How's it going?*"

"*Vogue's job is complete,*" she says. "*I'm going to get them.*"

"No, I don't see him," Nemora says as she manipulates holos.

"*It's me. Come on. Quiet now.*" Misty's with them. I let out a long breath. Now they just need to get out.

Nemora stiffens. "He wouldn't."

Oh God, do they know I'm involved?

"*Clover, we can't. You're the only ones covered, and we need to leave now.*"

I'm torn between the scene in my head with Misty and trying to decode Nemora's conversation. "*Misty, what's going on?*"

"*This is a bad idea,*" Misty says to someone other than me.

Everything feels like a bad idea. I should have just gotten as far away as possible. Will Nemora count herself lucky for having me in the same room when they realize they need to arrest me?

A new holo flashes before Nemora, and her jaw drops. "Mother, we do have a problem in the prison."

Here it comes.

"No, not ours," she says. "The Kaycian."

My chin jerks back. "What are you talking about?"

She ignores me and springs to her feet. "Yes, I'm on my way."

"Nemora! What is going on? What Kaycian?"

"Moving and talking." She gestures for me to follow her, and we hurry out of her office. "We couldn't find Rocco. Now we have an escape on our hands."

Blood pounds through my ears. "He got Clover out?"

"No. Clover, Priam, and their cohorts are contained." Or so she thinks. "There's a Kaycian imprisoned here who seems to be misplaced at the moment." We get into the lift, and it plunges along with my stomach.

"When was I going to be informed that one of *my* citizens was locked up here?"

She eyes me in a way which tells me I need to tread carefully. How dare I think Kaycie is mine just because Ismene says so in front of my face.

"Misty, you all better be gone. Nemora is on her way there."

Silence. Hopefully that means they are off the grid and on their way to safety.

Ismene catches up with us as we make our way toward the prison. Fortunately, the tree-walkers aren't going through the door. My being with Ismene and Nemora is either going to serve as the ultimate alibi or get me thrown into one of the now-vacant cells with startling efficiency. I fix an unreadable look on my face and continue to play the part.

Ismene throws the door open and stops so abruptly Nemora runs into her. It's as if time has stopped, and sound has been sucked into a vacuum. Finally, Ismene enters with slow, intentional steps. Nemora lays a hand softly on her mother's shoulder in the greatest show of affection I've witnessed between them. I follow and see what shocked Ismene into this state.

Rocco lies dead on the floor.

Chapter Thirty-Three
SERENITY

It's dark out by the time I leave the hospital. I didn't even see the sun today. Bram strokes my shoulder as he walks me to the hotel. He's been at my side since I woke up.

Vogue greets us in the lobby. "How are you feeling?"

"I'm all right."

"I got you moved to a bigger room with a bathtub so it's easier to keep that hand dry." She hands me a card.

"It can get wet actually."

"*Shh*, don't tell them that." She winks. "Do you need help with anything?"

I manage not to glance at Bram as I consider her offer. "No, I think I've got it. I'll be in bed soon."

"I already put your things in there." She hugs me extra tight. "I love you."

"I love you, too. Thank you."

Bram accompanies me to the sixth floor. I don't bother pointing out that I can get there myself, because that's not why he's escorting me. If not for the insanity of the day weighing on me, the same waves of tension which kept me up a few nights ago would make my entire body tingle. It's not until we get to my room that the awkwardness of wondering what we do takes over. I open the door but stop halfway through it.

Snowflake jumps at my knee, and I scoop her up. I look from her to Bram, wondering if he's thinking the same thing I am. *She can't replace you.*

"I'll just…"

"Come back?" I get the words out despite the tightness in my throat. "After you get cleaned up." Neither of us should stay in these blood stained Montican uniforms.

He nods. I hand him my key. "In case I'm still trying to shower one handed when you get back."

Bram presses his lips together, and I wouldn't be surprised if the look in his eyes lit me on fire. "I'll see you soon." He turns and walks away.

It's a moment before my feet remember how to function and bring me into the room. Bigger indeed. This room has an added sitting area and a four top table. The large soaking tub is inviting, but I don't think I want to take that long, so after I peel off my clothes, I turn on the shower and step in. Maybe I did need Vogue's help. Washing my hair with one hand is not ideal, but my fingers are mostly numb on my left. At least the challenge keeps my mind from what I am eagerly yet nervously waiting for.

I pull on leggings and a T-shirt and step out to find Bram on the sofa with Snowflake curled up next to him. It's not *so terribly* bold of me to sit on the bed instead. We've slept next to each other before. Plus, it's getting late and neither of us are willing to part ways.

"Are you okay?" I figure since I'm the one who got stabbed, the rules don't really apply to me today.

He shakes his head. "Only you would ask that in this situation."

"I know how you worry about me." Today rattled him. Some terrible part of me brightens at how much he cares about me.

He rises and approaches me. People weren't meant to look so beautiful in a T-shirt and jeans. How did I fail to notice for so long? He gets down on both knees in front of me, and my heart jumps into my throat.

"That was so far beyond worry, Serenity. When I heard you scream..." He drops his face and kisses my bandaged palm.

"It's numb," I say. "I can't even feel that."

He slides his lips up to my wrist and presses a kiss there. "Can you feel that?"

I shake my head. "Keep trying."

He must know I'm lying but continues kissing his way up the inside of my arm to the crook of my elbow. "Still nothing?"

My toes curl. "Not a thing."

Calloused fingers slide up my arm. In one fluid and gentle motion, he rises from the floor and kisses my collar bone. Heat rolls through me in waves. We sink down onto the bed as his mouth makes a path to my neck. I tilt my head to give him better access. My heart speeds out of control as his lips brush my ear. "Serenity."

"Hmm?" I can't manage words, but the rest of my body picks up while my mind shuts down. My leg wraps around his. My fingers press into his back, and it's the most beautiful music they've ever played.

"I just like the way your name feels on my lips."

I turn my head to bring our faces together. "I like the way your lips feel on me."

Our kiss is full of simmering longing rather than the searing want of last time. Kissing him again is almost enough to make me cry. The idea of him regretting the egg incident seems ridiculous now. My hand roves down the planes of his chest and stomach to grip the hem of his shirt. He pulls back to let me yank it off. I marvel at his body, but it's his eyes that consume me. How he ever hid the life from his eyes, I'll never know. They smolder and gleam so fiercely... It's a wonder I saw anything but him when I first walked into Sophos' office a lifetime ago.

With a gentleness entirely at odds with his strength, he pulls my shirt over my head. I will my eyes to remain on his face, even as I blush wildly. He kisses me again, and his hand slides down my side, coming to a stop when he grips my hip. My chest threatens to explode. He holds himself over me like I don't *want* to feel the weight of him.

Why weren't we doing this all along? Months sleeping on the other side of a wall from him, and I could have been doing this. I'd mourn the lost time, but we can make up for it now.

"This," I say, "is the happiness I couldn't even imagine."

Mischief dances in his eyes, and I wonder what he's imagined. "I'd give anything to make you happy." He kisses me again, and my back arches. "What do you want?" His voice is a warm breeze against my ear.

"More of you. All of you."

He grants my wish... and several I didn't think to ask for.

Chapter Thirty-Four

ADWIN

The chaos caused by Rocco's death and the discovery that the tree-walkers were gone made me even less important than I usually am. Moving through the fortress unnoticed allowed me to arrive first at my meeting spot with Misty. Darkness has settled over the forest—deep and solemn. Or maybe it's me. The urge to get to the tops of the trees and stargaze is there, but mental exhaustion wins. I sit and wait.

"I didn't expect to see you here again."

Of course she'd come herself. I take a deep breath before I stand and turn to face Clover. The judgment and disappointment she looked at me with last time are still there albeit subdued. Her dark hair is slightly longer, and the earrings that curled up her outer ears are gone, but she's otherwise unchanged. The suspicion radiating off her is well deserved. "Hi, Clover."

Her shoulders rise and fall with a breath. "Throughout Misty's explanation, I thought of a hundred things I'd like to say to you, but I find myself speechless."

"I don't want to get in your way. I'm sure you don't want me around, and I deserve that. Just tell me how I can help."

"They don't know you were involved?"

"No."

"It's still dangerous to come out here. They may be watching you." She looks around as if she'd see some sign of their surveillance, but she could be using it as an excuse to admire the forest.

"They're preoccupied."

"What could be more important than finding Montica's most notorious fugitives?"

"You might want to sit down."

She shakes her head, then pulls herself onto a tree branch. She may not take my warning seriously, but she'll take any excuse to be in a tree.

"Um, there appears to have been a struggle with the Kaycian team, and…"

"Who died?" Her tone exudes acceptance. Her face is tilted toward the sky, eyes closed.

"Your father."

Her eyes snap open, but her expression remains blank when she turns to stare at me.

I rake my hand through my hair. "I'm sorry, I don't—"

"Misty said you were sending a few girls in?"

"Well, our marshals couldn't pass for Montican, so yes—"

"No." Clover hops down and lands silently on the ground. "There's no way two or three Kaycian girls took down Rocco Agnar."

"I don't know what to tell you. Carista has two marshals for brothers, and Serenity used to fence—"

"Jase's Serenity?"

I give my head a quick shake. I must have heard wrong. Nothing about that makes sense. "Pardon me?"

"Are you talking about Jase's girlfriend?"

"How on earth would you know Serenity Ward as *Jase's girlfriend*?"

"He was the only person I was allowed to speak to *in prison*." She shoots me a sardonic smile, but my head is spinning. "I make friends in prison now. Isn't that something? But anyway, what you're saying still doesn't—"

"Jase Delgado is alive?" I blurt out.

"Yes. Can we get back to the topic at hand? You're mistaken. There is no way they could have—" Something in my eyes stops her. Her eyebrows draw together, and her lip quivers. "Is he really?"

I nod, and tears gather in her eyes. I pull her into a hug as she starts to cry. "I'm sorry."

We stay like that for some time. She absorbs the loss of her father, and I try to wrap my mind around Jase Delgado being alive and right under my nose all this time. Clover straightens and takes a step back. "Okay. Well, what are you going to do now?"

"Whatever I can to help you get Ismene out of office."

Clover rubs her forehead. "You'll need to give me a minute to plan. And Jase is going to want to return to Kaycie."

"I can't believe he's been alive this whole time. Is that who you had to take out with you?"

She nods. "They wouldn't let me talk to any of the tree-walkers for security reasons, but I guess they took pity on me being alone."

I'd wager she was the only one given the luxury of companionship. "We all thought he died in the EC."

"Our agents had collected him."

I could have gotten Serenity and Vogue to help *much* sooner had I known. "Where is he? Where is everyone now that your hideout is obliterated?"

"The treehouse wasn't our real hide out."

"What?"

She sniffles and composes herself. "Come on."

Even in daylight, there wouldn't be anything to demarcate the trail Clover leads me down. She stops, and I swivel my head, not seeing anything. She rubs her eyes and sighs. "Bringing you to us *again* is probably the stupidest thing I've ever done." Her stare asks the question she won't voice—*Can I trust you?*

"You've heard about what happened in Kaycie, right?" She nods. "I'm sorry I didn't believe you before. I didn't understand the magnitude of what Ismene was capable of. You were right."

"You can't change teams again. We're getting to the end, and win or lose, it's time to pick a side, for good."

"I'm with you," I say. "But the Clover I know would never entertain the idea she might lose."

One corner of her mouth turns up in a grin. "Getting a loss under my belt adjusted my expectations." She turns and presses her palm to a tree. A section of it depresses, and a large rock slides a few feet over, revealing an opening into the ground. Clover gives me one more heavy look before dropping into it. She's trusting me after everything I've done. Everyone else who has bestowed responsibility on me has done so with the knowledge they can simply take it away if I don't work out. The Kaycians who helped get us here didn't do it because they *trust* me, they did it reluctantly and hoping for the best, but I doubt they'd have been surprised if I had double-crossed them. But Clover, who I've betrayed worse than anyone else, is truly offering trust again.

Determined to earn that trust, I take the plunge into her hidden underground world.

Green light glows around us. We are at the end of a hallway or tunnel of some sort, but it disappears into darkness. Clover starts down it, and lights engage with each step. The lights behind turn off as we pass, allowing darkness to trail us closely.

"Why did you stay in the treehouse when you had this stronghold?"

Clover looks like a fantasy creature in the green glow. "Isn't it obvious?"

It is. Underground is a last resort.

Other tunnels split off from this one—black holes in the illuminated walls as we pass them. I have so many questions but don't dare voice them. How far does it go? Does it connect all the way back into the Breck? I don't deserve to know more details than she volunteers. Finally, we arrive in a utilitarian living room of sorts. Tree-walkers are scattered across sofas and in a kitchenette. All eyes dart to us. Misty lays a hand on Knox's arm in a decidedly *don't hurt him* kind of gesture. Aspen, Juniper, and Willow avert their eyes, and Priam puffs out his chest as he crosses his arms over it.

In the corner, Jase Delgado lowers a mug and his jaw ticks. "Is she okay?"

Chapter Thirty-Five

BRAM

Before I open my eyes, I wonder if last night was a dream. But Serenity's head rests on my shoulder. My hand is on her bare back, rising and falling with each breath she takes. *It was real.* If only the memory could be bottled up. It would be a hit of pure serotonin I could keep in my pocket.

The bliss that rolls over me is quickly replaced by panic. What if this ruins everything between us? What if she feels so guilty about what we've done, she can't even stand to look at me? What if this was just a one-time thing like Tori? I don't know if I can handle that with Serenity. The thought of that being the last time makes my heart turn to lead. Shit, was this a terrible mistake?

It didn't feel like a mistake. I was so relieved to have her safe and whole... I've never felt terror like that before. Hearing her scream. Seeing her hurt. After all that, I couldn't get close enough to her. The urge to hold her and never let go took over. It was all so much more than I could have imagined. Every touch, kiss, sound.

The flutter of eyelashes tickles me. Serenity's back arches in a slow stretch. She looks up at me and blushes as she grins. "Good morning." The light rasp of her sleepy voice is enough to make me wish I'd die. Right now. End it on a high note.

But my heart beats on, so I say, "Good morning," too. I lift her bandaged hand from my chest and rub the spot where a blade protruded from it yesterday. "How are you feeling?"

"Amazing." She props herself up on her elbow. "Are you going to kiss me good morning? Is that something we do now?"

"It can be something we do now... if you want."

Her smile within the frame of her tousled hair is so perfectly imperfect. She's so much better like this than when the perfection was intentional. My smile is untamable.

"I want."

The slow kiss dissolves the rest of my worries. Good thing I didn't die after 'good morning.'

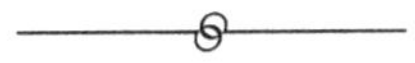

Instead of being awkward and embarrassed, Serenity is more relaxed and comfortable than ever. After yesterday's excitement, we decide we deserve a day off and shut ourselves away in her room. But it's not the same as when we hid in Eudora—at least not for me. That was avoiding people for the sake of avoiding them. Today it's about wanting Serenity all to myself. What is it for her?

I follow her lead on how affectionate we want to be with each other. We don't spend the day tangled up together, but we find ourselves always touching in some way or another. That's not even new but feels different now. Our knees will touch, or her hand drifts to my arm, or she puts her *freezing cold* feet under my leg to warm them. It feels natural... except the cold feet. That was mean.

She brushes her fingertips over the tattooed number on my forearm. "Will you have it removed?"

"I don't think so. It's part of my story now. I can't erase that time, so this shouldn't be erased either." I'd suffer it all again to get here.

"Have you ever thought about what the numbers could mean?"

"I assume it means I'm the 954,407,813th marshal."

"Because obviously they started with one." She rolls her eyes. "The numbers should have some personal significance. That way it isn't just the Establishment erasing you. Like the nine... You were nine when your father died, right?"

"You remember that?" She nods. I continue, "Yeah. I guess five four could be my birthday."

"See? It's better like this. The next four could be you and your three siblings." She looks at me with apprehension in her eyes because she gets it—toeing the line between remembering and despair.

"I like that."

She grins and touches the numbers again. "What's the rest of it?"

"I don't know yet."

Eventually, we need to eat, and I need fresh clothes. I go to my room to shower. The hot water rains down on me as I stand there in disbelief. We messed up most of our plans, broke the world, and shattered our lives. How did so many wrongs make a right? I can't decide if we deserve this after everything we've been through, or if we're lucky karma has forgotten all our mistakes.

I stop at the cafe and grab sandwiches to go. As I walk back into the hotel, I run into Vogue.

"Oh, he lives," she says. "Have you spoken to Serenity today? She's been ignoring us."

It's hard not to feel cocky about the fact that she chose to spend the day quietly with me. "She did get stabbed yesterday. I think we all need some rest."

She runs her tongue over her teeth and her eyes narrow. "Okay. We're going to the bar later if you'd like to join us."

"Maybe."

Her suspicious gaze follows me to the elevator. I contain my snicker until the door closes. This is hands down, the most fun secret I've ever kept. When I get back to Serenity's room, seeing her again makes me float. I feel like a complete idiot. She's making me an idiot. My brain doesn't function around her—or at least it functions very differently. Being the reason for her smile is now my greatest achievement.

While we eat, I tell her I ran into Vogue.

"Oh? What did she have to say?"

"She was wondering why you've been ignoring everybody."

"And did you tell her I have not actually been ignoring *everybody?*"

"Of course not."

She bites her lip and nods. "I think we... I'm just not..."

"No one has to know anything. It's nobody's business."

She looks at me with wide eyes. "You're not offended? I promise I'm not ashamed or anything, I'm just not ready for that."

"S, I am perfectly content to keep this to ourselves and avoid Frey's commentary."

Her smile is more thanks than I need for something I really don't care about, but she says, "Thank you," anyway. "S?"

My neck and face flush with warmth. "You signed the note that way when you gave me this." I tap the leather band on my arm. "Is that okay?"

"It's perfect. I am disappointed in you, though."

My shoulders tense. "Why?"

"You already took a shower." She smiles wickedly, now. "That bathtub beckons, but I was waiting for you..."

A breath puffs out of me in relief. "That was specifically a pre-bath shower."

"That's not a thing."

"It absolutely is."

She shrugs innocently. "I mean, if you want."

I lean in close to her face. "I want."

Chapter Thirty-Six

ADWIN

"I need to get back to the fortress before they become suspicious." Plus, there isn't enough coffee in the world to keep me awake much longer. I rub my eyes. "They'll only be busy with everything else for so long before they remember me."

Clover shoots me a sharp look. Maybe downplaying her father's death isn't ideal, but my mind has melted from lack of sleep.

It was nice to see that Clover and the rest are well, but they have a lot to figure out before I can help them do anything. Mostly the day has been spent avoiding Priam's glare and catching up on the last five months. Well, me catching them up. They didn't do much in that time.

"What you *need* to do is get ahold of Serenity to make sure everyone got out all right." Jase has a one-track mind. It's growing tiresome.

"Checking on them when I'm not supposed to know they've left Kaycie isn't an option. Once I'm re-connected, the death of Serenity Ward would be the first news I'd hear if it happened." We know they all got away. We just aren't sure what state they're in. The blood left on a knife and the wall wasn't Rocco's.

"That's not good enough."

Clover offers Jase a reassuring smile. "We'll go. As soon as possible."

I groan. "Clover, you can't go to Kaycie."

"Then you take him."

"I am even less able to go to Kaycie! I can't afford to be away from Nemora and Ismene's sights any longer than I already have been."

Jase shakes his head. "What's it like only caring about yourself?"

"That's not what this is."

"Yes it is." He pushes his hair out of his face—scraggly from months of confinement. "I can't believe it took so much for Serenity to break up with you."

His distaste for me because I 'dated' Serenity was never a secret, but this is pathetic. "She didn't break up with me. I broke up with her."

He smirks. "No you didn't."

"Perhaps she told you otherwise to save face, but you weren't there. I was—"

"You don't remember it." The satisfaction is thick in his voice.

"Of course I—" Wait. We were at the symphony's spring gala. Everything was fine—as much as Serenity and I could be which was bland. We broke up on the roof, and she had left by the time I got back down to the party. I don't remember the details, but ending the farce was always on my mind. And I was drunk. I narrow my eyes at Jase.

"She gave you amnesia."

I tap my teeth together. At the time I would never have believed it, but now I know she was involved with Sophos' uprising. And how would I have chosen what I wanted over what my grandfather told me to do. "Okay," I admit with a sigh. "That makes sense." Not as if it's the first time I've been surprised by her. She may have just killed my uncle. "Anyway, I'll work on a way to get you back over there, and I'll send word when I confirm everyone made it out in one piece. But I need to distance myself from everyone involved as much as possible."

Unsurprisingly, no one seems upset by this idea.

Chapter Thirty-Seven
SERENITY

How is it that even as Bram has me coming undone, I feel more whole than I've been in a long time? It has to be too good to be true. The guilt is bound to come for me any minute. But for now, all I feel is Bram's hand as it rubs my back. The beating of his heart under my hand creates a pulsing shield, protecting me from negativity. I fall asleep so thoroughly content and secure that nightmares seem like a distant memory.

He's still sleeping when I wake. In a completely unfair, but unavoidable move, my mind starts to draw comparisons. I had always liked Jase, but I never thought of him as more than a friend until he confessed his feelings for me. We fell hard and fast, even though we restrained ourselves from physical intimacy. Bram hasn't ever *told* me anything about how he might feel for me in a romantic sense, but the intensity of the attraction that started to buzz between us as we scaled the unthinkable mountain of misery was too much to resist. I would think it cheapens it—to not have some sort of commitment agreed upon—but in fact it's almost a relief. It feels pure. Like being together was unavoidable and we've finally given in to it.

If anything, I feel a twinge of guilt about *not* feeling guilty for this. It seems like I should, but who am I hurting? Who would my guilt benefit? No one. I've been my own harshest critic and worst enemy, but those nagging voices in my head have quieted. It's so peaceful without them.

We *are* going to have to rejoin the rest of the world, though. Reluctantly, I slide out of bed. After I get leggings and a T-shirt on, I look in the mirror and stand a little taller than I have been. I'm done picking myself apart. The world has done plenty to try to break me; I don't need to help it along. I come out of the bathroom to find Bram sitting up with his face in his hands.

"Are you all right?" I sit on the edge of the bed next to him.

He nods and lets out a breath. "I'm good."

I hold to the bargain about not asking, but I let my eyes inquire as I brush my fingers over his jaw.

"It's stupid and embarrassing," he says. My chin dips, and he groans as if I'm ruthlessly interrogating him. "When I woke up and you weren't there—I panicked. Only for a second. I'm fine. Please don't think I'm some needy loser."

"Since when do I judge you that way?"

"You could easily start after that."

"I'm not going to start now." I kiss him softly. "I'm sorry I startled you. It's understandable. These last two mornings, I've woken up a little surprised this is real."

"Good surprised or bad surprised?"

"You're fishing for compliments." Another little kiss, then I pop up to my feet. "Okay, vacation is over."

<hr>

Hiding out yesterday was... blissful, but it feels good to be out in the fresh air. Our shoes pound out a steady rhythm against the pavement. This run feels different than the countless ones we've gone on together. Even though we aren't being affectionate out in the open, having him by my side actualizes our new dynamic. We still exist outside the confines of our—*my* room. Not in the same capacity, but it's comforting.

Deep in the wooded trail, Bram slows to a stop. I follow suit, reaching down to my toes to stretch and catch my breath.

"I think you're in better shape than me, now," he says.

I straighten and enjoy the hungry way he looks at me. "I've started a new workout routine recently." My eyes remain locked on his as I press my palm against his chest. "It's *amazing.*"

Freedom from the what ifs, hesitation, and worries that had us wrapped up tight is glorious.

Fire dances in his eyes. Not the flame of rage that contorted his features for so long, but smoldering embers. His lips crush onto mine. *This bliss exists outside the confines of my room, too.* He swings me around. My back presses against a tree and my hands are pinned up over my head.

The memory of a hard arm pressed against my throat makes it close up. A phantom blade makes my left-hand clench into a ball. I shudder as every muscle in my body tenses and ice shoots through my veins. A gasp that is in no way impassioned, shocks Bram. He drops my hands quickly.

"Did I hurt you? Are you okay?" His gaze scans me for an injury he won't be able to see. "I'm so sorry."

My chest heaves with shallow breaths. He holds my shoulders, backed up to arm's length. I shake my head and lean against his chest.

His arms wrap around me, and he waits, ever patiently, for me to settle down.

"I... I'm sorry. It was..."

"Deep breaths." His hand rubs up and down my back, and I pace my breathing to its slow rhythm.

"Being pinned like that. It reminded me of..." The words stick in my throat, so I hold up my bandaged hand, tapping my palm with my little finger.

Bram turns to stone and sucks in a sharp breath. "God, I am so sorry. I wasn't thinking." His arms tighten around me. "You're safe. I'm so sorry."

I nod against his chest and arch back to look at him. The ice melts away. "It's okay. Hopefully it won't trigger me someday, because I really liked where you were going with that."

He relaxes and leans his chin on my head. The pieces of me that were poised to fall apart, settle back into place as I press against his steadying heart.

This is a routine I could get used to—running, sparring, and peppering in some *extra* workouts.

Chapter Thirty-Eight

BRAM

The sunshine and rainbows couldn't last forever. Rejoining the world includes dealing with the aftermath of our mission in Montica. And of course, it wouldn't be us if we hadn't botched it big.

"Yes, I'm *sure*. How do you think he knew me?" Cary paces the Establishment boardroom. "I can't believe we killed Rocco *freaking* Agnar."

We don't mess up in small ways.

The Campbells and the Kaycian crew coming together to be the center of this could have made me feel secure—not being outnumbered, having more people I can count on in a fight—but it's just more people with targets on them. My isolation used to feel like a punishment. Compartmentalizing everyone was used to deceive. But it was safer too. The more people involved, the further the shadow of danger stretches. And the person who's been the light for me is terrifyingly close to epicenter.

Serenity's gray eyes have gleamed with every positive emotion I couldn't have dared to hope for in the past few days. But now they're dark as she looks at me from across the table.

"Did you leave anything they could use to trace you?" Dixon asks.

Vogue gasps. "The knife. Holy shit, I dropped the knife. It has Serenity's blood all over it." The image turns my stomach.

Frey drops his face into his hands. "Come on, Vogue."

"Doesn't matter," Krisalyn says, "the wall was covered in blood."

I really need everyone to stop talking about Serenity's spilled blood before I get sick.

"They aren't going to like us if they find out." Serenity's wide eyes on me bring me back to the issue at hand.

"Me," I say. "They're not going to like *me.*"

"*Us,*" she repeats. "*We* killed him."

"We didn't do anything. I killed him."

It's odd how offended she looks at the idea of not having killed someone. She taps her fingers on the table. "I definitely had a hand in—"

"To claim you had a hand in killing him is like if you gave me a jar to open, and when I opened it easily, you claim to have loosened it."

She gasps, but before she can go on a rant Frey cuts her off. "Either way, let's hope they don't figure it out."

"Here's hoping." Serenity pops up to her feet. "Wouldn't want them coming after Bram and only Bram because it was obviously all Bram's doing." She slams the door on her way out.

An awkward silence descends on the room. I drop my head forward then stand. "I'm going to go... deal with that."

In hindsight, that wasn't the best way to put it. But the issue itself is obvious. Spreading the blame won't lessen the consequences, it'll multiply across all of us.

I knock on Serenity's door, and she opens it just enough to look at me with one eye. "If I only open the door this much, and you open it the rest of the way, did you open it by yourself?"

"Really?" I push it open and follow her into the room. "Have you considered I might not want people to think you had anything to do with Rocco Agnar's death because I want to protect you?"

"Don't protect me at your expense! I don't want you to be in danger either!"

"I would be anyway. If you don't have to be in it too, you shouldn't!"

"I'm the only one who left DNA. And has it occurred to *you* that you wouldn't have been able to take him down if I hadn't skewered him first?"

"I could have."

"I don't think so. His skill level was—"

"Excuse me, are you questioning my skills?"

She drops her chin. "Not in everything."

Her grin sends a heat wave up my chest. "You can't possibly think us killing someone together is sexy."

"Sexier than you rescuing me." Her gaze trails over me. "I prefer to take a more *active* role."

If all our arguments end up in this way, I'll be picking fights more often. I wrap my arms around her waist and sink my face closer to hers. "How active do you want to be?"

"That depends." Her lips brush up the side of my neck and stop at my ear. "Are you going to take back that stupid remark?"

"What if I don't?"

She pulls her hand up my thigh. Shivers run down my spine. "Then I may start something else and leave it for you to finish."

"You... are so mean."

"Am I?" It would be unsettling that she can sound so innocent when she's torturing me, but since it's unbelievably sexy...

"Do you want me to apologize?"

"What I want…"—she pulls back and her eyes lock on mine—"is a sandwich." She whips around and gets a couple of steps away from me before I snap out of the shocked daze she threw me into.

"I don't think so." I grab her arm, and her laughter as I spin her back to me is a song I could play on repeat forever. But I don't mind cutting it off when her lips meet mine. With Serenity pressed against me, and her kiss making the rest of the world a distant memory, I barely remember what we were arguing about. But I don't want to see how far she'll go to torture me for it.

Between kisses, I manage to say, "You're right… Sorry… I'll never… downplay anything you do… ever again." How could I when every moment with her becomes the new best moment of my life, and every touch redefines ecstasy?

"I hope not." The spark in her eyes alone could undo me, but she doesn't only give me her sly looks. She gives me all of her, and even though it's more than I ever could have wished for, I know I'll never be able to get enough.

Chapter Thirty-Nine
ADWIN

Awareness comes in pieces. Where am I? The bedroom I keep at my mother's house. What day is it? Could the prison break really have been two days ago? Two days since Rocco died.

Nothing can be easy, can it?

At my silent command, a cup of coffee rises out of the nightstand. There's no way it'll be enough to help me make sense of this mess. Rocco wasn't supposed to die, and Jase Delgado wasn't supposed to be alive. Clover can't really think getting Jase back to Kaycie is a priority. Once she stops to think about everything going on, she'll reconsider. We can't smuggle someone out of the country now that her escape and her father's death have caused a strict lockdown.

My body resists the idea of getting out of bed, but I muster the energy and get to my feet. There's so much to deal with—I have no idea where to start. My heart picks up to a painful race, and my lungs rattle with the effort of slowing down to get enough oxygen. Forget the list. It'll never end. One thing at a time. One thing is doable. Especially when the one thing is just to get in the shower.

With that done, I feel somewhat put together—enough to continue with the day. The house is quiet. I find my mother outside in the swing she wishes I had grown up with. "It's about time," she says. "I thought you had given up the Kaycian lifestyle."

If only I had woken up in the middle of the day because the night was spent drinking. Wishing that was an option is precisely why I still hold firm in my belief that people are better off sheltered. Ismene may be too extreme, but Clover's ideas are no less extreme for being opposite. "It's just been busy." It's an understatement, but there's no need for her to know the truth. Even the parts the Breck is aware of.

"Yes, the life you've chosen always will be, I suppose." She sighs. This is the life she tried to keep me from. The life her father had, which destroyed her family. "I'm proud of you for it, though."

"Since when?"

Her shoulders slump. "It's not that I've ever not been proud of you, darling. Worry tends to overshadow it, but you are so strong to be able to deal with all this. Stronger than I ever was."

I lay my hand on hers. "Well, I never had anything bad happen to me. You protected me well enough that it was an adventure to become involved in such things. I never had to fear for anything like you did."

"If I didn't think you could take care of yourself, I'd regret that. But you know what you're doing."

Do I?

An avillipse comes into view and lands at the edge of the sprawling property. Mother's calm evaporates. Her hand clenches underneath mine. Visitors aren't supposed to come here. I rise and approach the craft Nemora is exiting.

"What are you doing here?" I wouldn't normally be so assertive with her, but Grandfather and Ismene agreed Mother would be left alone here.

"You and your mother need to stay at the Breck. We can't guarantee your safety out here with a pack of convicts running loose."

This house will be far safer from the tree-walkers than the fortress will be. "I appreciate your concern, but—"

"It's not a request."

"Nemora, you can't *make* us leave."

"I could." Her gaze is steely. It's true, of course. How would I stop her? "Adwin, you're the one who got them arrested. In the shuffle we failed to think of it, but you're not safe."

My jaw clenches. "That may be true, but my mother will not be made to stay at the Breck. I... I'll take her back to Kaycie for a while."

Nemora presses her lips together before giving me a stiff nod. "Fine. I'll send a plane for you in an hour."

"I'll just take my avillipse."

Her eyebrows pull together, but she doesn't argue. It's a slower option, but not terrible. She turns on her heel and gets back into the avillipse.

All right. I can go to Kaycie without looking like I'm running from the events I plotted. Mother won't love this idea, but she'd hate it even more if she knew we weren't going alone.

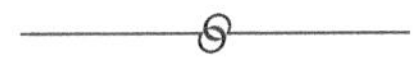

One task—that's not so bad. It's nothing new for me to sneak off into the forest to meet a fugitive. I'm certain my approach is announced to the underground bunker well before I arrive. When I arrive at the entrance, Clover slips down from a tree branch.

"You shouldn't be out here," I say.

"Neither should you." She shrugs. "I can't resist being outside after all that time, Adwin. Anyway, what brings you here?"

"I have to go to Kaycie. I figured this would be a good opportunity to get Jase out."

She straightens. "That's great. Have you confirmed that Serenity is all right?"

The urge to roll my eyes at Serenity managing to become important to people here too is strong, but I resist. "I haven't heard she's dead, which—again—would be an immediate update situation."

"Come on, then." She leads me down into the underground base. Her footsteps are silent as we traverse the glowing green hallway. "Could I go, too?"

"You just got back into your trees, and you want to go to Kaycie's concrete jungle?"

"I can't exactly be up in the trees right now anyway. And I'd like to find out who killed my father."

I stop short. "Clover…"

"I'm not going to seek revenge. They were trying to get *me* out after all. But I need to know what happened."

This sounds like a bad idea, but I owe her. "You can't exactly pilot us out of here, Clover. My mother is coming, and I have to fly the avillipse. Would you be okay holed up in the back?"

She lets out a slow breath. "Yes. I can do it. I've gotten used to confined spaces." Accusation is thick in her voice.

"Fine, if you insist."

We get to the living space, and Clover says, "Jase, it's time to get you home."

He drops his head forward and lets out a sigh. "Thank you." He rises from the table and comes to squeeze Clover's hand. "I'll come back. I'll do whatever I can to help you, but I have to—"

"I'm coming with you actually." Clover's voice is sunny. She steps away to grab some things from a cabinet.

"Oh." A surprised smile stretches across his face. "Thank you."

"We have to get going," I say. "There is no good reason for me to come out here before leaving, and I don't want Nemora returning to my mother's to send us away."

Clover slings a small bag over one shoulder and rejoins us.

"How are we leaving?" Jase asks.

"I have an avillipse. We have to pick up my mother, and she can't know you're there. So you two will have to hide in the trunk."

Jase's eyes widen, and he turns to Clover. "Are you going to be okay?"

"I'll be fine." She offers a thin smile which does nothing to convince me she can handle this, but it's her choice.

"Let's go then." I lead the way out.

Clover takes deeper breaths outside like she can store up the fresh air. With each step, I resist trying to talk her out of this. We reach the avillipse, and she hasn't changed her mind. I've seen her do many incredible things, but making herself so small in the available space ranks right up there with tree-gymnastics. She seems so much bigger than her body. It's difficult to imagine this is possible.

Jase curls in opposite her, and I push down nausea at the thought of shutting her in like this. I tell myself to stop questioning her every move. Maybe we could have waited and come up with something better, but I don't want to miss the opportunity to get out when it's what Nemora is *telling* me to do. It's only a few hours. By tonight everyone will be where they need to be.

Chapter Forty

BRAM

Serenity's smile from a distance is almost as good as being the reason she smiles. She laughs with her friends, and she's whole again. I can see it. It's not just me holding her together anymore—not that I mind being that. For her sake, I don't want her to depend on me. That she can feel whole on her own means I'm not a bandage. The idea of her not needing me is a little scary, but I'd rather her want me.

Preferably, in a more significant way than how I want her at this moment. Seeing her dance shouldn't stir this much in me, but here I am. It's not like I don't know how smoothly she can move. So why does watching the perfect swing of her hips as she twists around Dixon make me squirm? At least now I don't have to berate myself for thoughts like this. The struggle of trying *not* to care for her was exhausting. Even if we haven't decided what we are to each other, we're enough that I can let myself feel this. Knowing that I'll have my hands on her soon enough drops the sensation from torture to anticipation.

Serenity and Dixon part ways and she saunters over to where I sit at the bar. "Dance with me." She takes my hand and tugs.

"You shouldn't be drunk yet." She pouts when I don't move, but I go on. "We haven't even opened the champagne." Leave it to the Kaycians to throw a party when it looks like we might have initiated our doom. Of course, if Montica finds out it was us, we might as well have drunk the stolen champagne. Can't exactly take it to the grave with us. And commandeering a restaurant is child's play after a prison break.

The warm flush of Serenity's face reminds me of other things that leave her looking that way. "Oh, come on."

"Have you given up on discretion then?"

"I have nothing to hide. I just don't feel like I owe it to anyone to tell them. Do you want me to?" She leans in close to whisper against my ear. "Will you dance with me if I tell them? I'll stop the music right now and announce to everyone that we share a bed, and a bathtub, and—"

"You're about to show them rather than telling if you keep talking like that."

Her nose crinkles when she smiles, and she tugs my hand again. "Come on."

"I don't dance."

"I'll teach you."

This time I let her pull me with her. Why did I even pretend I could deny her?

"It's easy," she says turning to me. "Just mirror my feet. When my right foot steps back, your left foot steps forward toward it."

I do as I'm told, but in a much more stiff, awkward way than she does.

"Yes. Forward and together. Then your right foot goes back as my left goes forward, and together."

We repeat that several times. She takes my hands into hers and holds them just below her shoulder level.

"Okay, so keep your feet moving just like that." She switches our hands so they're crossed and raises them up to spin underneath them, falling right back into the rhythm of our steps. "Easy right?"

"You make it look easy."

"Years of practice will do that."

"Not for me it wouldn't. Could you try to be less graceful, so I don't look so ridiculous in comparison?"

"Sure." She lets go of my hands and throws her arms up over her head, jumping around and wiggling playfully. Even goofy is sexy on her. She goes back to trying to teach me. "See? Easy. But you might recall that you don't have to act like a robotic marshal anymore. Sway into it."

She demonstrates those mesmerizing movements of her hips.

"My hips don't do that," I say.

Not that smile, S, you'll break me.

"Oh, I beg to differ. I know what your hips can do."

Chapter Forty-One
SERENITY

Bram's embarrassed agitation is too fun. Getting under his skin when he was always such a stoic badass is impossible to resist. I enjoy watching him squirm.

"Oh, that reminds me of when you said you knew what my mouth could do." My shoulders shake with suppressed laughter.

He presses his lips together and shakes his head. "I didn't think you noticed that awkward phrasing."

"I noticed, I just chose not to be a twelve-year-old about it and didn't giggle."

"How kind of you. Glad you've moved past that whole 'not wanting to embarrass me' thing."

The music changes. Slower. Softer. I drape my arms behind Bram's neck, and his hands find the spot on my lower back they fit perfectly on.

"I prefer this 'anything goes' phase of our relationship. We shouldn't have to tiptoe around each other." I tap out gentle notes on the back of his neck.

"Me too." A coy grin pulls up one side of his lips. "Plus, it was a ridiculous thing to say *then*. Now, it's actually true."

He enjoys making me blush too. The words almost come out as a laugh, but I want him to know I mean them. The three words which keep dancing through my mind when I'm with him. He needs to know I don't mean it lightly. It's not just something to say—it's consuming.

Even though I said it in a teasing way, I meant it when I said I'd tell everyone. We're not a secret, but I have to tell him how much he means to me before anyone else. I pull myself closer to him. His warmth envelops me. His clean scent draws me to nuzzle into his chest. It's perfect, and if I could only find it in me to deliver the words as perfectly, they'd be out already.

A cork *pops*.

So it begins. Someone opened their bottle.

Then Krisalyn screams.

Bram and I both snap our heads toward the sound. I drop my hands from Bram and take one shaky step. My body shuts down as I gape at the sight. Everything stops working. My heart, my lungs, my brain.

It's a miracle I'm still standing.

Krisalyn sobs into Jase's shoulder. Still holding her, he searches the room. His eyes meet mine, and my knees buckle.

Bram catches me by the elbow. My entire body shakes uncontrollably. My chest is going to explode. I'm going to die. I'm dying. Maybe I'm already dead.

Maybe a bomb fell on our festivities, hence we're being reunited with a ghost.

But being dead can't possibly be this painful. My eyes see nothing pointed to the floor. My heart goes from its full stop to a frenzied race, as if it might be able to run right out of me.

Two hands support my shoulders, and I look up to find that I'm face to face with my dead boyfriend. "Serenity?" Jase's face is wet with tears, and I realize mine is too. He's different than I remember. The golden eyes are right, but his hair is longer, and his face looks thinner, harder.

"How... I... Are you real?" My sputtering sends me shaking even more. My hands hover near my face, half covering my gaping expression.

"I'm real. I'm here. I'm sorry it took me so long to get back to you." He pulls me in to a firm embrace.

I can't breathe. *I can't breathe.* I push back from him, and my face crumples as his eyes scour it. Every unsavory feeling I thought I had rid myself of—I can't hide from them anymore.

"I've missed you every second." He leans toward me, but I turn my head aside and his lips brush my temple. *Oh, God.* Does he still love me? He can't. He shouldn't.

"I'm... sorry, I..." I clench my chest as I step back and out of his grasp. "I just... I need..." I don't know if I'm going to throw up or faint, but as quickly as my trembling legs can carry me, I dart to the bathroom.

Chapter Forty-Two

BRAM

Silence grips the room, squeezing us. Nervous glances pass back and forth between everyone left, but I stare at the now empty hallway Serenity disappeared down.

"Um, Jase?" Krisalyn sounds mousy as she approaches him.

Barbed wire wraps around my heart, tighter and tighter. Some part of my consciousness is aware of people moving, talking. Explaining. Grouping off and trying to figure out what's going on. Glances are thrown my way.

My legs are lead, but also magnetically drawn toward her. Before I can stop them, they carry me after her.

In the bathroom, Serenity leans over the sink, chest heaving, head down. I can't tell if she hears me come in.

"S?" *Shit, no. Don't call her that.*

She looks up and meets my eyes in the mirror. Her body quakes before she buries her face in her hands. Sobs rack her, and my throat tightens—threatening to suffocate me. Every cell in my body aches to wrap my arms around her. I *need* to hold her. To let her cry against my chest like she's done so many times before, but now... I approach slowly.

The first thing she did was step away from me. What am I supposed to do with myself? Maybe I shouldn't have followed her.

When I get close enough, she whips around and throws herself against me—curling into me as she gasps for air. I'm probably not very soothing when I'm shaking as badly as she is. We stand there like that for I don't know how long. I'm thrust back to the memory of her crying like this when she realized Jase was dead—when she *thought* Jase was dead. I knew then that I'd rather see her happy in Jase's arms than feel her crying like that in mine. But that was never supposed to be an option again.

When she seems to have control of her breathing, I try her name again, but it chokes me. She looks up, and those gray eyes I'd be happy to drown in are puffy and red. I'd give anything—*anything*—for her not to feel like this.

"Serenity," I start again, forcing my voice to work, "I will never be a source of guilt for you. I'll understand... no matter what you want to do." Her eyebrows pull together, creasing the space in between them. At another time I'd have kissed that little worry-wrinkle away. "Really, I'll be fine." It almost feels like a lie. For her happiness, I mean every word. "We were both broken. We were mourning. We needed... a distraction."

She jerks back from me so hard I almost fall toward her. A storm flashes in her eyes, but only for a moment. She takes a deep breath. Then, despite the puffy red eyes, her face is a sea of calm. *Shit, here we go.*

"Well, thank you for being so *sensible*." She says the word like a curse, even in her most businesslike voice.

"Don't do that."

"What?"

"Put on your damn mask when I'm trying to talk to you."

She rolls her shoulders back. "This... is an extremely uncomfortable situation. I appreciate your... honesty... and understanding."

Honesty? Maybe in some points, but... "I didn't mean to make you angry."

"I'm not."

"Don't lie to me."

"Oh, I'm not lying. I am, most definitely, *not* angry." She stalks past me and through the door.

My fists clench so hard I might break a finger. I drop my chin to my chest, fighting the urge to roar with every ounce of self-control I have. Is it possible that this hurts even more than finding Emrys' dead body? Than hearing about my mom's murder? Am I a horrible person if that's true? Their deaths burned me in a fiery inferno. I had someone to blame for those. This... this is just dark and cold and empty. And who do I have to be angry at but myself?

Chapter Forty-Three
ADWIN

Clover grips my arm. "Everyone scrambling around and slamming doors isn't what I expected."

"Welcome to Kaycian drama." Of course, this is a subdued version. There isn't the city glamour to make it really look like a spectacle, but these people are making do with what they've got. Serenity was the first to go running. Vogue wasn't the one to go after her. She's still with Krisalyn, who is crying and talking to Jase at the center of their circle of friends. Frey and Carista break off from the group and come toward us.

Frey doesn't even look at me, just continues straight out.

Carista's gaze catches on Clover. "You're here?" she says. "I'm glad you got out, but I need to go check on a friend right now."

Clover nods. "Why is Jase's return causing such a stir?"

"Serenity is seeing someone else now." She drags her fingertips across her forehead and sighs.

"Oh." Clover frowns. She glances toward Jase and worries her bottom lip.

"That's... awkward," I say.

Carista rolls her eyes. "Yeah, so, if you'll excuse me." She walks out.

"He spent the entire time wanting to get back to her." Clover's voice is more breathy than I've ever heard it. "How could she forget him like that?"

"She thought he was dead. I didn't see firsthand how she was, but I know it was rough."

Clover's lips pinch together. She's always planned to live a life free of romantic love. Will this prove Ismene's plans for that are rational?

Vogue leaves Krisalyn and Dixon with Jase. Her eyes lock onto me, and as she approaches, I remind myself I've been punched by *Priam* so this can't be as— She swings her palm toward my face. I catch her wrist before it makes contact. All those attacks from Misty are paying off.

"How *dare you* not tell us Jase was locked up there!"

"Vogue, I didn't know. Don't you think I'd have used it to convince you to help me?"

She huffs and plants her hands on her hips. "What the hell were they doing with him all these months?"

"Interrogating him, at first," Clover says. "He doesn't remember what they asked him, of course. Then he was my companion—someone who I couldn't very well conspire with, so they let us talk. I'm Clover Agnar."

Vogue takes a deep breath. "I'm sorry about your father."

"Who killed him?" Clover asks.

"I did." Vogue doesn't miss a beat. It would convince any Kaycian, but I know the art of lying too well.

"No you didn't," I say. "You were busy. It had to be Serenity or Carista, but you'd only lie to protect one."

Vogue gets close enough for me to see every shade of her green eyes. "You wouldn't recognize what lying to protect someone else looks like, Adwin. You only ever do it for yourself." She takes a step back. "And

I don't owe you anything. You asked us to get her out,"—she gestures to Clover—"and we did. You said you could keep us safe. Do it, or I will happily serve you up to Ismene." She storms off.

Clover looks at me with amusement glittering in her eyes. "That's exactly how Jase described her."

I doubt he described Serenity as the kind of person who'd kill Rocco, but I have to guess that's what happened. I shouldn't have pushed Vogue on the topic in front of Clover. I owe it to Serenity not to incriminate her. After all, she was there at my request.

Somehow, I don't think Ismene will find Serenity to be any less guilty for that.

Chapter Forty-Four
SERENITY

A distraction? A distraction. Really? Babysitting Libby was a distraction! The egg incident was a *distraction!* Making love to me was more. I thought it was more. Maybe it should be rephrased. Apparently having sex with me would be the more accurate description.

I get to my room and dive onto the bed. A pillow muffles the sound of my scream, but it smells like Bram. Not helping.

What kind of wretch am I that this is what I'm thinking about right now? Jase is back. He's *alive.* That's amazing, but... Tears pour down my cheeks. Did I move on too quickly? I *loved* him. But now I... I can't breathe. I can't think. My shoulders quake as more tears come and all I want is to be in Bram's arms. All the seams where my pieces were put back together are coming apart again.

How did I get it so wrong? We weren't defining what we were, but after everything we went through, I thought what we had was real. I didn't feel broken with him. He never looked at me that way. He looked at me like... like he loved me as much as I love him.

He joked about showing everyone we were... whatever we were. But I thought it would really happen. He'd have kissed me when I told him I love him. Not for a second did I think he would respond with anything other than 'I love you, too.' I was so sure. God, I know he can hide his feelings, but this...

No. *No!* I refuse to believe that was a lie. That was infinitely more elaborate than pretending to be a marshal. There is *no way* Bram Eros would *fake* vulnerability. He'd fake being impenetrable any day, but not this. He was too gentle, too tender. It wasn't just about sex. Regardless of verbalizing a commitment, we were no more casual than a golden ballgown.

Fuck this. We've been fighting the entire time we've known each other. I'm not going down now without a fight.

At the sound of a knock, my head whips toward the door. *Please,* don't let that be a well-meaning friend. Or worse, Jase. Please, please, please let it be Bram here to admit he was an idiot.

Out of habit, I wipe my tears away. Not like he hasn't seen this mess before.

I open the door.

The last person I'd expect stands in the hallway: Lanelle Kemp.

"Hello, Serenity."

Before I grip reality enough to know what's happening, I feel a prick on my neck. I hold onto consciousness long enough to feel myself fall.

Chapter Forty-Five

BRAM

Walking outside is like wandering through a nightmare. It doesn't feel real, but it's still horrible. Carista and Frey fall into step with me.

"What happened?"

Why is it always Cary when shit hits the fan? I'm really close to not being able to look at her without remembering all the times I wished I was dead. I keep walking in silence. Where to, I don't know. Tonight won't be ending where last night did. Or the night before.

"Bram!" Cary grips my arm to stop me. "What happened?"

"What *happened* is that *yet again* anything good that comes my way is ripped away the minute I get comfortable with the idea of being happy!"

Cary and Frey look at each other and then back at me. Frey is the one to speak. "She wants to be with Jase?"

"Well, fuck, she only *wasn't* with Jase because he was *dead.*"

"Did she *say* she wants to be with Jase?" Cary asks.

How is this confusing? "The first thing she did when she saw him was move away from me."

"She was shocked, you ass." Cary shakes her head like I'm an idiot. "A fucking ghost walked into the room."

"He's not a ghost. He's alive. And guilt is going to devour her because we were..."

"Fucking."

"Frey, I swear you're not going to look pretty anymore with a black eye."

"But you are. Were. Whatever."

My fist clenches, but Cary grabs my wrist. "Don't talk about her like that." My voice is practically a growl.

"It's not an insult," Frey says.

"Yes it is!" My self-control is shredded and blowing away in the wind. "She wouldn't fuck around. She's... We..." I press the heels of my hands to my eyes. *Fuck.* "*I'm* in love with her."

I knew I'd have been better off dying that first morning with her.

"Then we're back to, what happened?" Cary crosses her arms.

Air scrapes my lungs on its way out. "I told her she didn't have to feel guilty for my sake. That she could be with Jase, and I'd be okay." How that could even be believable, I don't know.

"And she..."

"Got pissed and left."

"Of course she was angry," Frey says. "You don't sleep with a woman and then tell her you don't care if she walks. It never goes well."

Why is Frey here? I look at Carista, but she presses her lips into a hard line. "He's right. And he's talking about one-night stands. It's much worse in this situation."

I tried to do the right thing. I wanted her to be able to do whatever she needs to do. She couldn't possibly think I don't want her.

Did I say that?

Shit.

⸺⸺ &⸺⸺

"Serenity, please. Talk to me." Vogue leans her head against Serenity's door. When I walk up to her, she turns her tear-streaked face toward me. "This is insane. Maybe she'll talk to you."

One can only hope.

"Krisalyn and Dixon are explaining to Jase..." Vogue's voice drops so she isn't heard from the other side of the door.

"Explaining what?"

"That you two have been together for a while."

"We haven't... We never said we were *together*."

She wipes her eyes and smiles. "Whatever you *said*, you've both been over the moon happy since we got back from Montica. And pretending it was some secret was so annoying. I didn't even get to give you the protective best friend, *if you hurt her, I'll kill you*, speech."

"Well, I'd rather cut off my arm than hurt her."

"I know. Hence why I restrained myself." She pats my shoulder and says, "Good luck," before leaving me alone at the door.

After a deep breath I knock.

There's no answer.

"S, it's me. I won't let anyone come ask if you're okay. I won't ask you anything. I just need to tell you..." I can't tell her I love her through a damn door. "Please let me in."

Eventually, the weight of tonight's events is enough that I drop to the floor with my back against the door.

"I'll be here whenever you're ready."

I'll wait here as long as it takes.

Chapter Forty-Six

ADWIN

Clover insists on staying at Leavenworth for the time being. Her fondness for Jase is the only reason I'm not worried about her exacting retribution on Serenity. Although, with Serenity having moved on that might get twisted. As I get into the avillipse, I shake my head at how complicated everything always gets.

"The Establishment still giving you trouble?" Mother asks, oblivious to the real reason for our detour.

"I keep telling you, they're nothing to worry about." Not all of them, and not in the way she suspects anyway. The rebels won't be held down, but as long as I'm on their side, that'll work out just fine.

"Don't underestimate people who have always known power and had it taken away. They won't simply accept that."

We rise and make our way across the dark expanse between the former islands. Her statement makes me worry more about Ismene than the Establishment. Was Priam right? Is killing the holder of the power the only way for it to pass on?

The sound of my mother's gasp hits me when the lights of Kaycie's skyline come into view. Colors splash across the city like a glowing painting—back to its former glory. "Even though you said it was done, it was impossible to envision the city whole again after all that." Her words drift through the craft. "I never thought I'd be grateful for Ismene."

My heart sinks to my stomach. The masses have no idea what kind of monster Ismene is. They don't know their suffering was at her hand, so for them to accept Montica as savior is one thing. But if my mother—whose entire life has suffered for the Agnars' spite—is grateful for their aid, then they've sunk their claws in too deep. I can't argue now, though. There's no need for her to continue to fear them, and she'll sway whichever way the winds of power blow. They all will.

Below us, the city bustles the same as ever. An atmosphere of fun, the calm of being carefree. We pass the new EC, which now stands for Equality Capital, but will always live in many minds as the Establishment Center. There's a hovercraft on the roof, not the dark blue of Kaycie's now-scant fleet, or the forest green of Montica's.

Who is in my city?

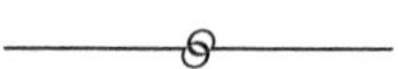

I remain outside while Mother goes into her building. A cold breeze whips between the buildings and sends a chill down my spine. Anger will suffice to warm me up. The security office doesn't even get a full greeting out before I cut in. "Why is there a craft on my roof without my knowledge?"

A mousy male voice trembles through my comm. *"Mr. Lebeau, the council has only—"*

"What council? We are no longer governed by a council. This country is governed by *me*." Ismene can't blatantly walk all over me. This kind of behavior doesn't maintain the façade of my power.

"The Collective Council."

The Collective is here? Does the entire world brush off my position then? They come here without contacting *me?* "And why hadn't I been informed they arrived?" To save a little face, I can at least act like I was expecting them.

"Lieutenant Governor Agnar was with them. We didn't think we—"

"Thank you. I'll take it up with him."

I end the call and take a slow breath. He's here, after months of silence, not even telling me where he is, he pops into my capital like he owns it. I am so *sick* of him relegating me to the sidelines after *he* dragged me into this life.

Kaycie taught me to expect everything I want. Montica taught me to portray power. It's time to put both of those to use.

This city is mine, even if I had to lie, cheat, and steal my way to owning it. It isn't as if anyone else has ever earned power by noble means. There's not a thing wrong with me entering the EC like I own it—because I do. Guilt has no power over me, and there's no room for fear. I've stood against more frightening people than these.

I throw open the door to my office. My jaw flexes at the sight of Casimir sitting behind my desk.

"Adwin, what are you doing here?" It's not often that Casimir Agnar is surprised. I'm embarrassed by how much I enjoy this little victory.

"You are the one in *my office*. I didn't know you were in the city, and you brought in the Collective without my knowledge?"

"It isn't safe for you to know everything."

"Don't pull that shit with me. Save it for everyone else. I'm on this side of it, and I need to know what's going on."

I expect him to get angry at me for standing up to him this way, but he only raises his eyebrows in a patronizing expression. This is worse.

"You have to remain near Ismene, so we must take the utmost care with what you know."

I've done just fine keeping secrets from Ismene, but since I don't think he'd approve of the prison break, I don't bring that up.

"I told you," he continues, "keep your head down. Hold your position. Do what you need to do to remain in her good graces. Let me take care of the rest."

"You think you can control everything, but you can't. While you're off *taking care of things*, Clover and her team escaped, and Rocco was killed!" Of course, that's all because I *didn't* keep my head down, but since I don't regret the first part, I won't feel guilty for what happened to accomplish it.

His eyes go from light blue to steely. "Rocco?"

I scrape my bottom lip with my teeth. With anyone else, I'd never use the death of a family member like that, but I'm not sure Grandfather even has emotions. "He died on Wednesday."

"No one thought to inform me?" His voice is still cold, business-like. I was right. He doesn't have feelings; it probably affects him for some political scheme.

"That can't surprise you." He hasn't been a part of that family for a long time.

He folds his hands together. "What are you doing in Kaycie?"

"Nemora and Ismene didn't think Mother's home was safe enough after these events. I brought her here rather than subjecting her to the Breck."

"Good." He nods. "Now we can go back to Montica."

I attempt to keep the surprise from my voice. "You're coming to Montica?"

Chapter Forty-Seven

SERENITY

I can't open my eyes. Not like when waking up is miserable, and I just don't want to. I literally cannot open my eyes. Or feel them at all. I feel nothing. I smell nothing. But do I hear... rain falling?

"You can wake up now."

I can see now, though I didn't feel my eyes open. The ceiling above my bed is dimly lit in grayish hues. It is raining. *Who told me to wake up?*

"It's me, sweetie. Look at me when I speak to you."

Against my will or ability, I sit up and turn toward Lanelle. *What's happening?*

"Well, you see—"

Did she hear my thought?

"Yes, isn't it amazing?"

I'm not talking to you!

"Oh, but you are. In fact, I could talk to you without moving my lips too. Would you like to see?"

No! Get the hell out of my head!

"You've changed, Serenity. You used to be so sweet."

Hearing Lanelle's voice in my mind makes me want to vomit. If a consciousness without a body could throw up. *What are you doing, Lanelle?*

"I need your help with something."

You could have just asked.

"You'd have said no. At least, I'm fairly certain you'd have said no." She stands and glides toward me. "But maybe"—she deigns to speak out loud—"you're as disappointed as I am that Jase didn't die. Looks like it's complicating matters for you."

Emotions are so strange without feeling my body. My heart should be racing, my stomach twisting, but none of it happens. *I am* not *upset that Jase is alive.*

"I wouldn't judge you if you were. I *am* judging you for the clothing selection you have here." She clicks her tongue. "You used to be more fashionable. You should be *furious* about the crimes committed against you. Dragging you into this has made you dreadful. And I want you to look pretty today."

I *see* her hand as her fingers brush down my cheek, but I don't feel it. I hear the slap she lays across my face, but... nothing. *You extirpated me.*

"That took you too long. Come now! There are things to do. I'm letting you borrow my dress,"—she holds up a skimpy black and red shift—"like the good friend I am. Go get dressed and ready."

Like a puppet on strings, I do as she says. *Where is my dog?*

"Just taking a nap. I'm not heartless, Serenity. I wouldn't hurt an innocent little dog."

While my hands style my hair and apply my makeup, Lanelle busies herself with talking my ear off. If only my hearing went with my autonomy.

"Did you all really think you could take everything from us without repercussions? Even after you learned of your birthright! You can't fathom how it feels to be betrayed like that."

Yes, I can.

"Oh, silly me. Of course. This isn't the first time you've had your mind toyed with. Except, I'm smarter than Jase. My method gives me more control."

If you stop now, you might walk away from this.

"You're in no position to make threats. No one will ever know about this."

People are going to notice. It's an odd thing that happens when you let people in—they know when something is wrong.

"There won't be much opportunity. Unfortunately, yours and Jase's complicated love story ends in murder-suicide."

I should be heaving quick breaths; I should feel a chill down my neck. *You won't get away with this.*

"It isn't so hard to believe. Jase, faced with the reality of your gut-wrenching betrayal, ends you both in a fit of jealous rage."

No one will believe Jase would hurt me.

"Except he has before. This is more permanent, but he's been through *so* much. It's tragic, really. You should be thanking me. You'll be more famous than ever. I wonder who will play you in the movie?"

Shut up!

Lanelle glances at her cuff. No wait, *my cuff*. "All right, Jase has agreed to meet you." She looks me up and down. "I'd have put you in something more form fitting, but you're too small to fit in anything of mine. Did Jase ever suggest you get implants? He's always been a breast man."

Go to hell!

Her voice in my mind is like dragging a knife on a plate. *"After you."*

How did the marshals survive years of this without going in-sane? It's like watching a film of myself as I finish getting ready and open the door to leave.

Bram tumbles into the room. "S?"

The sound of his voice should make my heart flip right now. Instead, I step right over him and start down the hall.

"My, my. He stayed at your door all night long?" Lanelle muses in my mind. *"You must be very gifted. Even more reason for Jase to be infuriated now."*

Bram! I walk away from him without a word. *Bram, follow me. See me!*

"Serenity, stop. Please." He sounds broken. Not being able to do anything cracks my sanity. He follows me down the hall. "I need to talk to you. You have every right to be pissed off at me for last night. We need to talk about it."

In the elevator he says, "Would you look at me?"

Fight with me! Take my face in your hands so you can see!

"Not yet," I say, my voice detached from my control.

Lanelle croons. *"Don't want to risk him figuring this out, now do we?"*

You fucking psycho!

"This is what I'm talking about, Serenity. These people have even degraded your language. I can't believe you've lowered yourself to this rabble's level."

He will rip you limb from limb.

"So we agree then that he's a savage?"

I take it back. He won't have the opportunity to kill you. I'll do it before he has a chance.

While Lanelle and I fight in my head, I pass Vogue and ignore her completely. I hear her stop Bram behind me. They're discussing what's wrong with me. *Ugh. Follow me and see for yourselves!*

In the main office building's elevator, I'm alone with Lanelle in my thoughts. *Lanelle, there's still time to stop this. I won't tell them what you were trying to do.*

"Oh, I'll tell them myself. You and Jase are only the beginning. Your entire group is going to be slaughtered by the time I'm done. The timing worked out gloriously. Testing has been fun, but now it's perfect, and I couldn't be happier it's for the two of you. The rest will all watch as one-by-one, tragedy befalls them. They'll find out how you and Jase went out, and they'll learn what's in store for the rest. Are you a religious person, Serenity? Perhaps you'll all be reunited soon.*

"Oh! Will your story repeat in reverse? It wouldn't really be heaven if you couldn't have sex, so when your new boyfriend isn't there, will you start sleeping with Jase?"*

You soulless bitch.

From the top floor, I go up a stairway and exit onto the roof. Jase stands there in the rain—dark circles under his eyes.

"This reminds me of the plaza fountain." My voice sounds sad.

"Nice touch, right?"

Jase doesn't respond. A storm roils in his golden eyes.

"I'm sorry about last night," I say against my will. "It was such a shock, and I… A lot happened when you were…" A sniffle. *Am I crying?* "I thought you were dead." It's barely a whisper. *Lanelle, you are a master puppeteer. My congratulations on your last achievement.*

"I heard." Jase's voice is heavy.

"Serenity?" Bram arrives behind me.

Good luck now.

"I can work with this."

"Bram," I say. "I'm sorry, I needed to tell Jase. I owe him that much."

"Don't you think Jase deserves this after you walked in on him kissing me?" Lanelle asks as if she didn't orchestrate that too.

I approach Bram and see my hands wrap behind his neck, his face comes closer to mine, and I'm blinded behind my eyelids, left with no idea how this kiss is going.

How. Are. You. Kissing. This?!

My eyes open and Bram looks at me like he's never seen me before. *Ha! You've lost, Lanelle. He knows me too well for this to work.*

"I guess we have to make this quick then."

Like lightning, my hand snatches the gun from Bram's holster, and I swing around toward Jase. He's ghostly pale and wide-eyed. If I could cry, I would sob. But my arm is thrown down and I'm spun around into Bram. I can barely tell what's happening as we fight. My surroundings swirl and flash past me so quickly, I don't know what my body is doing. There's one thing I do know. Lanelle's fury ruined her own plans. The smart thing to do would have been to drop Bram first, but she went for Jase, because she hates him. Her critical error will save us all. Or it should.

It's taking longer than necessary. Even if my feelings can't stop me from truly fighting him, he should be able to take me down quickly. But he can't fight me either.

"What the hell is going on?" Jase shouts.

"It's not... her!" Bram gets the words out as he struggles against me. "Some help... would be nice." The gun skitters away, but our scuffle continues.

Just knock me out! I can't feel it!

Jase finally intervenes... by pushing Bram away from me. "Get the hell off her!"

Bram sends Jase sprawling with a shove and steps cautiously toward me. I step back in equal measure—slowly. It's like the dance I taught him last night. Our steps mirror perfectly.

This is what it feels like to mentally cry.

I stop moving, and Bram's eyes widen.

"I think he'll jump with you," Lanelle purrs.

Bram! My fingers wave.

The sky takes over my vision as I fall backward over the edge of the roof.

Chapter Forty-Eight

BRAM

Nothing exists. The world vanishes. Straight as a board—with that perfect posture I used to be so annoyed by—Serenity tips over... and falls.

I dive forward as she disappears over the edge of the roof.

No no no no no no.

I catch her ankle. She flips upside down, knocking her back and head against the wall. Screams bubble up from the ground below. Rain trickles down onto us, and I tighten my grip to keep her from slipping. Then she increases the difficulty level.

Every twist and kick makes holding her damp skin a more impossible challenge. Her other foot comes to kick my hands away, and I catch that one too. Jase appears at my side and takes one of her legs. Small as she is, it would be easy to pull her up if she wasn't fighting us every inch of the way.

Her body writhes. The moment she's back on the roof, she rolls around and springs up. Jase and I are still kneeling, and she throws her knee into his temple. He hits the roof, and I dive for her again. We roll on the roof in a tangle of limbs. Even though she can't feel anything right now, she's going to feel the after-effects when we reverse this. It kills me to hurt her.

Finally, I get her pinned down. Holding her hands back over her head is nauseating. This would terrify her. My body weight holds her down as she squirms. Even as her body tries to continue to fight me, I whisper to the girl trapped inside. The girl who can hear me, who watched in horror as this happened, who I almost lost.

"We're all fine. You're safe. I've got you. It's going to be okay."

Footsteps rush toward us. Krisalyn appears and injects something into Serenity's neck. Her eyes close, and she goes still.

I relax my grip on her wrists and support my weight over her. My arms shake underneath me as I pant against her neck. I could have been grieving over her dead body right now. *Too close. That was too close.*

When a hand lands on my shoulder, I tense instinctively, still protecting her.

"It's okay." Vogue's voice has never been softer. "Let's get her fixed up."

I nod, taking another moment before I peel myself off Serenity. On my knees, I look at Krisalyn as she tends to Jase. Vogue hugs me and whispers, "Thank you."

This isn't the first time I've carried Serenity's unconscious form. Last time I was kicking myself for the feelings it provoked in me. Now, holding her against me is perfectly familiar, and looking at her face stirs up even more emotion.

After I lay her down on the hospital bed, she's wheeled away. Being separated from her aches. Like my body knows it narrowly avoided the worst pain imaginable—losing her forever—and has to keep holding her to be assured it won't happen. In a daze, I sit, every muscle trembling.

Vogue sits next to me. "Serenity can confirm when she wakes up," she says, "but we have a theory on who did this."

I turn my head slowly. Does Vogue know that even without a name, I'm debating how to kill this person? Whoever locked Serenity away in her own mind so she could watch as she hurt or killed us and herself, is going to suffer in ways previously unimaginable.

Unaware or unconcerned, Vogue continues. "They're going to see if she has any injuries to tend to before giving her the antidote. Don't want her to wake up in too much pain." Vogue's face contorts in agony.

Regardless of whatever medical attention Serenity gets, she's going to wake up to pain. Today has been its own trauma, and she still has to reconcile Jase being back.

"Where was Jase this whole time?" I ask.

Vogue sighs. "Montica. He was captured and taken from the EC before it was destroyed."

Shit. I don't want to think about how guilty Serenity is going to feel about this. To know that while he was imprisoned, she was... Well, she was suffering too. She suffered so much, but she survived. Is it really so terrible? She might think so, but I need to give her the chance to decide for herself.

Chapter Forty-Nine
ADWIN

The flight to Montica is quiet. Grandfather still insists he can settle all the continent's issues diplomatically if I keep my head down and shut up. He won't divulge any more information, so I maintain that I have no way to contact Clover. How could I find her if the Breck can't? I couldn't hand her back to the family again, and I won't presume to tell her what she can or can't do for her own country. I've made those mistakes before.

Everything and nothing has changed since the first time I arrived here with Grandfather. I've made it more my home than his, even if my position is tenuous at best, a sham at worst. We make the familiar walk across the atrium. This time the boardroom door opens to my face scan.

We enter, and Ismene's head snaps up. Her jaw clenches at the sight of her father. Nemora's gaze bounces between all three of us.

"Ismene," he says with an uncharacteristic softness, "why didn't you tell me?"

Her shoulders heave. "You didn't deserve to know."

"But what do you deserve?" He walks around the table, and she rises slowly. I've never seen Ismene physically violent—she never gets her hands dirty—however, I wouldn't be surprised if she took a swing at him. Instead, she drops her face into his shoulder as he pulls her into an embrace. She quakes with sobs, and he whispers, "I know," near her braided hair.

I stare in disbelief, unable to process what I'm seeing. Nemora grips my arm and pulls me out of the room. Whereas I'm confused, she looks uncomfortable when we stop in the atrium. "Not what you expected either?" I ask.

She plants her hands on her lower back and paces short loops. I don't know how Ismene has been handling Rocco's death, and I don't know why this show of emotion has rattled Nemora so much. Does she expect her mother not to mourn her own brother?

"Nemora?"

Her eyes meet mine, and something flashes in them I can't quite pinpoint. "I don't want to think right now."

A laugh bubbles in my chest. "Oh, and I gather as a Kaycian, I'm expected to specialize in *not thinking*?"

Her lips turn up. "You said it, not me."

"What am I supposed to do?" Nemora's hand gestures alone are enough to mark her unnatural ease. But that's the least of it. Talking seems to be quite acceptable even if thinking isn't. "Don't raise me to be untouched by emotion, then be disappointed when I'm not emotional!" She goes for a sip and finds only ice in her glass. She lacks the agility I've come to expect from her. At the counter, she refills her drink and brings both it and the bottle back to the sitting room. The bottle slams onto the coffee table.

"She said she was disappointed in you?" I sip my own, not affected thanks to years of built-up tolerance.

"She doesn't have to say it." Nemora leans over the back of an armchair, cradling the glass in two hands. "Disappointment is one emotion well established in this family. I can spot that from a mile away."

"It's probably genetic. Grandfather's disappointed face is pretty obvious, too." I'm not sure if it would have been any better if I knew Serenity had broken up with me. He'd still have been upset with me for not being able to keep it up.

"We are their own creatures. It isn't as if they can blame us for how we turned out."

"Wouldn't that apply to Clover and Priam then?"

She snorts a laugh—or I'm hallucinating. Both are equally improbable. "No. Priam and Clover exist to contradict our parents' efforts. *I* am the perfect Agnar specimen. I'm the only one who is what I'm supposed to be. Then she acts like I'm *broken* because I don't cry over someone dying."

"She's dealing with something different than you are. I'm sure you would if it was your brother." She shoots me an incredulous look. Okay, maybe she is broken then. "Look, I can't presume to understand how sibling relationships work. Families are complicated."

"Ours has to be the most complicated."

"I hope so."

She rounds the chair to sit on it, and pushes a hand through her hair, tussling the braided crown. "Didn't your mother always hate Casimir for it, too?"

"Yes. She kept me away from him. We didn't meet until I was sixteen."

"You'd think our mothers would have bonded over that."

"They didn't have a chance."

"That's true." As she tips more whiskey down her throat, I can't help but wish Nemora had joined when I first got here and bonded with Clover and Priam this way. Just like Ismene shunning my mother, Nemora was determined to do the same to me, but all four of us could have gotten along. We could have figured out a way to fix things in a way that everyone could be happy with. Instead, we each set off on our own paths and have to hack away at everything in our way. When those paths cross, it's hard to avoid hitting each other.

A dark laugh slips from her. "Of course, if Rocco's claims had any truth to them, I don't suppose our mothers could have ever been friendly."

Is she drunk enough to share? I'm afraid to ask, sure she'll close up if I show too much interest. "He was desperate. He may have even been trying to sneak Clover out of prison, so he was obviously unstable." *Because who would do that?* His presence there does lend to the assumption that he tried to take advantage of the commotion we caused. "I wouldn't worry about it."

"I hate him for planting the idea in my head." Her gaze goes distant. "Maybe that's why I don't mourn him. Perhaps I should tell Mother the horrible things he said. She wouldn't deign to *cry* over someone who would claim she reveled in torturing someone."

I suck in a sharp breath. "He said she *what?*"

Chapter Fifty

SERENITY

This time when I wake up, I can feel my body—every last ache and pain. Being able to feel is thrilling. My eyes open to my mother's face.

"You're back?"

Tears cascade from her eyes. "How are you feeling?"

I sit up slowly. I'm back in my room, in a short, cotton night-gown. It's still raining outside, and night has fallen. "I'm okay."

She hugs me, and my eyes meet Bram's. I wince as her embrace aggravates the soreness in my shoulder. "Oh, I'm sorry," she says.

"No, it's okay. Feeling anything, including pain, is a relief."

She brushes my hair from my face. The skin behind my ear in tender under her touch. "Do you know who did it to you?"

"Lanelle Kemp."

My mother nods, and her gray eyes swirl and darken like storm clouds. "I'll go find her then." She kisses my forehead. "I'll be back soon." On her way out, she pats Bram's shoulder.

The door closes, and our eyes lock onto each other.

"Thank you." Even those two words threaten to crack me open and send me into a fit of sobs. Screaming for his help in my head was a unique torture. He did it though. He saved me.

He moves from the corner he was brooding in to sit on the edge of the bed. "Does this mean you aren't angry at me anymore?"

"I already told you I wasn't."

"That was bullshit." He says it casually. Not hostile, just a fact.

"It wasn't *bullshit*. I was not angry, Bram. I was *fucking furious*." My voice cracks as I say it, and his dark eyes widen like I might still not be quite myself. "A distraction?" The tears start to spill over. "Is that all I was to you?"

He drops his head. "Of course not."

"I mean, if that's what it was, okay. I'd have been that for you. I just felt like it was…"

"You were *not* a distraction. Don't you know anything? That was the most ridiculous thing I've ever said."

"What's the truth then?"

His chin quivers as he looks at me. "The truth is, everything else has barely been a distraction from you. I've loved you since before the uprising even started. I spent the whole time in Lawson kicking myself for letting you go to Martel's office. Then every time we almost died, my first thought was how glad I was you weren't there to die too. Aren hated you because he was sick of me putting you above everything else. It killed me when you didn't remember me, and it killed me when you were devastated over losing Jase. Even though being with you saved me from sinking into a place so dark I couldn't name it… I wished he hadn't died. I wished you'd never known that kind of pain and loss. And I have to be grateful for part of that wish coming true."

"Then why cut me loose?"

"Because you had no feelings for me until Jase was gone. If he's back…"

"So you think since you fell in love with me first, I don't love you as much?"

"You...?"

I crawl out from under the blanket to kneel next to him. "Bram, you were always beating yourself up about saving me from physical perils, but you saved me from something so much worse." His shoulders buckle, like he might sob right here, and there's no way I'm finishing this if he does. I sniffle and push on. "I was going to that dark place too, and you saved me. You took my broken pieces and built me back up into something new. And that something is yours. All of it—all of me. I'm yours. I love you."

He looks at me with wonder—amazement. His dark eyes glisten, and tears finally overwhelm his eyelashes to spill over. I wasn't sure he could cry. Even after all he's been through, I've never seen it. Words escape me. All I can do is pull his face to mine. Our tears add a salty edge to the kiss as we fall into each other. Lying here in his arms is so familiar, and we almost never got to do this again. Before I pull back, I kiss away a tear from his cheek. I don't point out that his crying is mind blowing, but he explains it anyway.

"Hearing you say you love me is... indescribable."

"Wasn't it obvious?" I ask. "If you couldn't see that I'm in love with you, I must not be doing a good job of showing affection."

"You've been perfect." He takes a deep breath and lets it out slowly. "I've never been able to believe this is real, because this isn't how my life goes. I don't get the good things. I don't know if I deserve it. Falling for you seemed like the ultimate guarantee of my own misery, because there was no way you'd ever feel that for me. When you started showing that you did, I couldn't get my hopes up—everything I hope for shatters."

Are there words to convince someone he deserves to be loved? "I don't think anything I say will change the way you feel, but I'm going to try to show you—every day—that my love cannot be shattered." I kiss him deeply then whisper against his lips. "You can count on me. I'm not going anywhere."

One hand weaves into my hair as he kisses me harder. The other slides up my thigh. I break our kiss only long enough to pull off his shirt, and he wriggles out of his pants. Even though this isn't the first time he's laid underneath me, being forthright about how much it means gives it a new feeling. Our mouths move together, and I bite his bottom lip softly.

"This is real. I want you to feel it bone-deep that I love you."

"I do." He clutches my face as he kisses me. Our bodies move together and against each other and when my bones have melted, and I lie panting on his heaving chest, he says, "I love you."

It's the best way he's ever said goodnight.

Chapter Fifty-One
BRAM

Last time I saw Grace and Anton Ward, we were leaving a decimated Kaycie with a heartbroken Serenity, a huge surprise from Governor Martel, and a plan to revive the marshals. We came to Leavenworth, and I was sure I'd be able to focus on helping Serenity cope as soon as we took care of business. But the plan broke me, and Serenity and I spent months in darkness before we healed together. There are endless *what-ifs* of how things might have gone differently, but here we are. And though I've already met them, officially being introduced to Serenity's parents in this way is unreal.

"Papá, you know my boyfriend Bram."

His smile for Serenity is only rivaled by Grace's. There wasn't enough time for me to worry about what they'd think of their daughter being with me, but some part of my subconscious must have tucked away the concern, because it's a relief to see they're happy about it.

"Of course." He shakes my hand. "We can never thank you enough for catching her yesterday."

"Well, he already knew I was quite the catch." Serenity smiles at her own maneuvering of the mood. The whole thing is still hard to think about, much less talk about.

Words are on the tip of my tongue—*I'm sorry it got so close*—but she doesn't want to talk about it, and it's nothing we don't all know.

We go to the back corner of Leavenworth's main restaurant and take our seats. Serenity hooks an ankle around mine, keeping her hands folded on the table. "Where have you been all this time?"

"Serenity Eve, don't make it sound as if you'd have listened to us before we left." Grace manages to sound firm and gentle at the same time. She knows why Serenity was checked out, but she's still not going to let her daughter use that against her.

I tilt my head at Serenity, oddly amused to learn her middle name.

She peeks at me from the corner of her eye. "I'm just asking."

"We were in Asia," Anton says, "appealing to the Collective to intervene on Kaycie's behalf."

Kaycie was the whole world, but then there was also Montica. Except, we're only two of eight countries. It's bizarre to think of six others out there. "How did that go?" I ask.

"Good." Grace waves a hand in the most elegant lazy gesture I've ever seen. "Eventually. There was a lot of back and forth between each country before we approached the Collective. I'm sorry we were gone so long."

"It's okay," Serenity says.

"Why did it take so much convincing?" I ask. "Montica practically flattened our capital. I wouldn't think they'd stand for that. Montica is obviously a threat to everyone."

"Kaycie has been cut off from the Collective for a long time." Grace pauses to order a bottle of wine and returns to the topic at hand with a newfound tension in her shoulders. "Our marshal program made us ineligible to be a part of it. The ocean wasn't all that isolated us."

It was bad enough to shun the country, but not enough for them to do something about it? The whole thing makes me doubt the Collective's intentions.

"The marshals' revival finally got them on our side," Anton says. "You all made it possible. You've saved Kaycie in many ways."

Serenity's foot bounces against my ankle. Quick and nervous, not an intimate touch. Because saving the marshals ended Emrys' life? Or is she thinking about how unsafe we still feel in the aftermath of Rocco Agnar's death?

"We heard you spent some time in Eudora," Anton says as he fills our four wine glasses.

Serenity only nods.

"We both needed a change of scenery," I say.

"Eudora is a good option for that." Grace smiles. "Gardner too. That's my favorite. But it's lucky you were back before Jase returned. It must have been a little strange, but God, I'm so happy for him and his mother."

Serenity smiles weakly. "An incredible surprise. I can't believe we didn't know he was imprisoned in Montica this whole time." That's the only part she can respond to—not the timing of being back when he returned. Because of course we had nothing to do with his escape...

Grace's expression hardens. "Do not get tangled up with Montica. Between their own internal turmoil, and the Collective's support, they'll be taken care of. Do you understand?"

We both nod. I cover Serenity's hand with mine and give it a light squeeze. "It's been good to be out of the game. We need to stay that way."

Chapter Fifty-Two
SERENITY

Brunch with my parents made things feel almost normal. My next task will probably be less pleasant. I have to face Jase.

I can't imagine how hurt I would be if our roles were reversed. We walk down the boardwalk lining the border of the base. My arms are crossed tight around me—a foreign feeling when I've gotten so used to that being Bram's job.

"Are you okay?" Jase asks.

I nod. "I heard they can't find Lanelle."

"She took off, apparently. I'm sorry she came after you. It was because of me."

"Her madness is her own fault." I suck in a shaky breath. "What happened to you?"

He stops and leans his elbows on the handrail. This is where we first saw that the sea had receded. His reappearance is just as much of a world-shifting event. "I was on the craft that blew up the EC. They had caught up to me, and I watched as..." He drops his head. "I didn't know who escaped. If they told me anything that would have clued me in, I wouldn't know. I don't remember anything except being in the dark alone. Food and water showed up, but I didn't hear another person's voice for, I don't even know how long. I thought I was going to lose my mind. I didn't know what happened to you, Krisalyn, my mom, anyone. I was scared. And I missed you." His gaze drifts off.

"Eventually they moved me to a cell where, periodically, I got to spend time with Clover. It was for her sake, not mine, but I was grateful. She told me they had probably interrogated me, but I wouldn't remember. We discovered a shared distaste for Adwin."

I rub my eyes, unsure if I want to laugh or cry. "We thought... *I* thought you were dead."

"And I thought..."

I bite my lip to keep it from trembling. "What?"

"I thought you loved me." He drops his head. "I know I had messed things up before it all happened, but I didn't think you were really done with us. Clover figured if you were all dead, there would be no reason for Montica to keep me. So I had to believe you were okay. And I had to think we'd be reunited, and that you'd still..."

My hand flutters to my bare neck. I haven't worn the forget-me-not necklace in some time. I can't keep a reminder of him on my body anymore. The truth might be harder to take than a lie, but I can't lie about this. It was only a missed opportunity—bad timing and disasters we couldn't control broke us apart. Though now, I can't regret where it all brought me. "I wasn't done with us. I was going to tell you that morning, but you weren't there yet, and then..." The familiar nightmare of the EC crashing down plays in my mind, and a shudder runs through me.

"So it all comes down to, 'what if I hadn't taken a sleeping pill the night before.'"

Our eyes meet, then he glances down at my wringing hands.

"Jase, there are a million little things—a million what ifs—that could have changed our trajectory. A lot of them could have resulted in us never being together. And"—tears sting my eyes—"if those options would have meant you would have been safe that day the city was attacked, I'd have preferred one of those. Even though there were times with you I'd never want to trade. Even though I loved you."

"Loved..." he whispers.

I tremble as the tears escape. How many times did I regret never telling him? Now it's past tense. "I couldn't..." What? Couldn't be in love with a dead person forever? Couldn't let myself be eaten alive by grief? There are plenty of reasons, but none of them will make a difference. All I can say is, "I'm sorry."

He leans his head back and sighs toward the sky. "I just can't believe I spent all that time thinking about nothing but you, and you were falling for someone else."

"We thought you were *dead*."

"And how can I argue when you have an excuse like that?"

I bristle. "I don't need an *excuse*. Would you have liked to come back to a half-dead husk of me? Because that was the direction I was going."

"Of course not! God, Serenity, no, but why did you need to get laid to survive it? We hadn't even ever—"

Heat explodes over my face and neck. "First of all, it was your idea for us not to sleep together. Secondly, I did *not* need to *get laid*. I needed understanding, and love, and patience, and Bram gave me all those things long before anything else happened. He saved my *life*."

"He saves you and he's a hero. When I tried to save you, it made me the bad guy."

"You were never the bad guy. Don't go down that road."

"Why?"

My mouth aches with the words I haven't voiced, even to myself. "Because you weren't saving me! If you hadn't given me that amnesia shot, we wouldn't have been fighting, you wouldn't have been captured, and I wouldn't have thought you were dead!"

I drop to the wooden planks and wrap my arms around my knees. I can't believe I said that. It was too awful to think, and I say it to him? What kind of person blames someone for his own death or misfortune?

"So you spent the whole time blaming me?"

I look up. Jase sits opposite me, now. His chin dropped to his chest.

"For the record," he says, "so was I. Knowing I landed myself, and more importantly *you*, in that nightmare was a unique torture. But I hoped—I had to hope—that you'd be waiting for me when I got back. That you were missing me as much as I missed you." He takes a breath. "That is selfish."

I press my fingers against my temples. "I didn't blame you. I blamed myself. I focused on everything I could have done differently that would have saved you." My throat aches as I swallow. "I did miss you."

After a moment, he says, "I don't want us to be like this. I want you to be happy; I'm glad you're doing well. It's just hard to see you with someone else."

"I understand that."

He drops his head back then looks down at my hands. "I heard about what happened. Can you still play piano?"

"I haven't played in a long time."

Jase takes my hand, his thumb tracing the scar across my palm. This time apart has done a number on us both. Those sweet as honey eyes look like hardened amber. Does he see the same person he knew when he looks at me now?

"I'd like to have something meaningful to say, but I'm at a loss." His throat bobs. "I'm glad you're all right. I worried about you... constantly." He stands, offers me his hand, which I take to stand as well. And he walks away.

Did he mean to imply that I was far less thoughtful about him? Or is that the guilt creeping in? I lean my elbows onto the rail. The ache in my chest that Bram loved away is back. It's not as overwhelming or consuming as it used to be, though.

I don't know how long I've been standing here frozen when Bram appears next to me. The simple act of looking into his dark eyes eases the pain. He doesn't touch me; he doesn't ask questions I might not be ready to answer. Always taking my lead, always letting me set the pace.

"You know," I say, "I've been thinking if you and I had happened sooner, it would have prevented a lot of the disasters." I chew the inside of my cheek. "If I hadn't been fighting with Jase he wouldn't have been in the EC—or captured as we now know. Even before that, if I hadn't been with Jase, I never would have taken the amnesia. It seemed like it would be really horrible to say I wished I had never been with him."

His hand warms my jaw, his thumb brushing back and forth over my cheek. "It's not horrible to want to go back in time and stop bad things from happening."

"I'd never be willing to change things in a way that resulted in us not being together, though." I sniffle. "That's so selfish."

He pulls me in, and we hold each other like space between us is the cause of every heartbreak. "That's not selfish. That's very generous to me."

I soak up the feeling of his heartbeat against me—the steadying beat that's kept me grounded so often. "How did you know it wasn't me?" I ask. "Was I a bad kisser when I was extirpated?" I rub the spot behind my ear where the chip was and groan a little "Was I better?"

His chest bounces against me with a small laugh. "No. Neither really. It was actually that there's no way you'd kiss me in front of Jase like that. You'd never be cruel."

"Well…" Am I ready to test how unconditional his love is? "I might have been cruel." Bram waits patiently again. "I told him if he hadn't given me the amnesia none of it would have happened." A tear rolls down my face. "I basically blamed him for getting himself captured. I tried to bury it, but some part of me had been blaming him for his own death." My face crumples, and I bury it in his shoulder.

"Why didn't you tell me?"

"I already hated myself for thinking it. I didn't want you to think I was terrible, too."

He pulls me back far enough to see my face. His eyes lock onto mine, and the idea of him judging me is debunked. "Do you think I don't know the misery of blaming someone for dying?"

Oh, Bram. "Do you want me to tell you?"

His throat bobs. He nods with his lips pressed together.

"If I had watched myself kill you or Jase, I don't know how I could have lived with it." I hug him tight, and he bows his face into my hair. "Emrys was put in an impossible situation. I wish he was with us, but I can't blame him for the escape he took. It's not fair to you, and I'm so sorry."

A moment passes. "Thank you for telling me that. But you shouldn't know how it feels. I let that happen."

"Hey." I arch back to look at him. "It's not your job to protect me all the time. Just to love me."

"Well, that's easy." He smiles, and I let myself feel hope.

Chapter Fifty-Three

BRAM

Serenity fights me against her will. Gravity tries to claim her. Even the rain works against me. All the world is determined to take her from me. Even if she thinks I deserve her love, the universe won't allow it. To love her only puts a target on her, because everything I love is taken away or destroyed. I grip as hard as I can. Can't karma take her in a way that doesn't kill her? I hold on to save her, so I can let her go—save her from the shadow of misery that I can't escape. My hand hurts with the effort.

Bram.

"Bram." *Her voice is soft but scared. She should be. I can't protect her.*

"Bram!"

My eyes snap open.

Her face is inches from mine. She cups my cheek with a hand. "Relax." Her voice washes over me, slowing my speeding heart and relaxing the tension from my muscles.

Particularly— *Shit.* I let go of her wrist as I suck a sharp breath in. "Did I hurt you?"

"Just uncomfortable. No harm done." She holds up the hand and rolls her wrist to prove it, but I'll be keeping an eye on that to see if it bruises.

"I'm so sorry."

"No need." She means it, I can tell. She's not worried about herself, she's worried about me. Completely backwards. No questions come. She doesn't even move to hold me closer. She just waits.

I let out a long breath and rest my forehead against hers. She looks like the small fragile one, but I'm the one falling apart. "I had a nightmare. You hanging off the side of the building. I was trying to hold onto you…"

"And you did."

"I'd rather not break your wrist when my subconscious replays it."

"But hey, you dreamed." I pull back, and her grin is faintly visible in the dark. "I told you dreams were overrated."

"Yeah, this isn't the kind of dream I'd like to have of you."

"It's a start." She kisses me softly. "How about I give you some good dream inspiration."

I smile against her lips, the stress of waking up almost forgotten. "You already have. This wasn't the first time I dreamed of you."

"Oh really?" The smirk is audible in her voice.

This kind of sharing might be the best way to fully recover from the nightmare. I run my fingertips up and down the bumps of her spine. "Last year, Vogue told me you had a hand on an amnesia shot when I found out about you telling Adwin everything."

"Okay?" Of course she doesn't see the link. Because I am deranged to have linked it like this.

"Afterward, I dreamt you took the shot out, but I caught your wrist as you swung for me. And then I kissed you."

A breathy laugh. "How did that kiss compare to reality?"

"My dreams don't do you justice."

Not in what it feels like to touch her. Not in what it's like to lie here in the dark and know I'm not alone for the first time in recent memory. Everything about being with Serenity is more than I could have imagined.

Time is a constant pull between panic and calm. Everything drags me toward the former—memories, all the loose ends, my insecurities. But Serenity settles me every time. Except when she causes it.

"This is exactly what you refused!" I squeeze fistfuls of the blanket where I sit at the foot of the bed. "You wouldn't let me protect you by excluding you, so how the hell do you think I'm going to let you do it to me?"

She plants her hands on her hips. "You were just making rude comments in front of people who know the truth anyway. This is entirely different."

"It is different. This actually matters." And when it matters, there is no way I can stand back and toss Serenity to the wolves.

"Exactly. It *matters* what Clover Agnar thinks. It's not as if we can claim none of us had anything to do with it. She knows I was there; she knows Vogue was trying to cover for me, so I'm already incriminated. My blood was left behind. Nothing places you there."

I scrub my hands over my face. "If this conversation goes badly, and she comes after you, I'll have to be responsible for multiple Agnar deaths." Neither are the one I wanted for so long.

She steps into the space between my knees and rubs my shoulders. "Better to have her attention on me then, I guess."

"It's not funny."

"I know." She takes my hands and pulls me to my feet. "We'll all be there today. There's nothing to worry about."

But there is always plenty to worry about with our group. Even with her hand in mine, the walk across the base feels ominous. Adwin trusting Clover Agnar doesn't do anything to recommend her. Apparently she's friends with Jase now, though. That helps.

As we walk into the administrative offices, I release Serenity's hand so she won't have to feel bad about doing it herself. Her chin tilts up, and she smiles when we make eye contact. Go figure as soon as we started to call this what it is, we have to tread carefully because of Jase's feelings. There's always something.

The boardroom is uncomfortably quiet. Clover's eyes dart around, scanning everyone, making me wonder if she has some sort of computer embedded in her eyes. We all take seats. The already odd grouping of my friends from Lawson mixed with the Kaycians is made even more strange with the addition of an Agnar. She's the first to speak. "I haven't met you all, but I feel like I know most of you. First, let me apologize for everything my family has done to you."

My jaw clenches. It's not like she's responsible. It only makes the apology more pathetic. Serenity's hand finds my knee, and she brushes her thumb back and forth in slow strokes.

"I had a team in place to strip Ismene of her power," Clover continues, "but we waited too long. If we had acted sooner, we might have avoided a lot of the turmoil."

The attack on the city might not have happened. Serenity wouldn't have been broken. My family probably still would have, but even with the current state of things, I wish Serenity never had to deal with any of it.

"I'd like to take care of it now, but even with the tree-walkers free—"

"The what?" Frey's face twists.

"Our group," Clover explains. "We're tree-walkers. We—"

Vogue's gasp cuts her off, and a chorus of groans erupts. "I. Told. You." Vogue accentuates each word by pointing at one of her friends. Serenity shakes a little with laughter at my side. "Team names *are a thing!* You all mocked me. We are long overdue!"

"All... right?" Clover sighs. "Well, as I was saying, now that we've been found out, I need a little help."

"It's already coming," Vogue says. "Our families have sought assistance from the Collective. They can't turn a blind eye to Ismene destroying our capital, and they won't let her hold control over us through Adwin."

Clover takes a fortifying breath and clenches her jaw. "That may be true, but they can't take Montica from her. The Collective will cut her off, but Montica will always see our family as the rightful leaders until they see proof we shouldn't be."

Just like what happened in Kaycie. The Collective left the Establishment to do whatever it wanted within their borders, probably making it worse.

"I need to show the country what kind of people the Agnars are," Clover continues. "And her brother's murderer would thoroughly disrupt Ismene's ability to keep on a cold façade."

I go rigid from head to toe. Serenity grips my knee.

Clover looks at the woman I love, and even that is enough to make me want to pull her behind me, away from all of this. But Clover Agnar is just beginning. "I know you killed my father."

Serenity holds up her hand and turns it to show both sides. "He stabbed me." Her voice betrays no fear, no regret. I thought I'd hate to ever see or hear her with her Kaycian mask on again, but to show no weakness here, I'm grateful she has these skills.

"And it assured *you* got away." My voice is controlled too, but in an angrier way. I've never felt Kaycian, but Serenity and I presenting this strong, calm front here when I know we're going to have this conversation in a much more honest, anxious way later, makes it clear I can fit into that life.

Clover's shoulders rise and fall with a deep breath. "I understand that, but Ismene, of course, will not."

"Ismene doesn't have to know," Vogue says.

"She'll find out." It isn't a threat, just a matter of fact, the way Clover says it. "She won't let it rest until she uncovers the truth, and there will be no safety for anyone involved once she does. But if we can get Serenity over there—"

Krisalyn gapes at Jase. "You can't actually think to use Serenity as bait?"

"She would be kept safe," he insists.

A cacophony of chatter rings out.

"That's not something any of us can ever guarantee," Dixon says.

Frey talks over him. "We'd be separated again. We can't keep trying to do this stuff split up."

"Not happening," Vogue says.

Krisalyn's mutterings are all disbelief. Carista points out that Serenity wasn't alone in this.

It's all mostly drowned out by blood pounding through my ears.

But Serenity's voice cuts through it all. "What exactly do you have in mind?"

Chapter Fifty-Four
SERENITY

I was prepared for yelling. A fight to rival all our others combined. Maybe one so bad it wouldn't even transition into make-up sex. But instead, there's just silence as Bram stands unmoving against the wall of our suite. The silent treatment on the way here was—I thought—just the buildup so the yelling could explode when the door shut. But it's still going strong. Time stretches in torturous misery. The pressure increasing with each passing second is un- doubtably worse than whatever the fight could be.

If I break the silence, it might be like a balloon popping. The pent-up yelling will erupt, but the silence has me too scared to do that. If I don't say anything, will this last forever?

I take a deep breath to fortify myself for it. "We can't spend our entire lives looking over our shoulders." I have more words, but I didn't think I'd get that many out, so it takes a second to remember my point. "I want us to know safety and peace—to no longer be afraid of anything. We have enough scary history to fuel our nightmares without leaving loose ends to worry us about potential futures."

Bram's gaze is distant. I haven't felt so shut out from him since before we gave up our stalemate and became friends.

"I know it's terrifying, but it'll only be terrifying once and then it'll be over."

Now his eyes meet mine. Dark in a way that has nothing to do with their color. "Your parents said they were going to take care of it."

That's... unnervingly calm after I braced for so much more.

I clear my throat. "They're taking care of Montica's crimes against Kaycie and their continued influence. That won't do anything for the vendetta Ismene will have against *us*."

"Maybe it can. See if your parents—"

"I cannot tell my parents." I swallow hard. "I can't tell them I killed someone."

Bram finally softens and moves to wrap me in a hug. He holds me there against his chest, and this time the silence isn't torture. The weight of the horror settles over me, but Bram is here to hold me up. Everyone else I care about was close enough to know as soon as it happened. But to tell my parents? They'll never look at me the same. I haven't done much in my life to disappoint them, and this would be so far beyond anything I ever thought I'd have to confess to them.

"What about the Collective?" Bram asks. "Go straight to them."

"They might side with Ismene. We broke into their fortress and killed a leader." I pull back enough to look up at him. "If Clover can take all of Ismene's resources from her, we're free from all of it."

"Do you really trust Clover Agnar?"

I press my lips together before saying, "Jase does. And I trust him." *Enough.* He's made some horrible choices, but he wouldn't consider this to be an option if he didn't thoroughly trust her. He wouldn't knowingly put me in danger.

"Okay." Bram doesn't sound as defeated as I'd expect. "Not alone, though."

My eyes sting. "Please don't make me be the reason you go into a fire."

"If it were the other way around, would you let me go in alone?"

Kaycie taught me how to lie. Bram would see through it though. Or worse, he might not. If I tell him I could actually let him do this alone, would he believe it as further proof that I couldn't possibly care for him as much as he does for me?

"No." A tear falls from my eye as the truth slips from my lips.

He swipes it away and leaves his hand on my jaw. "We agree then."

Before I can argue, he kisses me. I shouldn't agree. I can't drag Bram into danger the same way I thought I did with Jase when the uprising started. But all I can do is lose myself in this kiss. It's not a ploy to shut me up. It's a reminder we're a unit that cannot be divided again. Guilt has no place in this matter. There's no room for it when every bit of me is filled with love.

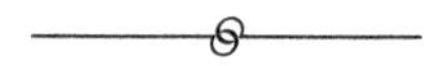

Vogue is less accepting than Bram. Or at least, I have less tools to work with to calm her down. The chance to catch up on missed time is worth a shot though. Even in a cardigan and leggings, she could strut down a runway and look just right, but instead she cradles a glass of wine and glides between rows of vines.

"I can't believe Lanelle didn't see the beauty of this place." I sip my own wine as I take in the scene. Open space and fresh air remind me of Eudora, and the thought finally occurs to me: Bram and I could have come out here instead. I was really out of sorts to not consider staying near a winery. But then we'd have missed out on the messiest first kiss ever. I wonder how the chickens are doing?

"If anyone could miss it, it would be Lanelle," Vogue says. "I hope she's stuck hiding in a dank hole somewhere."

I sigh. "Maybe roughing it will make her even more dangerous. Look what the perceived hardship of being trapped in Leavenworth did to her. The struggle strengthens, indeed. And she was already brilliant when she was irrigated."

Irrigated vines make bland wines. A saying I can't help but replay in my head while walking through a vineyard. These scraggly vines are forced to work to survive, and the result is delightful in my glass. When I first learned about these 'islands,' I worried I was always pampered and pruned and wouldn't be able to do what people needed of me. But the past year has certainly caught me up on struggling.

"Can't argue that it didn't make her more resourceful," Vogue says. "Also psychotic. But she's not a grapevine working to make the best possible wine. She's a weed trying to choke out all the growth around her."

A laugh bubbles in my chest. "Well, not everyone can be Vogue Taylor, using the past year to grow into the best possible version of herself."

"I haven't changed." She takes a self-satisfied sip of wine.

"Of course you have. Your restraint is a particularly impressive change."

"That's Krisalyn's doing, not revolution."

"That makes it even better." I bump her with my hip. "Love tamed the wildest vine."

"That one! That could be the title of my biography."

"Biography? I thought you were going to write an autobiography?"

She scrunches her nose. "Writing a book sounds hard."

"Never did I think I'd see the day." I lay my hand on my chest in faux shock. "Vogue Taylor declines a challenge?"

"Part of that growth you claim I achieved—I know I don't have to be the best at everything."

"That is growth. I'm proud of you."

"You did too. We all did." She gasps. "That's it! Vines! That could be our name! What does it stand for?" She bites her lip, and her eyes dart back and forth as her mind works. "Visionary... Infiltrators... Empowering Society!"

"You missed the *N*."

"Infiltrator is the *I* and the *N*."

I shake my head. "That's not how that works. Also, it doesn't need to stand for anything. Vines themselves are symbolic."

"Fine. You know what else vines do? Twist together. Unite. I'm not letting you go to Montica alone."

"I won't be alone."

Vogue loops her arm through mine. "I like Bram for you."

"Me too," I say with a laugh. "Does it make it awkward for you now, though? Jase is back, but the group dynamic is... tense with us split up and me with Bram."

"It'll be fine. Jase feeling weird about it is a given, but he'll get over it. And the rest of us love you two together. We just want you to be happy."

"Kris is okay with it?"

"Yes. If you two hadn't so awkwardly hidden your relationship from us, she could have told you that."

A weight lifts off me. One less thing to worry about. "It's not like we had been together long. Nothing happened until we got back from Montica."

"Really?"

"Well... a little something had happened."

Finally, we settle into our natural state of sharing and laughing together and I tell my best friend about *the egg incident*.

Chapter Fifty-Five

ADWIN

A call from Lanelle could be anything from complaints about living in Leavenworth, to demanding more involvement in government, to... I don't know. She can find anything to be upset about, but it's almost certainly negative. Answering it is a chore I have no desire to do, but I pop a pod in my ear. Communicating with my Kaycian cuff feels cumbersome and inconvenient now.

"Adwin." Clover's voice comes through, and my mouth falls open.

"Oh." I probably shouldn't say her name out loud through this channel. How much of a conversation can I have without drawing attention? I pull on gloves and go out through my fortress suite balcony and into the trees. It's a false sense of security to be out of the Breck, but at least it's something.

"The line is secure. You can speak freely. The technology is so archaic no one in Montica cares about it, but I cloaked it anyway." Clover is always ten steps ahead.

"Great. How are you enjoying Leavenworth?"

"It's... fine. But it's time to plan the return trip to Montica."

"All right. Now that my mother is in Kaycie, it's not unreasonable for me to travel back and forth."

"It'll be slightly more difficult than that."

"Why?"

"We won't all fit in an avillipse."

I sit on a high branch with my back against the tree trunk. "How many people need to come to Montica?"

"Eight." Her tone isn't the high nervous one I might expect from someone asking for the impossible, just exasperated.

"You're joking."

"I wish I was. Do you want the why or just what I need you to do?"

"The why may not be particularly vital, but knowing would be nice before I die doing something idiotic."

Her sigh whispers through the ear pod. "The entire plan hinges on Serenity Ward and Bram Eros, so they have to come."

"What's the plan?"

"When presented with her brother's killers, I'm counting on Ismene showing her true colors."

Serenity's marshal boyfriend being at least partially responsible for Rocco's death makes more sense than her doing it on her own. But... "You're using Serenity Ward as *bait?*"

Unintelligible murmurs are out of character for Clover. Was it imprisonment or being surrounded by Kaycians that brings it out? "She happens to be one of the people who killed my father. I assure you that Ismene is unfamiliar with her renowned. Why on earth do you still talk about her as if she's more important than everyone else?"

"Old habits I guess."

"As I was saying,"—not for the first time by the sounds of it—"if we let Ismene think she has a chance to kill those who killed her brother, she will jump at it. No matter who or what she'd have to destroy in the process, she would take her vengeance. If we can show the Montican people that her only care is for our family rather than them, she'll lose her supporters. With no one left to take orders from her, she's powerless. She could be locked up and no one care."

I rub my temples. "You have no idea how right you might be." Or I hope she doesn't know. No, she couldn't. "There's... a possibility that Ismene is worse than we thought. If you put them in front of her, they could be in serious danger." I don't want to expand on comms, and Clover seems to understand that.

"They'll be perfectly safe." Her reassurance doesn't quell my anxiety but questioning her hasn't gone well in the past.

"There's room for argument, but aside from that, I'm counting three people to bring into Montica."

"Vogue, Frey, and Dixon are claiming to be useful enough to help. Since Vogue and Frey were instrumental in my rescue, I can't exactly argue. Clearly they all just want to stay together, but since stopping them would require me to kidnap Serenity, and since everyone acts like she's made of gold, I have to accept their terms. Krisalyn doesn't even have a valid excuse, but I'm stuck with her too."

"That's seven."

Is her pause due to her frustration with this demanding crew she's inherited? "Jase just got his friends back. He doesn't want to lose them again. And since he's been with me the whole time, he feels a part of it."

"That is an impressively long list of bad reasons."

"Does that mean you aren't going to help me?"

"Of course not. What do you need?"

———— Ⓢ ————

It hadn't occurred to me that entering tree-walker headquarters without Clover would make it more intimidating. Without her, the chances of Priam and Knox trying to kill me grow significantly. Who could blame them? This shouldn't be the hardest part of this scheme, so why is it so nerve-racking?

Misty leads me to the communal space where at least I only have to face Priam and Aspen for now. Misty hops into a chair so quickly I think she'll squish January, but the fox is just as fast and maneuvers out of the way and onto her lap. "He's spoken to Clover," she says in a casual explanation for burdening them with my presence.

"How is she doing?" Aspen asks. Strands of straight, dark hair frame his face where they're loose from the knot at the top of his head.

"Well enough to come up with crazy plans," I say.

"It's about time," Priam mutters without looking at me.

If I were bolder, I'd point out that they've all only been out less than a week. Priam has enough reasons to hate me without picking that fight. "You'll be able to communicate with her now." I place my cuff and ear pod on the table in front of Aspen. "What she needs now is to be hidden as she flies a Kaycian hoverPlane here."

Priam deigns to glance at me, a smirk on his lips. "Always upping the ante in hide and seek. Okay, well at least that's fun."

Their ideas of fun never cease to amaze me.

Aspen drums his fingers on the table. "We'd need to get in the Breck."

"I was feeling a little homesick," Priam says with a shrug.

"I know you're about as smart as Clover," Aspen says, "but you aren't as stealthy."

Priam leans back against the wall and crosses his arms. "Clover isn't even the stealthiest person on this team."

Aspen's eyes dart to Misty and back to Priam. "Knox isn't going to let Misty go in." This first glimpse of doubt seems late. How are they confident about the rest of it?

"It isn't his decision," Misty says, her voice ripe with indignation.

Priam grins. "Next issue."

Aspen sighs. "It's going to take very precise scheduling."

Priam turns his head toward me and his jaw ticks. "We've waited this long."

Chapter Fifty-Six

SERENITY

Vegetation is starting to come in across the dry seafloor. The land is taking advantage of the first spring it's seen in centuries. The idea makes me smile. Humanity held back life as long as we could, but it's come back as soon as it got the chance. We can grow and thrive once we're free too. And that chance is coming soon.

We *will* have that chance. It's something I repeatedly remind myself of, along with: *We're not saying goodbye.* That's not the point of this excursion to Lawson. I meant it when I told Vogue, and I mean it when I recite the words in my head. But it feels ominous all the same. Waiting to go to Montica gives us too much time to think.

I can lie to myself that this is about getting away from it all for a day.

Bram's left hand at the top of the steering wheel puts the tattooed numbers on his forearm on display for me. "Have you thought of what any of the other numbers mean?" I ask.

He glances at it and back to the path ahead of us. "Seven is the number of nights we slept next to each other platonically."

A giggle bubbles through me since I think that included the night on the sofa. "I slept so much better with you next to me."

"Me too. But it was also torture." He squeezes my thigh, and I wrap my hand around his. Part of me hates that he suffered with unrequited feelings for me so long, but we came together when we were supposed to, I guess.

My fingers press against Bram's palm—slight changes of pressure where they already sit intertwined with his. The song my fingers play is beautiful, but a little heart breaking. That's probably just me. I've never thought it was sad before. But I never really understood it either.

"I should warn you," Bram says, keeping his focus ahead. "Aren and everyone had assumed we were... *together* from the get-go. The popular opinion being it was the reason we went to Eudora to begin with."

A smile tugs at my face. "So, I should expect some *I told you so* type sentiments to float around?"

"At least."

"Not surprising since Reid planted the idea in my head to begin with."

He groans. "I was so pissed at Cary for pulling that."

"I'm not complaining. It is a little embarrassing that we were the last to see it, though."

"*We* weren't. You were the last. I was first. Actually, that's not true either."

"Who was first then?"

"Tori."

I squeeze his hand. Tori was his first friend in Kaycie, and the first of many deaths he suffered during this conflict. "I bet she had some opinions on that. She hated me."

"At first... yeah, she wasn't a fan. She approved in the end."

There are so few people in Bram's life whose opinions matter to him, that even this little hypothetical approval feels good. The Campbells all seem to be on board. Libby will be thrilled. That just leaves Aren.

Lawson seems relatively unchanged by all the upheaval in the country. Minor improvements, enough to appease people and keep them quiet. It's such an Adwin move to think a few new modern buildings and fresh paint are what the uprising was trying to accomplish.

Libby runs headlong into Bram's arms as we approach the house. Maybe seeing how he is with her was what started my inevitable fall for him. I have plenty of experience with his tender side, but this big strong man turned softy for her melts my heart. When she turns her attention to me, I soak up the sweet affection. It took Bram and me months to even tolerate each other, and I was mortifyingly slow to realize how well we fit together. Unlike us, Libby gives love quickly, openly, and without condition.

She pulls my hand, leading us inside. Bram and Sophos greet each other with uncomfortable coolness, then my former mentor gives me a light hug.

"How are you doing?" I ask.

"Getting better." His eyes still reflect a sad weight, but he does look brighter than the last time I saw him.

The four of us have a simple lunch, and I quip about my experience with food preparation in Eudora. Neither of us ask where Aren is.

When our conversation reaches current events, Sophos nods with a bemused smile. "Grace Ward would be the one to get the Collective back. I shouldn't be surprised. Your mother has always been one of the best of us."

Pride flutters in my chest. My mother *is* incredible. I can't believe I ever thought she was among the silly, blinded masses. All of Kaycie knows she's a great actress, but her best performance was the one no one knew she was putting on.

"I suppose everything is about settled down then." Sophos' contentment is shadowed by grief. We've nearly arrived at our intended destination, but the journey was more costly than any of us ever imagined.

Bram nods his agreement with the false statement. Things aren't settled down—not for us. But we're almost there.

"Then you can live here again?" Libby's wide eyes and excited smile are hard to say no to. I'm glad they're pointed at Bram.

"Maybe not *here*," he says. "It's easy to get around now. We can live anywhere near Kaycie and see each other all the time. I'm not sure where we're going t— I mean *I*. I'm not sure where *I'm* going to live." His gaze flicks to me, and my lips tug into a smile.

An hour or so later, we peel Libby off us and make our way out to meet the Campbells and Aren. According to a message from Cary, they're all next door.

I squeeze his hand as we head in that direction. "I don't mind, by the way... the living situation being a matter of *we*." I tuck my hair behind my ear to better see him from the corner of my eye.

He closes his eyes for a breath, then stops and turns to face me fully. "Do you remember being on the plane when we left Montica?"

My hand prickles at the reminder. "The combination of adrenaline and pain killers makes it a little fuzzy. Why?"

"I told you we were going home, and that home could be wherever you wanted it to be. You said, *'your home,'* and I mean, you were on pain killers, but why the hell would either of us want to live in Lawson?"

The scene replays in my head. Bram and I had finally shared our first kiss only to be thrown back into chaos instead of having time to explore what we could be. Bram promised we'd talk afterwards, but would I get out alive? Rocco Agnar was terrifying. Through the blinding pain in my hand, my only comfort was knowing he was there with me. Even in the worst danger, Bram made me feel safe.

The connection snaps into place. "Oh." My cheeks warm. "I think I was being a little bold, and *you* misinterpreted."

"What?"

"I wasn't saying *your* home. I meant *you're* home. As in, *you are.*"

Something flashes in his eyes, and I worry it's doubt, so I rise up to my toes to kiss him. How many times do I have to kiss him, hold him, tell him, love him, to convince him that this is real, and he deserves it all? Fortunately, I'm happy to provide all those reassurances.

He releases a slow breath and hugs me to his chest. I am going to spend weeks tucked into his arms when this is all said and done. It's not time for that yet, so we continue on.

Aren and Carista are in the kitchen when we walk in. Reid and Travick sit at the table. Aren's face snaps toward us before redirecting a sharp look at Carista. She whispers through gritted teeth, and I give Bram's hand another squeeze. It doesn't seem like Aren is in much of a mood to see us.

I'd bow out if I didn't think that would be abandoning Bram. Instead, I do my best to make myself scarce—sliding into the seat next to Reid and meeting his smile with my own. Without him getting the idea in my head, how long would it have taken me to find my way to Bram? It would have happened eventually, I'm sure of that. But the egg incident would never have happened, and honestly what would our story be without that?

"Yeah, I heard." Aren's voice is far louder than whatever he's replying to.

Reid leans back with a sigh. Travick tenses like he's going to have to jump into a fight.

"It won't be long," Bram says with a steadiness he has to be fighting for, faced with his brother's hostility.

"Doesn't really matter." Aren crosses his arms. "You won't be around."

"Things have been crazy, but—"

"Cary's kept me in the loop. I know." Aren's lips twist into a spiteful smile. "Since you don't talk to me."

"Well, last time I did talk to you,"—Bram's cool is melting away—"you were a jackass."

"I was *right*." He nods in my direction.

"No, you weren't." Bram's voice rumbles. It's a sharp reminder that the sweet, funny, loving side I get is just that—one side of him.

"Well, I guess that's true." Aren throws his arms out in surrender. "Because I thought fucking her would get your head screwed on straight, but instead you're somehow now okay with running off to get yourself killed for her!"

Bram's knuckles pale as he clenches his fist. The fact that he hasn't swung it into his brother's face astounds me. I hold my breath, sure that any movement will shatter the tenuous grip on Bram's self-control. "We don't have a choice." Each word rips out of him slowly.

"It sounds like *she* didn't have a choice, but you volunteered!"

"I can't just let her—"

"Reid's not going!" Aren waves a hand toward us.

"Not exactly by choice," Reid says.

"Okay, Reid," Aren says. "Even if you wanted to be as stupid as my brother, at least your boyfriend doesn't want you to risk your life. *This bitch*—"

Bram's fist finds its mark. Blood sprays from Aren's mouth as he's knocked against the refrigerator with a force that teeters it. The room is a blur of movement. Bram pinning Aren by the neck. Carista trying to push herself into the sliver of space between them. Travick, Reid, and I jolt into the kitchen.

"Stop it!" I yank Bram's shoulder back. I'm not strong enough to pull him away, still he yields to me. We move a few steps back, and his fury melts to agony as he looks at me. I couldn't care less about the insult thrown at me. I just wish Aren would open his eyes to see he's tearing his brother apart. Bram has already lost so many people, and those of us he has left can't stand to be in the same room together without a brawl breaking out. It's so incredibly unfair. I take his face in my hands. "Are you okay?"

The shouting fades to the background. Bram shakes his head. "I'm sorry."

Whether it's for Aren's words or getting violent, I don't know. My response is the same either way. "You have nothing to apologize to me for. Would it be okay with you if I try to talk to him?"

His chin drops, and he looks at the floor between us. "You shouldn't have to deal with so much shit because of me."

"I've brought plenty of my own to the table." My ex-boyfriend's ex-girlfriend did try to kill us, after all. "And not to brag, but I *did* bring an Eros man who hated me over to my side once."

He smirks and cocks an eyebrow at me. "Well, don't go making this one fall in love with you."

"Damnit, that's my go to." I sigh dramatically. "Fine, I'll improvise." I wink and turn away. "Aren, can we talk? Please."

Carista and Travick fix him with hard glares. He holds a cloth to the side of his face and stomps off. I follow him outside, and he turns on me in a rush. "Do you want a fucking apology?"

"Not for me." I brace my hands on my hips. "Bram is the one you should be apologizing to. You don't have to like me, but for God's sake don't point it out like that in front of *him*! I don't want to come between you."

"You've been a wedge between us from the start. Do you have any idea what it was like to have him come home after *five years* and all he cared about was getting back to you?"

My heart twists. "No, I don't." All the strength has left my voice.

"You probably never will. Must be nice to have everyone always put you first. Being important to the entire shit city wasn't enough? You needed to be the most important thing in the world to *my* brother, too?"

I wasn't important to the city. The idea of me was. But that would sound like an excuse—a champagne problem. And this isn't about me. "Bram worries most about the people he can't protect. When he was in the city, before the uprising, it was all of you. When I was ripped away from him, it became me. Now that we can all be together, we don't have to fight for his attention. You're not any less important to him because I am too."

"He just made it pretty damn clear whose side he's on." He pulls the cloth away to reveal the red mark which will no doubt turn to an impressive bruise.

"Don't *make him* choose a side. You were being an asshole for the sake of being an asshole. How would he *not* side with me in that particular situation? You want him to choose you, but your tantrums aren't ever going to get you what you want." I press my fingers across my face as dread slithers through me. "You've both already lost so much. Please don't make me the reason you lose each other."

Chapter Fifty-Seven

Travick and Reid disappear through the back door. Cary drops onto the couch and presses her fingers into her temples. "Bram… could you not—"

"That was not my fault! Did you hear him?" She should be commending me for not hitting him sooner.

She sighs and shakes her head. "You're careful not to rub your relationship in Jase's face, but the first time you see Aren in months, it's with Serenity at your side."

"Aren was never in a romantic relationship with either of us."

Cary is not amused by my sarcasm. "He hasn't had any relationship with you! That's the problem." She waves me over to sit with her, mumbling something about billing me for therapy. "He doesn't blame you for the years you had to spend in Kaycie, but when you finally came back you were clearly preoccupied by Serenity's absence, then you chose to go to her again and again instead of being with your family."

I open my mouth to respond, but she raises her hand to stop me. "It's not that I don't understand it. I encouraged the idea to reunite you two. But Libby is a baby, so you're the only family he really has. You're the only person who has lost just as much as he has, and that would be lonely enough even if you were around to share it. But you haven't been."

Weight presses down in my chest. I lean my elbows on my knees, unable to pull my gaze off the floor. "I couldn't have been there for him. I couldn't even think about what happened without wanting to burn the world down. That wouldn't have changed without her. Serenity wasn't a bandage; she was a heart transplant."

Once, I thought of Serenity as a little wrecking ball. I was sure she was going to ruin everything. Instead, she smashed through the walls I had built around myself and led me past the rubble, back into the world. Reality still hurts. It has to, or I'd have forgotten my family like Aren thinks. It doesn't go away, though—not even with Serenity. There are moments when I'm so consumed by her, I can't feel anything beyond her touch, her love. Of course I cling to those moments. They're like diving into an oasis on a trek across a desert. And afterward, the desert is manageable because she's there. It doesn't feel like a complete wasteland. The heat becomes a tolerable warmth instead of scorching. Things might even be able to grow in it.

"I know," Cary says. "I do. You need to make an effort with him, though. You can do that now. Don't miss the chance." I nod, and she stands. "I'm going to take Serenity for some girl time. Talk to your brother." Those four words are accentuated like she's explaining something to a child. It's offensive, but when she walks out and is replaced by Aren, I realize my preferences for when I can and can't handle being apart from Serenity are a mess. Gun fight: definitely want to be alone. But talking to my brother without her is daunting.

He goes straight to the refrigerator and turns back with two beers in hand. That's a good start.

I take a deep breath before standing and joining him. He hands me one and leans back against the counter. There is no comfortable way to start this, so might as well dive in face first.

"I'm sorry I haven't been here." I look up to find him staring at me. Avoiding eye contact when things are hard is another trait we don't share. "I will be. I promise. Everything will settle down soon. We've almost ended everything."

"And what if *you* end with everything? I'll be the only person left who knew Mom, and Dad, and"—his voice cracks—"Emrys. At least the way we knew them." Aren was the one who kept it together when I left for selection, but there have been too many losses now for him not to cling to me.

"I'm not going to die." The words are empty, and we both know it.

"You don't know that. How many times can you rattle death's cage before it snags you? And our family has given enough! You don't need to be the hero."

I press the heels of my hands over my eyebrows. "I'm not trying to be the hero. I'm not trying to save the world anymore."

"No, you're just trying to save her." There's no venom in it this time.

"It's not just her, I—"

"This is one hundred percent for her," Aren says.

"Yes, *this* is. But she's not the only person I'd do this for. I wouldn't think twice to jump in front of gunfire for you. And you know what, Serenity would probably be at our side, too."

"Yeah, to protect you."

"Protecting you is protecting me. She knows I can't lose anyone else. She knows how much you mean to me."

He stares at nothing and takes a swig of beer. When his eyes return to me, he says, "I don't hate her, you know?"

"I know. Just... maybe keep it directed at me next time. I'm the one you're pissed at, not her."

He rolls his eyes. "You already know you're an asshole. Where's the fun in telling you?"

A smile pulls at my lips as I raise the beer to them. "We're okay then?"

"Come back in one piece from Montica and we'll be okay."

"Deal."

"I mean,"—he shrugs—"you could lose one or two of those goddamned perfect teeth, but nothing important."

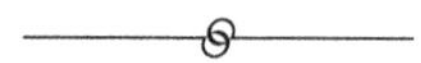

We have to be ready to leave for Montica at a moment's notice. On the way to see Aren, I wasn't exactly upset about that. A quick visit and leaving seemed like the safest option. But as Serenity and I drive back, I wish we'd had more time. Avoiding Aren was stupid and only made things worse. It'll be over soon enough.

Serenity's fingers wiggle between mine, tapping my knuckles. Her hands were always her tell, her nervous tick, but it's only recently come back. She had kept them pretty still since we reunited. Did Jase's death leave her too numb for that, and now it's back? I lift our hands and kiss her fingertips. Her smile is genuine. She doesn't look stressed. But her fingers keep tapping away.

When we get back to Leavenworth, she brushes off her parents, making it sound like we had a nice relaxing afternoon with my family. They think we're still staying in Leavenworth because Kaycie has too many terrible memories, not because we're waiting to run off to Montica with a Montican fugitive. Serenity doesn't seem to mind keeping that secret. I guess it's better than the alternative.

She goes into the bathroom of our room to change, and it strikes me that I've already gotten used to her dressing and undressing in front of me. Maybe not *used to*. The sight of her always burns me up in the best way. Still, this seems off. Is she more upset by Aren than she's let on?

I'm sitting on the bed when she comes out. Before I can ask, she sighs and starts talking. "Just one more adventure together, then we get to navigate normal life?"

I don't know if I'm relieved she isn't upset about Aren or if this is worse. "We don't have to do it," I say.

"I think we do." Her lips twist to the side. "But that's okay. I've got one more adventure in me."

"Are you going to retrieve your adventure wear?"

It takes a moment but understanding flashes in her eyes. Followed by a blush as she calls to mind the thigh-high boots and tight skirt she wore for our *adventure* to the train station so long ago. "As I recall, you didn't approve of that outfit."

I shrug. "It wasn't practical. I might have a new appreciation for it, now."

Serenity steps over to me with an exaggerated slow swing of her hips. She stands between my knees and drapes her arms around my neck. "You like me in leather?"

How is it possible that I'm the person she looks at like this?

"I love you in anything. Leather, jeans, T-shirts, sweaters, covered in egg, even those ridiculous Kaycian dresses you always used to wear."

Those perfect lips turn up in a laughing smile. "I like how the dresses were worse than being covered in egg."

"They were. In that stuff, attention was drawn to the glitter and ruffles." I brush my thumb over her cheek. "But even in all that, I'd just see you now."

She blinks away a glassiness from her eyes. "I can't believe I didn't see you before."

"We've both opened our eyes. I'd like to see more of you right now." I slide my hands up her back, her skin like silk under my fingers. She stiffens, and I lean back a little. "Unless you don't want to."

"No, it's not—" Her shoulders drop forward. "I don't know why I thought I could hide it, or what I thought I was waiting for."

My chin pulls back. What is she hiding from me?

She sits on my lap and fingers the end of her left sleeve.

"Is it bruised?" I hurt her. That's what she doesn't want me to see.

"No. Or barely." She pulls up the sleeve, and there is some discoloration in her wrist, but higher up are nine black numbers. Like the marshal ID numbers.

I can't tear my eyes from it—her perfect skin that she voluntarily marked the way the Establishment marked us as their property. Her voice pulls my focus back to her face.

"You're keeping yours. And how different are we really? They tried to control everything about me, too." She shrugs, but her eyes bore into mine. "It hurt—not much—but at least I was able to react. I winced and hummed and tapped my feet." Her hand slides up my tattoo. "You had to act like you didn't feel it at all."

I swallow past a lump in my throat and nod.

"You spent years unable to show that anything hurt you in any way, that you could feel anything. I know you think your response to all your tragedies made you think you were broken, but it was how you survived. Of course it would bleed into you."

All the aches and pains I ever endured didn't compare to how much I feel from her words. And I don't have to hide it anymore. I dip my face to kiss her shoulder. "Thank you." For understanding, for caring, for making me feel again.

She smiles, though I'm not sure she knows how much I'm thanking her for. "At least I got to pick the numbers instead of back peddling meaning into them."

I brush my fingers over it. "What do they mean?"

"Seven, twenty-four is my birthday, like yours has. Six is for the closest thing I've got to a sibling group. Ignore the fact that some of those siblings have dated or still are. Three is for my family—my parents and me. This six for the different ways I've known you."

"What?"

She enumerates the list with her fingers. "Marshal, thorn in my side, friend, stranger when I lost my memories, life support,"—after the fifth she slides her open hand onto my neck—"and lover."

Any of the numbers on my own arm representing her doesn't even mean that much to me, because I know she's tattooed on my heart anyway. But she's chosen to have a permanent mark of me on her, and it's so overwhelming I don't know how to respond, so I move on to the end of this unbelievable show of love and solidarity. "And eight-one-three?"

"You hadn't figured out anything for those on yours, right?"

"No."

She gives me a shy smile as she shrugs. "So, on August thirteenth we're going to need to do something worth commemorating, I guess."

Her lips meet mine like waves crashing on a shore—sinking into me, pulling me into her current. I thought of her as an oasis, but that doesn't do her justice. Serenity is an ocean. She's a beautiful view that reflects the sunlight into a million sparkling lights and depths that would take a lifetime to explore. I never cared much for swimming, but when Serenity is the sea, nothing on Earth could stop me from diving in.

Chapter Fifty-Eight
ADWIN

Full alert. All available personnel to perimeter meeting points.

"Volume down!" Why would this stupid thing be capable of going off while I'm asleep?

The message quiets in my head but doesn't stop. It echoes out loud in my room, too. I rub my eyes, and the alert sinks in. *It's happening.*

I jump out of bed and throw clothes on. Shouldn't it have taken them more time? I don't know the plan or the schedule. There's no way for me to keep in contact with them at this point. The extent of my involvement was to tell them what Clover needed and give them my *ancient,* easily masked technology so they could communicate with her directly. I forgot to ask why she has Lanelle's cuff, but that's the least of my problems.

Out in the hallway, I realize I have no idea what I'm doing. It's not as if anyone here considers me useful during a security issue. But surely staying in bed would look suspicious. I rush to the lift. Maybe if I go to the security office looking concerned, I might help to deflect attention from whatever Priam and the rest are doing.

The door is closing, but I thrust my hand in, and it opens instead. Nemora's eyes widen when she sees me. "Adwin."

"Glad I ran into you," I say as I step in. "I wouldn't really know where to go or what to do."

"Well, I..." The door closes, and the lift rises. Why are we going up? I cock my head, and Nemora answers my silent question. "I'm not needed for the disturbance. It's a simple prank. Fireworks and the like."

The doors open.

"So, you're on your way to tell Ismene that?"

Nemora stops in the path of the door. "She's already out there dealing with it, actually."

"What are you doing up here then?"

Her face gives away nothing, but I have no doubt she's calculating all possibilities of what she could tell me and what might result. "I've been looking for something—supposed proof of Mother's derangement."

My knees buckle. "Proof that she tortured my grandmother? What kind of proof could there be?" I've tried to bury the thought. I've tried to only think about it as it related to Ismene—how dangerous she is in power. The idea that my grandmother wasn't simply executed for her relationship with the Director's husband, but brought to a slow, painful death at Ismene's hands is too much to think about. She'd have to have been about Nemora's age. Nemora is razor-sharp and unforgiving, but I can't imagine her doing something like that.

"I don't know." A flicker of vulnerability in Nemora's eyes tells me she's afraid of success. "You can't... Just, go back to your suite, Adwin. If it's true, it'll be too—"

"Difficult to handle? That doesn't only apply to me. I never knew my grandmother. This is worse for you."

She lifts her chin in a defiant motion, but to my surprise, she gestures me to follow her. We walk down the hall in silence to the suite where Ismene offered me the auspicious position of puppet-like leader of my nation. The door unlocks for Nemora, and she closes it softly behind us. Lights spark in the distance, bathing the room in brief washes of color. I'd think the tree-walkers would have a more sophisticated diversion, but I suppose if it does the job...

Nemora goes to the large table and digs into the glass stones from which the fire sculptures spring. "I tore this place apart while she was away. Recently, an anonymous message told me to look here." A *click* sounds, and Nemora removes her hands. The stones clack together with the movement. She bends down to a panel that's popped out of the table's side.

I take a knee opposite her, the newfound opening between us. She reaches under and pulls something out. The festive flashes illuminate the jar and the object suspended within it—a human hand.

Chapter Fifty-Nine
SERENITY

This will be the last time we slip away under the cover of darkness. Leaving without my parents noticing feels nearly as important as entering Montica without their leaders noticing. Except my parents wouldn't *actually* kill us.

We board the craft. It's smaller than the one we took the first time. This one is actually meant for a group our size, unlike the ostentatious Montican one Adwin tends to travel in. Today, Frey, Dixon, and Jase complete our team of vines, and Clover replaces Travick as pilot.

My unease isn't for myself, though my left-hand clenches at the idea of going back there. No, it's guilt that so many people I care about are going—for me. I could have gone alone, but we're a chain reaction of connections. Bound together. They're being put in harm's way for my sake. Clover's reassurances don't ease the gnawing at my gut. Although, I guess when it comes down to it this is actually all for *her*. She's the reason we were there in the first place and ended up killing Rocco.

The rest of us take seats, and relief washes over me when Jase follows Clover into the cockpit. I tuck in under Bram's arm, wondering if Jase did that on purpose to let me have this comfort. It's greedy of me, but I'll take it. Last time we made this trip, Bram and I weren't even speaking in the awkward aftermath of our first kiss. I could have been killed before we got together. Even after that one, I slipped in another near-death incident before I told him I love him. No matter how confident we are, I won't miss any opportunity to love this man. There's no way to know what's lurking beyond corners.

Bram keeps a hand on my arm, stroking the tattoo with his thumb. I wouldn't have thought I'd be capable of sleep, but when he gently shakes my shoulder, I wake to find we've landed.

Here we go.

Outside, I'm glad I wasn't awake to witness the landing. How this thing nestled into the forest without hitting any trees, I don't want to know. But it is incredible here. The view is worth the goosebumps raising on my arms in the crisp air. In fairy tales, dark forests are foreboding, but this is stunning. Trees are everywhere. Around, above, some fallen underfoot as we follow to the tree-walkers' headquarters.

"Is this what Greenwood was like?" I ask Vogue.

She, Krisalyn, Frey, and Dixon did some exploring when they were working for the uprising under Kolina and Sophos. They shake their heads, looking around in amazement.

"Not even close," Vogue says.

"This is so much bigger," Krisalyn adds.

"To think we all thought the world was so small all along." Bram's voice is a low murmur at my side.

When Clover stops to open the entrance, Krisalyn hands something to Frey. He pops it in his mouth and swallows it down. Dixon is the first one to drop into the tunnel where our sense of the world being so unbelievably big is ripped away by the narrow, dark passageway. Bram's hand is warm on my lower back, and through everything I find a good memory to cling to. Our first *adventure* together also involved a tunnel. When he took me to Union Station, I was still playing at spy in all black and sexy boots. He started to open up to me. A smile tugs at my lips.

"It's going to be tight," Clover says. "This place was never meant to hold so many people." The hallway opens into a living space slightly smaller than my old apartment in Kaycie. Six people are already here, and with our eight, tight is an understatement. We've met Misty, but the two other women scan us with curious eyes. The one standing in the kitchen is graceful and willowy like Clover. The time Vogue drunkenly whined her concern about Monticans being both smarter and prettier than her replays in my head. They aren't prettier than Vogue. But their beauty is different. While ours makes us look graceful and somewhat delicate, theirs is predatory. Their exacting glances and lean muscular limbs unnerve me, and if these are the people who can take down Montican leadership, that instinct is correct.

The men are intimidating in far less subtle ways. The two bigger ones look like they could rip a person in half, and the slender one has a sleek grace about him that makes me think he could kill before his victim knew he was there.

We're up against the people who caught *them.*

Jase floats into the room, not *at ease,* but certainly more so than the rest of us. It's mind-blowing to think of him here among these people. He made sense in our world. This one is so different. We've all been molded to fit new circumstances, but *this?*

"Who killed him?" The deep voice belongs to the burly young man on a sofa.

I swallow past the lump in my throat, but Clover answers before I can. "Allow me to introduce Serenity Ward and Bram Eros." She gestures to us, and he looks skeptical.

"If Adwin hadn't seen the body," he says, "I wouldn't believe it."

If fear wasn't churning in my stomach, I'd point out that Rocco Agnar wasn't even the first trained Montican to be taken down by Bram. Unfortunately, raising him in their esteem isn't likely to outweigh the anger for killing their own.

Interacting with people is usually the easy part to navigate, but I'm in over my head. I don't know what's important to these people or how to steer the conversation. I know they're proud, and supposedly Ismene instilled a *family first* conviction into the Agnars. Not the entire family, of course. She hates Casimir.

So many twisted webs. And we're no more than flies to her.

Clover leans back against the table and introduces everyone else. She thanks Misty and Aspen—the stealthy looking one—for their assistance in bringing us here. Then she explains her idea. How Bram and I can be used to break Ismene.

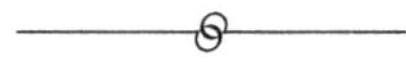

Time is stagnant below ground. I'm exhausted and clueless about my body's schedule. Is it night or day? Does it matter?

Clover sighs and says we should try to rest, and relief washes over me. Not only for the opportunity to sleep. I'm all too happy to get out of this room and away from these people who talk about us like we're pawns.

Misty shows us to rooms. There aren't enough, so we'll have three or four people in each. Before retiring to our assigned rooms, the seven of us squeeze into one to steal a moment to talk without our Montican *allies* around. Thinking of them as such doesn't seem right, but that's what they're supposed to be.

Krisalyn and I duck into the bed's bottom bunk, which takes up most of the space. Bram leans against the wall near me. Vogue, Frey, Dixon, and Jase pack tightly into the remaining space.

"You shouldn't all be here." My fingers tap a nervous melody in my lap.

"In this room?" Vogue says. "Agreed. Not ideal. But I—"

"No," I say, "in Montica. You shouldn't have come. I'm the only one they needed. Now that we're here…" I drop my face in my hands. "These people are terrifying."

"*These people* aren't," Jase says. "They're on our side."

I press my lips together. Is there any way for me to disagree with him without sounding like a resentful ex? I trust Jase, but what if *his* trust is misplaced? He could be wrong. Clover might be perfectly willing to toss us to the wolves.

"And anyway,"—Krisalyn rubs my back—"there's no you being involved without us."

"You insisted on coming when they only really needed me to get the tree-walkers out of prison," Vogue reminds me.

"That was necessary," I say.

"So is this," Dixon says.

"Everything fell apart when we were split up." Frey's knee bounces with the tapping of his heel. "We need to stick together and finish this."

My shoulders drop. I hadn't noticed they were tense. "Well, you're already here. Not like there's anything I can do about it now."

"Exactly." Vogue smiles like she's only talking me into going out dancing. "Just go with it. Vines are stronger when they tangle together."

Dixon rolls his eyes, and Frey puffs out a breath before saying, "There's only one *vine* here you tangle up with."

Krisalyn smirks and tosses her hair behind her shoulder. "That is correct. Come on. Tomorrow is going to be a long day." She squeezes my shoulder before standing and shoving Vogue, Dixon, and Jase out the door. Vogue blows me a kiss on her way out.

"And then there were three," Frey says.

Bram, Frey, and I are quite the trio, actually. Of everyone, we all handled the catastrophes from last year similarly. Frey and I hid out for months together until I left to be with Bram. Bram had cut himself off from everyone before I showed up. Frey was never as obvious as us with his pain, but it was there.

"Frey?" I say as Bram sits next to me. "I know we had an unspoken rule about not really speaking, but now..." Now that things are better, can we do that?

He leans back against the wall as he lets out a long breath. "Fine." He frowns for a moment. "Remember when we all started spending time together, and the buzzChains loved to speculate about you and me?"

Bram shifts next to me, and I bump him playfully with my shoulder. "That was always the way with me. Most people thought it was Jase, but some thought it was you." *Some people said both.* "I never cared about that."

"It was always the case for me too. Except, people romanticized you and enjoyed plopping you into a love story. In my case, I had to be sleeping with you because *Frey Dempsey doesn't have friends.*"

"We confirmed that," I say. "You couldn't name a heterosexual female friend you never did anything with."

"I know, but the reality was, I didn't have *any* friends. Even before Sophos set me apart from everyone else in the city, no one ever really cared about me or vice versa. I couldn't wait to move out at sixteen and live on my own. Everyone else only passed through." He rubs the back of his neck. "Our group was important to me."

I knew this, of course. He confessed to missing me when I had gone to Leavenworth, and he was disappointed when I reunited with everyone but him after I got my memories back. Even after that, it's not always easy to remember that these things run deeper for Frey than he lets on.

His voice gets lower. "I thought Vogue was going to die. Jase *did*, as far as we knew. Our little family was shredded. And call me cocky, but I'm not used to losing. We lost a lot, and it was hard."

"It was. But we're all okay now. What was the pill for?"

Frey rolls his eyes like it's silly. "Oh, that's for enclosed spaces." He looks to Bram. "Almost drowning on the train. How was I the only one freaked out by that?"

"We didn't almost drown," Bram says. "The ocean was dropping."

"We didn't know that. We thought we were going to drown in that train."

"Well, it turned out all right." I stand and cross the small space to him. "I'm glad we had each other for the hard time in between."

He accepts my embrace, holding me tight. "Me too." He lets me go and pulls his beautiful, confident expression back together. "But I'm not willing to lose again. So stop blubbering about us being here. We win as a team."

Chapter Sixty

BRAM

Serenity's slow breaths are almost enough to lull me to sleep. If only my mind would let me. Aren is afraid I'll die, but I dwell on a worse possibility. I've already come way too close to seeing Serenity's death. I've washed her blood off me. It makes the idea of her dying too visceral. Instead, I cling to the sound of her breathing, the feel of her heartbeat where she's pressed against me. I've held her through the entire range of human emotions. She has laughed, cried, loved in my arms. The one thing I can never face holding is her lifeless body.

The thought makes my throat tighten. My heart races. I hold her a little tighter. *She's right here. She's here and she's alive. She's going to be okay.*

And okay, selfishly I don't want to die either. Maybe it's not completely selfish. It would destroy her. She shouldn't have to go through that again.

She shifts, and I tense. Her face nuzzles into my neck. "Are you awake?" Her sleepy whisper is a warm tickle on my skin.

"Yeah."

"Have you slept at all?"

"No."

She stretches and props her head on her hand. "What's wrong?" My eyes are adjusted to the darkness, but I still see little more than her outline.

"I'm scared." The ability to be honest is momentous. I'd give her anything. Open my soul to her.

She sighs and lays her hand on my jaw. She knows the significance. "For me or yourself?"

"Both."

"Good."

Not good that I'm scared, but good that I'm not only worried about her. I know. I know she doesn't want me to care only for her safety and throw mine to the wind.

"Weren't you always willing to die for the uprising?" she asks.

I nod.

"I wouldn't think you'd ever feel fear for yourself anymore."

"Having something worth dying for is one thing." I comb my fingers through her silky hair. "But I've never had anything I so desperately wanted to live for."

She sucks in a breath, and I pull her in for a tight hug. "Do you know why most of our adventures have resulted in disasters?" she whispers near my ear.

"Because we never fully know what we're getting into?"

Her shoulders shake with a quiet laugh. "I was going to say something romantic, and you ruined it with facts."

"I'm an idiot to bring up reality with you in my arms. Tell me the romantic version." I kiss the top of her head. "Why isn't tomorrow going to be a disaster like the times before?"

"Because before, you and I were always apart, dealing with separate fires." She pulls back to face me, though we can barely see each other. "When the uprising started, I was out dancing while you were fighting.

You were on your way to Lawson while I dealt with the Council. Then you were saving Krisalyn while I was escaping the Monticans with our techs." She takes a deep breath—calm despite everything. "This time we'll be together. And that is why I'm not worried."

Chapter Sixty-One

ADWIN

"Adwin!" Ismene's voice cuts directly into my head. No ping first. No announcement. The sudden wake up makes my stomach tumble.

"What?" Damnit, I wouldn't be so short with her, but it caught me off guard.

"Do you know where Nemora is?"

"No." How the hell would I know where she is when I'm sleeping? "What time is it?"

"Five o'clock. I can't find her, and Clover has just resurfaced."

"Oh." Again, they're wasting no time. "Where is she?"

"She's asked me to meet her just outside the city." She takes a breath. *"Would you come with me? She told me to come alone, but you're not a threat."*

Thanks.

"I didn't mean it that way."

Did I think that clearly enough to be a message? I should not communicate this way half-asleep.

Ismene continues. *"I mean, you were her friend. She may be more willing to listen to you."*

"What am I supposed to say?"

"That I did not try to kill her. That we're trying to pick up the pieces of this family to hold our position."

This is more vulnerability than I've ever heard from her. If she was the one who almost killed me in the attempt on Clover, it makes sense. It would mean she does think her hold on power is tenuous. Of course, the real reason she shouldn't be allowed to rule had been hidden well enough that she must not worry about that.

While I get ready, I try to reach Nemora with no luck. She disapproved of the heinous memento her mother kept in the coffee table, but I don't know how deeply it affected her. She became instantly business-like, hiding the jar under her shawl as we returned to our floor. The order for me to go to my room wasn't even veiled as a request. I didn't argue. She had a lot to process. But I haven't heard from her since. What must it feel like to know the person you tried to model yourself after is a monster?

I dash the thought from my mind as I meet Ismene in the atrium. *Nothing has changed. Nothing has changed. Everything is fine.*

The avillipse ride is as nauseating as the first time. Priam and I were looking for Clover then, too. I thought they'd be all right if handed over to the woman next to me. All things considered, mountain bunker imprisonment *was* actually Ismene going easy on them. The unnatural angles of the fingers flash through my mind—broken before the hand was cut off, I presume.

I swallow back bile.

We exit the dome and land in a clearing. She's visible from here.

Clover sits cross-legged, wind blowing her short hair across her face. The large rock she's perched on looks like a stage. Or is it still considered a rock when it seems to be a continuation of the ground—laid bare and reaching toward a drop off? The tree line bordering one side of the area is close enough for her to escape into. Behind her, the capital city of Nyberg glows through a morning mist.

I used to create environments for movies, but this is a more dramatic setting than anyone in Kaycie could dream up. The familiar sense of inadequacy washes through me. What I'd give to create this.

Clover doesn't indicate she's aware we've arrived, nor is she surprised when Ismene speaks.

"Minea," she says, "I'm glad to see you're doing well."

Clover closes her eyes briefly, and I wonder if she'll even respond to her first name.

"There's something I need to tell you," Ismene continues.

"I know about my father." Clover's eyes flash toward us.

"How?"

"I've found his killers for you." It doesn't exactly answer the question, but it certainly does the job of redirecting the conversation.

Ismene bristles. "I suppose it was whoever aided your escape. Rocco was convinced Priam was the only one of you who would resort to killing a family member."

"He wasn't supposed to die. He wasn't supposed to be there." Clover takes it on like it was her plan. Not that my position with Ismene will matter here shortly.

"We can't allow these types of accidents."

"But the agents who died at the dam," Clover says, "those were all right."

"It was wasteful. Those deaths served absolutely no purpose. The accumulator wasn't even there."

"I'm sure their families would miss them less if their deaths were *useful*."

"Those families will enjoy a lifetime of their lost relatives' salaries," Ismene says.

"Would that be enough for the loss of Rocco?"

"I will get payment as well." She unsheathes a knife from her hip—the one Rocco stabbed Serenity with. "I'll cut it out of whoever thought they could spill Agnar blood."

A chill shoots down my neck like a bolt of lightning. I was once uncomfortable leaving Serenity in the hands of Lanelle Kemp. This is far worse. But Clover has guaranteed her safety.

"Why should his blood be worth more than anyone else's?" Clover asks.

Ismene's nostrils flare. "It's the only blood that matters! It's in your veins too, and you cannot pretend you aren't more—better than the rest. This place is nothing without us!"

"You're wrong." Clover's eyes glisten. "Montica exists—*Monticans* exist for their own sake, not yours."

"Some existence it would be without us," Ismene scoffs. "What do you want anyway? You should have taken *your father's* killers for yourself, but if you've brought them to me, you want something. What is it?"

"Freedom. For myself and my friends who you had imprisoned."

"You're smarter than that, Minea. You know freedom is the greatest lie ever concocted. But fine, enjoy life in the wild. I'll happily welcome you back when you realize it's not all playing in the trees and beautiful vistas." She slows down to annunciate the rest. "Who killed my brother?"

"Two Kaycians from the uprising."

Ismene swings her attention to me. "I told you to deal with those people!"

"I couldn't just—"

"Of course you couldn't! Because you're weak. Your only connection to this family is *him,* so you're as pathetic as he is."

"They are important to Kaycie," Clover says, "the people who killed Father. You can't kill them."

"Like hell I can't. You get your people, I get mine, Minea. Don't overplay your hand."

"It's a condition of my giving them to you. You can't kill them without ruining our relations with Kaycie. I'm trying to save you from yourself."

"Kaycie should appreciate not being wiped off the face of the Earth for having people who would dare come into *my* country and kill my brother."

"I won't tell you where they are."

"I'll order the obliteration of Kaycie then."

"They aren't even there!"

"Will that break your tender heart to let millions die for the two you absurdly want to protect?" She pulls the pad from her arm and starts tapping.

"No!" Serenity comes barreling from the trees in a sack of a white linen dress. She's a mess of bruises and smeared blood. On her heels is Aspen and... *Frey Dempsey?*

"It's only me you want!" Serenity shouts while Clover yells at Aspen for letting her go.

"I needed to keep them concealed longer!" Clover's fists tremble at her sides.

Frey shakes Serenity's shoulders. "You idiot!" His beauty is also marred by injuries. How did he replace Serenity's boyfriend in this?

"You?" Ismene's lip curls. "You couldn't have killed Rocco."

Serenity's shoulders heave. "I did."

"We did." Frey takes her hand in his.

"You want us dead? Fine," Serenity says. "I'd rather die to protect people than kill for hollow revenge." She steps backward, toward the cliff edge. Frey goes along with her.

"You think I'd let you off so easily?" Ismene twirls the knife. "No, you don't get to choose death, pretty girl. My brother drew some of your blood. I'll wring the rest from you slowly. You will beg for death, but I will choose when to bestow it upon you."

Did my grandmother beg for death? Would Ismene jar Serenity's hand too? She won't get the chance. I have to trust Clover to prevent it.

Serenity inches back farther, but Frey pulls her arm. Tears line her lashes as she shakes her head at him. "I'm sorry."

His own face is contorted in grief. "No."

"I'll still do it!" Ismene's voice reaches an ear-piercing level. "I'll destroy everything and everyone you've ever known. Are you so selfish?"

"Are you?" Frey asks.

"Ismene!" Clover shouts.

"Stop them or I'll crush Nyberg too!" She'd do anything to get the revenge she thinks she's owed. Not just their lives for his, but as much pain as she can wreak on them.

Aspen's eyes bulge. He lunges for Serenity and Frey, but they cling to each other as they jump off the cliff and disappear.

Chapter Sixty-Two
SERENITY

The breeze chills my legs. Adwin looks at me like he's never seen me. Ismene's rage is a parasite eating her from within. I wish I could apologize for Rocco. But it wouldn't matter. She's too far gone.

Aspen lunges, but we jump away before he would touch us. If that were possible.

Frey's hand—tight around mine—grounds me to reality. Everything feels so real. The jump is scarier than it should be. We fall. The sky still a gray blue above us in the early morning rays of sunlight. But the fall is brief. We bounce in the pit of squishy foam blocks, and I stare up at the image of wispy clouds.

Frey lets out a breathy laugh next to me. "That was fun."

I release him and rake both hands through my hair. "That was weird." I'd never have thought this room of cameras and projections could feel like the outside world. To have all this hidden away underground, connected to their stronghold and secretly linked to the fortress itself is mind-blowing.

"We're good at this." The screens that make up the huge box we're in, flicker back to their blank natural state. "Maybe we break into the movie industry after this. We'd make a gorgeous couple, and I'd be an amazing love interest."

"That'll just be me, thanks." Bram reaches in, and I take his offered hand. He pulls me out as Frey climbs out on his own.

"How was my performance?" I ask.

"Too good." Bram's dark eyes roam my face. The makeup job is incredible, so he hates it. "I couldn't watch on the screens. It looked too real."

"It felt that way, too," I say. "I don't know that I'm such a great actress. The set up was terrifying."

"Don't downplay our art," Frey says, his cocky smile betraying his lack of offense. "I still don't think Bram could have pulled it off."

I shrug and tuck myself into Bram's arms. That wasn't so bad. We had to come here for their tech and proximity to the real scene. I guess our history of catastrophes have made us paranoid, because this was never a terribly precarious situation. The rest is in Clover's hands—in Montica's. I'm so ready to go home. A deep breath against Bram reminds me I already am.

A wall explodes into a million shards of glass.

Screaming rings out from the other side.

A deafening bang.

Frey falls back into the foam pit, and Bram throws us both in next to him. He rolls off me and pulls a gun from his lower back.

What was that? The words don't form. My head spins. Bram peeks over the ledge which served as the rock we met Clover on. I want to pull him back. To tell him to stay down. Except, this isn't the kind of situation I know how to deal with. It's his.

Instead, I turn to Frey. He blinks wildly, and his chest rises and falls with quick, shallow breaths.

"Frey?" My eyes continue down his tall frame to where he clutches his lower ribs. Blood seeps between his fingers. A red stain blooms on the linen shirt. This wasn't supposed to happen in reality! "Frey!"

Every inch of me trembles as I press my hands over his. Ice in my veins makes his blood feel scorching hot on my hands. "Bram!" My throat constricts. My lungs burn with frantic breaths.

Bram moves my hands, then Frey's. "Fuck," he mutters.

"Frey!" His eyelids droop. "No!" I grab his face, my hands smearing blood on his cheeks. Real blood. Not the makeup. A desperate, high-pitched sound comes out of me. "Frey, stay with me."

His eyelashes flutter, and he finds my face.

"You've got more hearts to break," I say. Tears soak my face. "Let's go get 'em."

"You know me." His voice is flat—almost too quiet to hear. It misses the inflection the phrase needs. *You know me, I'll be breaking hearts again in no time.* But there is no time.

He closes his eyes. I don't know if he can hear me anymore. Not that there's anything to say. Just as he sat in silence with me while I grieved Jase, he lies here now. Silent and far too still.

Chapter Sixty-Three

Serenity is gone. My hand covers my mouth, but I don't remember doing that. She's kissed these lips that gape at her sudden absence from the world. I never cared about her romantically, but she didn't deserve this. What did Clover do? Was keeping Serenity and the others safe a lie? Did imprisonment change her? I wouldn't have thought her capable of betraying someone like that. Serenity came here of her own free will—to help!

"You fool!" Ismene lurches at Clover. She moves faster than she has any right to. She's as agile as Nemora who I've seen take down *Priam*.

I think Clover could still best her. Especially with Aspen's assistance, but after a few dance-like movements they stop with a blade at Clover's throat, and Aspen looks on with a calculating gaze. How far have they strayed from their plan? Does he know what Clover can accomplish well enough to give her the space she needs without risking her life? I'd think a blade at the throat would be the tipping point into *life endangering*, but what do I know?

"How dare you let the vermin who killed your own father get off so easily!" Ismene trembles as she holds Clover's back to her chest. "Have you learned nothing? Genius intellect without any sense of loyalty will get you nowhere, Minea."

Clover smiles in a defiant way her aunt can't see, but it creeps into her voice. "I didn't let anyone get away."

Ismene guides them both to the cliff edge and looks over. She sucks in a breath and drops her hand, still gripping the knife, to her side. "What are you playing at?"

What?

"I knew you'd scent blood like a shark when you saw them," Clover says. She spins away from Ismene with an easy grace. She could have freed herself all along, couldn't she? "I wouldn't have brought them before you."

"Where are they?" Ismene growls.

"They're hidden in Nyberg. Good luck finding them. You know your city about as well as you know these mountains."

"I would burn the city down if need be."

Clover's eyes widen. "It's your capital! Your own people!"

"Rocco was my only person. Rocco and Nemora. Even you and Priam are lost causes. So, *Clover*,"—the middle name she chooses to go by is a curse on Ismene's lips—"will you make me do that?"

Clover's fury melts away. She smiles. She's gotten what she needed. "Oh, Ismene. I'm so sorry life made you this way. But no one would follow that order. They know what you are. They won't follow you anymore."

"My word is *law!*"

"Not when the people who would execute it just saw how little you regard them. I love Priam, but he was foolish. We didn't need to destroy you. You've destroyed yourself."

Ismene's eyes go wild. She looks around like a caged animal—down to Nyberg and back to Clover. "You couldn't have."

"We were able to project people into the space," Aspen says. "I assure you we can stream your tirade."

"Except no one has seen it." Priam strides out from the trees. "Hello, Mother."

Chapter Sixty-Four

BRAM

I swore I'd protect her, and though there isn't a scratch on her... I've failed.

Her blood-soaked fingers are splayed over Frey's still heart. She shakes with sobs.

Tori flashes through my memory. This could have been how I reacted to her death. Except, I don't do this. There was no time anyway. We were in the middle of a fire fight, and we're in the middle of one now. Serenity can take this moment to cry over her friend—*our friend*, weird as it is to think that. She's physically safer down here, but I don't want to think about what extended time with a corpse will do to her psyche.

One thing at a time.

I look over the ledge. On the other side of the shattered screens, Knox is fighting off two men. One of the girls—Juniper or Willow—takes one down with a kick to his neck. Screaming fills the gaps between the sounds of battle. More shots fired. Shouts. I climb over the edge and hurry into the action. Two steps out of the room, a side impact throws me down. I turn and get back up to a knee, ready and looking for the next attack. But I'm not worth the Montican agents' notice.

Knox is built like a bear, but even he is out-muscled. He's taken down and restrained. The girls could be action movie heroes, but they're out-done too. Serenity's assessment that I couldn't have taken down Rocco Agnar on my own comes back to me. To say these fighters are on a different level would be an understatement. They are playing a completely different game.

I wouldn't have managed it if Serenity hadn't injured Rocco already. And back at the dam, Krisalyn's interference made our victory possible. Alone, I don't stand a chance against these people.

Maybe their underestimation of me can be an advantage. I lunge for one of the girls' opponents. He grabs my arm and swings me around into my ally. She grunts, sandwiched between me and a wall. "Don't bother," she says, shoving me away. Her adversary didn't take advantage of my interference because the other girl has looped an arm around his throat from behind.

Before I realize I'm moving forward, I'm stopped by the strong, lean arm of the tree-walker I smashed into. "Stop trying to help." She leaps back into the fray, a blur of limbs I can barely make sense of. No matter how far beyond me they are, I can't accept being dismissed like this. Fights are the whole point of my involvement. Without that, what's the point of me?

"Not again. Not again. Not again." Jase's voice pulls my attention to the Kaycians I'm failing to help.

Vogue and Krisalyn cower in a nearby corner with Dixon's—*shit*—hopefully just unconscious body. My eyes jump from him to Krisalyn. She nods and mouths *he's okay* through tears. Jase's expression is frozen in wide-eyed horror.

The three tree-walkers left are subdued and restrained, then the agents come for us. My fist is caught and wrenched behind my back so fast my head spins. I'm no more a threat to them than Serenity is when she play-fights me. Vogue, Krisalyn, and Jase don't put up a fight as their wrists are bound behind their backs. They all seem to have checked out with their distant gazes and trembling or slack jaws.

Then Vogue's attention snaps to me. "Where is Serenity?"

Right on cue, a screech comes from the screen room. "No!" She screams and thrashes as she's dragged in to join us. The Montican agent tosses her toward us like she's nothing, and Vogue whimpers.

The restraints cut into my wrists as I lean over her, desperate to hold her. These situations have always been the times when clarity sharpens me, but with Serenity right in front of me, all I want to do is grasp her and whisper that everything will be okay. It would be a lie, and we don't do that. But the urge is there—comfort her no matter what.

We need to get out of this. We need to get home.

Serenity covered in tears and blood.

No! That doesn't help.

"God, Serenity!" Jase blinks away his shock. "That's a lot of blood!" He looks around, suddenly ambitious about trying to get free. She lays unmoving by my knees.

"It's not hers," I say.

The unspoken fact hangs over us. Frey wasn't dragged in here because he's dead. It wasn't *because* he took a place in the plan that could have been mine, but the guilt is there just the same. Vogue shudders, and I think she might throw up. Krisalyn leans her forehead on Vogue's arm as sobs rack her body.

Chapter Sixty-Five
ADWIN

"What do you mean no one has seen it?" Clover looks daggers at Priam.

"We're Agnars," Priam says. "We don't air our dirty laundry."

"No, we shove it into the shadows and let it grow mold." She marches over to him, and even though he towers over her, she doesn't look small. The trees, the vista, the crisp breeze whipping through her hair—it's everything that looks and feels like Clover. She is a force here in her element, and even as everything we're doing seems to be falling apart around us, in *her* I have faith.

Priam only shrugs. "Better than having the world lose faith in the entire family when we only need to be rid of *her*."

Ismene sneers. "The prodigal son. Do you still want to take my place? You do realize it comes with *responsibility* and sacrifice?"

"I don't want any of it anymore. All I want is to leave and be rid of you." He crosses his arms and looks at me. "And to tell you he's betrayed you."

Blood drains from my face.

Clover gasps. "What are you doing?"

Priam shakes his head. "And to think, Mother, for all your insistence that we could only trust our immediate family... You didn't follow your own rules very well."

"I got you out!" Fear snakes through me.

"You put me in there! The other times you got in my way were coincidental, but *that?* I wish I had killed you with that EMP."

Clover's eyes meet mine, and the image of reaching for her as I fell flashes before me. This is just as hopeless. She's not going to catch me.

"You..." My mind reels. "It *was* to kill me? And it was *you?*"

"It was for Clover, but killing you would have been a fortunate accident."

Clover slaps him across the face. The sharp sound cracks between us all like a lightning bolt. "You tried to kill me!"

"I knew that wouldn't kill you! I'm not an idiot!"

"Why then?"

"So you'd finally get off your ass and do something about Ismene! Except I thought you'd know to include me. And then I idiotically brought Adwin along."

Ismene's jaw hangs open. "You speak of not following my rules by trusting someone from outside our family, but you've trampled the most important rule! You attacked your cousin. Our family comes *first!* You're willing to shred us, for what?"

"You deserve it for the way you've tried to cage us our entire lives,"—Priam points at his mother—"but you're right. The entire family shouldn't suffer for your mistakes. An idea which has obviously never occurred to you—that not everyone has to be punished for *one person's* treachery. None of this is Clover's fault. It isn't even Nemora's. Which is why I stopped the streaming of your rant. That downfall would mar the entire family. Clover or Nemora should be able to take over without the nation's contempt. Nemora might earn her own, but that's her problem."

"So do you still suppose my death is the only way to move forward?" Ismene twirls the knife between her fingers. Would she kill her son?

"Will you make it come to that?" Priam's pompous gaze falters. Maybe he doesn't want to kill her anymore. "Just because it hasn't already been shown to the country, doesn't mean it isn't recorded."

"Blackmail then?" Ismene's mirthless smile drips disappointment by this inauspicious end to her rule.

Clover and Aspen get the distant look in their eyes I recognize as listening to comms. They tense and scan the tree line. *What now?*

"Can I sweeten the deal with a parting gift?" Priam offers. "I've got Rocco's killers for you."

Her lips purse. It's not like she has an option to keep her position. Not with that footage. The option for revenge really is just a parting gift. A dark, twisted gift. Priam must know about my grandmother. The idea of Serenity stepping into that position turns my stomach.

"Was it really those cute little Kaycians Clover showed me?" Ismene asks.

"Yes." Priam maintains the lie. Why? "Although, the boy was killed when my people secured the group."

Frey Dempsey is dead, despite the death I witnessed being fake.

Ismene's eyes narrow. "What group?"

"The same Kaycians who destroyed the dam, stole the accumulator, and broke us out of prison."

Clover's lip curls as she looks at the cousin she considered a friend. She and Aspen drift into position with their backs to each other as if bracing for an attack.

"I want them all," Ismene says.

"They're marked for death, of course," Priam says. "They've committed plenty of crimes, and they know far too much. However, you only get the one who killed Rocco. The rest get clean deaths. Don't need you becoming a savage."

"You must already consider me a savage if you think I'll appreciate the gift of torturing a little girl."

"You thought telling me about what you did to your father's mistress would scare me," Priam says. "It only gave me a bargaining chip. I knew you'd never do such a thing to any of us. But this is a little girl who gutted your brother."

"Priam," I say, "you can't just—"

"Quick deaths for the rest?" Ismene confirms.

"Yes, Mother."

Her hand moves almost too fast for me to see. I feel it before I realize what's happened. Searing pain explodes in my neck. My fingers rise to it and come back sticky and warm.

Clover screams, and I try to respond, but only blood comes out. I don't know what I'd have said.

The ground is harder this time when I meet it, but it's only from my height—not so bad. And this time I have a great view. The mountains and the city. A vista like the painting Mother kept in her Kaycie apartment. Art I always wished I could create, but perhaps I should have just let myself enjoy it instead. Beauty doesn't need to cause jealousy. I got to see it, and that has to be enough.

Colors invade, not darkness. Every color in a stunning mural. I don't have to create such beauty; I can let myself sink into it instead. And I do.

Chapter Sixty-Six
SERENITY

Darkness so complete I wonder if my eyes are closed or maybe I'm blindfolded. I'm numb enough to not be sure. But I blink a few times, and—no, it's just a very dark place. Cold seeps through me, but there's no way to know if that's actually the environment. This chill is familiar to me, and even a summer day can't ward it off.

My hands curl into fists where they're bound behind my back, and dry blood cracks along my stretched skin. *Frey's blood.*

Sounds trickle into my awareness. Sniffles and whispers and shuffling. The walk here is a blur. Priam was giving orders. He betrayed us all. I wonder if Adwin, Misty, Clover, and Aspen are okay.

A weight settles onto my shoulder, and I know without seeing or hearing him it's Bram's chin. His breath is warm on my ear, and the cold creeping through me recedes. I tilt my temple to his forehead. "I'm so sorry," I whisper.

His nose brushes across my cheek as he shakes his head. He sucks in a shaky breath, and the need to wrap my arms around him carves cracks into my heart. Instead, I twist around to kiss his cheek. The taste of his salty tears focuses me.

"Hey." I swallow past a lump in my throat. I'm torn between not wanting to sound like this is the end and making sure that if it is, there's nothing left unsaid. This time I will not hold back. There will be no regrets. I have to hope my whispers will be a respite. "I want more time with you. A lifetime wouldn't be enough, but what we've had has been more than I ever could have hoped for. *You* are more than I ever dreamed of. I always wanted to love like this. It was just an idea, and I didn't know what it would feel like. It's consuming and crazy and comforting all at the same time." I nuzzle my face into his neck, having to find creative ways to embrace without my arms. "Thank you."

His cheek slides back along mine, and he finds my lips with his own. The kiss isn't desperate—it's accepting. When he pulls back, I drop my face to his chest. "We haven't done something for August thirteenth," he says into my hair.

"And you haven't determined what your zero means."

"Of course I did."

I jerk back. I wish I could see his face, but the darkness is infallible. "What is it?" I lean back in so he can whisper it.

"The number of people I have left to fall in love with."

A sob claws through my chest, but I do everything I can to stifle it. Now he's fairly guaranteed to be right, but he had decided that before today. I kiss him again. "I love you so much."

"I love you too." He does. He loves me completely. He's seen past every façade of perfection and all the crumbly mess—he loves all of me.

I could let myself drown in this for as much time as we have, but he's not the only person I care about here. "Vogue, are you okay?"

"I've been better." Her exasperated look is as clear in my mind as it would be with lights on. "Dixon is conscious."

"Unfortunately," he says in a gravelly voice.

"Jase?" I ask.

There is muffled mumbling, then Krisalyn answers. "We're fine."

Except we aren't.

"Is that all of us in here?" Bram asks.

"Think so." Vogue's voice is detached in the pitch black.

Light pours in, blinding me. I'm still trying to blink my eyes into focus when an unyielding grip snatches me off the cold, hard floor. I yelp and strain to see Bram as he pulls frantically but seems to be stuck to the wall. The person holding me reaches out and hits him in the neck with something gripped in his fist. That face I longed to see again goes slack and Bram falls to the floor unconscious. His bound wrists are still pressed against the wall.

"No!" I pull against my captor to no avail. "What did you do to him?"

I'm whipped around like a doll to face Priam. "You'll thank me. Come on." He pulls me out amongst a chorus of shouting.

Everyone seems to be stuck to the walls now. Were they the whole time? Could this be the last time I'll see these friends who have become family? "I love you all so much! I'm sor—"

My final apology for getting them stuck in this mess is cut off by the slamming door. I look at Priam, and my jaw clenches. "What's going to happen to them?"

"They're going to die." He says it matter-of-factly.

My chest caves in on itself. "I guess I'm first then?"

"You're last actually."

"Why did you take me first?"

"You killed Rocco Agnar. You have a very different death awaiting you."

My heart stops. My mouth goes dry. It figures though. But Bram... "What did you do to Bram?"

"Only knocked him out."

"Why?"

"He'd be the only one who would advertise his role in Rocco's death. Ismene still believes it to have been Frey with you."

My mind reels. What is he saying?

"The deal is," he continues, "the rest get quick clean deaths. Only Rocco's murderer shall receive a worse punishment, and she believes that to only be you now."

Tears sting my eyes. "So, you're trying to let him have a… less painful death?" My throat constricts. I can't believe I'm in a world in which any death for Bram would be a good thing.

"Yes."

"Why?"

"Because I'm slightly less depraved than my mother. Basically, I have a pet snake that needs to be fed. You're the mouse. I hold no ill will toward you; it's just a necessity."

My eyes close, and my lips press together. I don't want to ask what's coming for me. I suspect I should envy a mouse in a snake's enclosure.

"I can make it easier for you," Priam says, "if you wish."

My body detaches like when I was extirpated. My feet move me, but I'm numb. "How?"

"This would make it so you don't feel anything." He holds out a large capsule. "Your body would still react the way it should to sate Ismene, but you'd be gone."

"Like extirpation?"

He rolls his eyes. "No. Your mind wouldn't be trapped in your body. You'd effectively be dead."

"Is it reversible?"

We enter a small elevator and shoot up. "Even if it was, that wouldn't matter. But it's not."

It's a way out, I know. It's ease and comfort; a way to end on my own terms. But I'm still here, and even without anything to hope for…

I can't do that. "No." I shake my head. "No, but um, thank you." What's become of my life that I'm thanking the person handing me over for torture and death?

"I'll offer it again when I can." Priam leads me down a hallway I barely see. We stop at huge, dark wood double doors. "In the meantime, you can't remember the favors I've offered you." He holds out a smaller capsule.

God, I hate this. I take the capsule from him and step through the door he holds open for me. The room is a far cry from the medieval torture chamber I expected, but it blurs as I swallow the pill.

Chapter Sixty-Seven

BRAM

Cold stone against my face is the first thing my mind registers. It's soothing against the thrum of pain. "What the fuck?"

"Oh, thank God." Close by in the darkness, Krisalyn sighs.

Krisalyn. Not Serenity. I jerk up to my knees, bumping into her. "Where is she?"

"Bram, I..."

Choked sobs sound from farther away. The walls could be collapsing for all the weight crushing me. We were kissing, talking, checking on everyone. My wrists were pulled to the wall like they had electromagnets in them, and light flooded the room. She was wrenched away and— "Where is she!"

It's Jase's voice that offers an answer. "She's gone." He sounds as empty as I am. "Priam took her."

My arms tense against the restraints digging into my wrists. Every muscle trembles as I struggle for breath.

"Ismene wants her," Jase says—still flat.

My lungs burn like I'm drowning. "Okay. But Ismene didn't hurt you, right?"

"Ismene never even saw me. I wasn't important enough for her. But Serenity killed—"

"I killed him!" My voice is unrecognizable. More animal roar than speech. "It was me!"

"They can't hear you," Jase says.

"I don't care if she wanted to take the blame. We all know it was me. How could you let them *take her?*"

"None of us were in any position to stop him," Krisalyn says softly.

"You could have told him it was me he wants."

"It wouldn't have mattered." Dixon's words are followed by a sniffle. "Priam came back in. There's nothing to do for Serenity, but since Frey... Anyway, Ismene just wants Serenity."

"But it *wasn't* Frey. Why hasn't he told her it was me?"

"Because," Krisalyn says, "it wouldn't spare Serenity. It would only lead to you suffering when you don't have to."

"I won't let her face it alone!"

The weeping can only be the person who hasn't spoken up.

"Vogue! You know I'm right."

More sobs before she gets words out. "There's nothing we can do. Nothing any of us go through would help her."

"I have to try."

"Priam won't give you an opportunity to tell anyone," Dixon says. "That's why he knocked you out when the door was open. He'll silence you until you're killed."

"One of you do it. Tell anyone within earshot." The fire is gone from my voice. Desperation has suffocated my anger. "Please. I can't sit here imagining what happens to her."

"We can't, Bram." Krisalyn's words drip with tears. "She doesn't want you to suffer. None of us do."

My heart aches with a pain no torture could possibly replicate. "Jase. Tell them."

"I'm not going to do that."

"Why not? You can't possibly like me."

"Not liking you is very different from wanting you to be tortured."

My head spins. I *need* even the remote possibility of getting near Serenity again. Maybe I could convince them it wasn't her. Her friends may have given up, but I can't. I won't give up until I'm dead. And if Jase telling them the truth of my involvement makes my death worse, so be it. Just to see her again would be worth it. I let her go in the EC when the uprising started. I left her to suffer because I was too, and I won't do it again. Every thought of her death has made me feel like I'm drowning, but letting her die alone and afraid is the only thing that would be worse.

How to do it turns my stomach, but what do I care what they think of me? It won't be worse than how I'll feel about it. I just need him to hate me enough.

I'm so sorry, S.

"Don't you though?" Hopefully the rasp of my voice comes off sinister. "Do you want me to go to my grave picturing every pleasure I ever had with Serenity? I'm sure Ismene can make it so I don't remember anything that ever felt good."

Krisalyn gasps. "Bram!"

"I already listened to her say she loves you more than she's ever dreamed of loving a person," Jase says. "There's not really anything left to break me."

"Oh, but you don't know about all the other things she's only ever felt with me."

———————— ❦ ————————

I lick blood from the corner of my mouth. What did that even look like? None of us have our hands available, and we can't see. I don't know whose skull hit my face, but I deserved it. Darkness helped. I'm not sure I could have done it if I saw the shock and fury on everyone's faces.

There was a lot of yelling, but my words worked. I could tell because Jase finally welcomed me to enjoy every misery available on Earth before going to hell. At least none of them will feel bad about whatever's going to happen to me now.

How did I find the words to talk about her that way? Even the true parts were twisted to reduce us to lust, and some of it was exaggerated. My stomach rolls. I hate that I exposed us—*her*—like that, but we'll all take it to our graves soon enough. The most important things I kept for myself. The tears and cuddles, the vulnerability and fears, those are the most intimate things between us.

All I can hope for now is that someone comes in here soon. If the dust has enough time to settle, Jase might forgive what I said. He knows the real purpose.

Torn between never wanting Jase to ever think of Serenity like that and hoping it's playing in his mind on repeat to fuel his anger, time scrapes by with an agonizing slowness. It's nothing compared to what Serenity might be going through. My chest heaves, but I'm suffocating. Chills, but I'm sweating.

I need to get out of here. I need to get out of here! I. Need. To. Get. Out.

Blinding light illuminates the room. The metallic sound of blades being unsheathed.

My head is snapped back. For a second, I crave a quick death. Not to avoid physical pain, simply to escape my head.

"He killed Rocco Agnar!" Jase shouts. Everyone freezes.

Krisalyn screeches. "That's not true."

"I thought the other killer was dead already?" My eyes blink into focus to see Montican agents conferring.

"He is," Dixon says.

Priam presses his lips together and shakes his head.

"If Ismene finds out from the girl that it was actually this guy,"—one of them gestures to me—"and we killed him, we're dead."

"We already know it was the other one," Priam says.

"We should have them questioned first to be sure."

Priam's jaw ticks.

"It's true," I say. "It was me."

"Okay, we'll take him to Ismene then." Priam pulls me to my feet and hisses in my ear. "I tried to help you."

I believe him, despite everything. It's the only reason I'm not telling the others with him that Priam knew all along.

"Take him to Ismene if he's foolish enough to even claim such a thing. I'll get interrogation rooms for the others." Priam shoves me toward an agent, and there's a prick on my arm. I stumble into steel arms as a familiar dizziness washes over me.

Chapter Sixty-Eight

SERENITY

The grandeur of this space is beyond anything I've ever seen. I lean back and my hand finds a handle. A door then. It doesn't turn, but dizziness from shock or confusion or the knowledge that we're probably all going to die keeps me frozen here anyway. It would be a welcome change from the cold, dark cell, but now I'm alone.

What's happened to my friends? Why am I the only one here?

A wall of floor to ceiling windows showcases an incredible mountain vista. The furniture is dark and heavy for my taste, but stunning. The piece of me that still dreams of gin and opulence thinks it would be a great venue for a party—if not for the column of fire shaped like a scythe. That's certainly one option for a focal piece.

That isn't what draws me back to my predicament, though. It's Ismene Agnar prowling toward me like a panther that reminds me I haven't been saved.

"Serenity Ward. I've heard so much about you."

The phrase I know so well sends a chill down my neck when it comes from her. Ismene's radar is one I would've preferred to never have found myself on.

She approaches me with long, elegant strides like she can take her time and the world will wait for her. I'm always shorter than everyone, but Ismene looming over me makes me shrink into myself. My legs are water. I don't know how I'm still standing. A cold finger slides down my temple, along my jaw, and stops at my chin to lift my face. Her green eyes drill into mine, and my lip trembles.

"You're going to wish you had been there to jump off that cliff." She lays a hand on my lower back as gently as my own father would to guide me into the living room.

Mechanically, I obey her gesture to sit. Every inch of me is braced for whatever pain is about to come. The anticipation knots my chest. A tear slides out of my eye, and Ismene smiles.

"Waiting is terrible, isn't it?"

I drop my gaze to my knees, and her hand appears there—gentle again. I flinch. Time and silence tangle together into a noose. I thought the anxious quiet before fighting with Bram was painful. What I'd give to be so sheltered again. Ismene uses the wait as a weapon. My imagination runs wild. I'm torturing myself, and all she has to do is sit here.

"You're scared. That's good." Her voice is somehow simultaneously soft and sharp. A welcome change but still dreaded. "I will break you—body, mind, and spirit. But it won't be all bad. If every moment was pain, you'd grow numb to it. With a sprinkling of good... glimmers to remind you what happiness is, we can—"

I look up when she cuts her words off. Her gaze is distant. She's probably listening to that creepy implanted comm. The memory of Lanelle talking straight into my head makes me want to throw up. My fingers itch to rub the small scar behind my ear, but I keep still.

Her lips twist up at the corners, then she glances down at my blood-crusted hands balled in my lap. "So very lucky for your partner-in-crime to have died already. Was he your lover too? You Kaycian sluts have so many."

My eyes prickle. If she finds out about Bram before he's killed, she'll use him to hurt me. "Yes, he was." At least it doesn't take any acting to look mortified. Frey's death will haunt me until I die. Of course, that may not be such a long time.

"You've lost many an admirer here in Montica then."

My eyes snap up to hers. *Is he dead already?* My chest feels hollow at the thought.

"Adwin also died quickly."

My hand flies to cover my gasp. "Adwin?"

"You had been with him, too, isn't that right?" She slides one fingernail under another.

"Yes, we..." I'm blind and stumbling into horrors from nowhere. "He was your nephew."

"That's a technicality, and even then, only half." Her gaze sharpens. "He wasn't the lover you were worried about, though, was he?"

The onslaught of thoughts threatens to make me sick. Adwin had the best odds of any Kaycian—the best connections. If he wasn't safe, none of us are. Adwin and I were never really anything romantic, but I've found comfort in his arms. And he was trying to help—to fix his mistakes. He didn't deserve this. Now, Ismene lusts over my blood like— *Wait.* It's eternity in my swirling thoughts, but also only a second. *He wasn't the lover you were worried about.* She's baiting me.

The door opens, and Bram comes in.

Chapter Sixty-Nine

BRAM

Serenity's eyes flash from surprised, to elated, to horrified, to mortified, so fast no one else would notice each shift. But I can read those eyes the way some people predict the weather by the clouds. There's a storm, but the swirling grays won't rain for now. She's locking it down, being careful, because next to her is the woman who wants us dead. In some lower level of my consciousness, the grand space we're in registers. I'm not entirely sure how I got from that dark cell to here, but it's not enough to pull my focus from Serenity as I walk into the living room.

"Call me prideful," Ismene says, "but this makes more sense." Even when I knew it wasn't real, the sight of her prowling toward Serenity was unnerving. The way this woman looks over me like I'm a curiosity rather than a person—a child throwing a tantrum who doesn't need to be taken seriously—reminds me of Casimir's haughty confidence after he was arrested.

My fists clench at my sides. She feels no need to have me restrained. I'm no threat to her at all. "It's impossible for you to be any match for my brother either, but more likely than this." She waves toward Serenity.

Serenity rolls her eyes while Ismene is focused on me. Our argument over whether we both killed Rocco flashes through my mind. I wish I could laugh at the memory.

"I guess his skills didn't include surviving a bullet in the brain."

Ismene narrows her eyes at me, too controlled to show her fury, but still giving off the aura of a snake poised to strike. Her hand whips out to her side, Serenity yelps, and a line of red slashes across her ribs. She presses blood caked hands to her side and winces. Her eyelids and lips press shut so hard they tremble.

I lurch toward her but stop when Ismene holds the blade to Serenity's throat. "It wasn't her! I did it!"

"I don't doubt that." Ismene presses the blade where I've felt Serenity's pulse beneath my lips. "It's easy enough to guess the reason for your confession."

Serenity keeps her chin up. She's stronger than I could have ever imagined when we first met. Our eyes lock together, and a thousand thoughts hang between us. We said it all, but it doesn't feel like enough. It could never be enough with her. A hundred years wouldn't have been enough, but all we were given was a year to know each other, and a few weeks to love each other.

"I understand the need for revenge," I say. "I've wanted it on your father for months. But you haven't maintained control over a country by making rash decisions and taking out your rage on an innocent. You'd have to be insane."

Ismene pulls the knife away and twirls it between her fingers. "The greatest minds of all time were thought insane. People willing to do the things weaker people won't are made out to be monsters. Well, the dinosaurs were monstrous, and they lived far longer than our species is likely to. It's survival of the fittest, in mind and body now. I'm doing the world a service by ensuring my family's place and keeping us feared.

To fear us is nothing compared to the results of standing against us. But apparently there needs to be a reminder every generation or so."

Serenity closes her eyes, steeling herself. Ismene might strike at any moment. We both know Ismene is toying with us. I can't talk her out of killing Serenity. I can only hope she doesn't suffer. A quick death would be a mercy compared to whatever Ismene would have done otherwise. That isn't much consolation as I think of watching Serenity die, though. It's like she's hanging over the side of the building again in Leavenworth, and my hand is slipping.

"Letting you watch what I was going to do to her seems like a fitting punishment," Ismene says. "It seems more likely—"

Serenity whips her hand up, knocking the twirling knife away before Ismene could grip it. Her body follows the arc of her arm, and her knee thrusts into Ismene's stomach.

She wasn't steeling herself to die. She was getting ready to attack.

I sprint around the fire table as Ismene flips Serenity onto the floor with a *thud*. She's wrapped her hands around Serenity's throat when I barrel into her. The heavy couch slides with us when she slams into it. Ismene wastes no time getting to her feet and launching an attack on me like I've never seen. Serenity has slipped away, but I can barely stay on my feet as Ismene assaults me with every appendage available.

Just run, S. I can't look away long enough to know where she is. After an elbow to my face, I can barely see at all.

Then Ismene wobbles.

Serenity pops up at my side, knife in hand.

Chapter Seventy

SERENITY

Ismene teeters off her leg, and blood drips from where I cut her Achilles tendon.

Fury and horror warred in me when I realized what Bram was doing here, but maybe it'll work. He'd have been content to sacrifice himself, but if we can save ourselves instead...

She lunges at me, but Bram hits her from the side. Off-balance, she stumbles toward the table, and her hand lands in the fire. Her guttural scream doesn't sound human. Still, she dodges a punch. Bram's next finds its mark, but she stays on her feet, only shuffling backwards. She bares bloody teeth. "You're nothing, all of you. Compared to my family you are insects, and you *dare* to cross us."

"You're in this situation because your family broke," I say. "You war against yourselves."

"Only because of him. My mother actually loved that *rat,* and he destroyed everything. I should let you both go off into the sunset. You'll torture each other worse than anything I could do."

If we didn't still need to be ready for anything, I'd take Bram's hand or tuck myself under his arm. I pity her. She really doesn't know what it means to be loved. Bram's very presence here should be proof, but she's blind to it.

"Letting him live was the last time I make the mistake of mercy," she says. "His mistress wasn't the only one who deserved to anguish. I should have killed him and his bastard daughter a long time ago. Lesson learned. I won't let the infection of *you* fester."

There wouldn't be reason for caution or worry with most opponents in her state, but this is Ismene Agnar. Her body isn't her greatest weapon, even though it's enough to take down almost anyone. The shift of her eyes places me in a fencing match. She's calculating, planning. Bram is the more obvious threat, but I have a knife. I squeeze the handle and the slice on my palm stings. Ismene would have noticed if I looked at the knife she was twirling, so I had to swat it away blind. I could have been cut worse, really.

Before the next move in this game can be played, the doors fling open. "Mother!"

I look up to see the sandy haired woman who must be Nemora Agnar storm in, towing Emmaline Lebeau.

Ismene pays no attention and lunges. Bram, still ready, crashes into her to block me. They tumble together, coming to a stop with Ismene on top. Nemora and I both rush in.

Shit, we're no match for two of them.

But Nemora pulls her mother off Bram, with the added help of me trying to get in between them.

"Enough!" Nemora roars. She pushes Ismene away from us. "Look what you've become!"

A verbal battle ensues, and I collapse onto Bram. "You idiot." I catch my breath against his heaving chest as he wraps his arms around me.

"You said... we'd be okay... because we'd be together," he says between pants.

I sigh and push up on my wobbly arms. This isn't over yet. Ismene and Nemora are yelling over each other, and our safety is *far* from guaranteed. "We'll have that fight later." I wince as I get up to my knees, and Bram springs up to a seated position to hold the cut on my side. "It's okay," I say.

I wish we had more time for a reunion, but now at least we might have that chance. We stand, and I spot Emmaline huddled by the wall like she could disappear there. I never spent much time with Adwin's mother, but I know enough to know she is nothing like her fierce Montican family. Does she know yet—that Adwin is dead? They're a poor excuse for family, but her son dying at the hands of her sister is horrible.

Nemora points to Emmaline with a trembling arm. "She's not even his daughter!"

The air stills. Emmaline gapes and says, "Of course, I am. He's my father. He raised me."

I lean back into Bram, suddenly less terrified and more uncomfortable. If only we could slip away unnoticed.

"He may have raised you," Nemora says, "but genes don't lie. He isn't your father."

Ismene looks from Emmaline to Nemora. "What have you been doing?"

"Research. Like *you* taught me."

The door opens again. Casimir and Priam enter and eye Bram and me curiously. "Ismene, what the hell are you doing?" Casimir rubs his temples like his daughter has broken a toy, not like she was trying to break humans.

"What have *you* done?" she retorts. "Nemora says Emmaline isn't even your daughter!"

He pales. "Izzy..."

"Don't you dare!" The nickname is far too sweet for this woman, and she seems to agree. "You lost the right to call me that when you destroyed our family. And for what exactly?"

Casimir sighs. "Would you sit down?"

"No." Ismene's jaw is clenched tight.

Bram and I inch our way to the wall. I just want to get out of here. Priam is too close to the door. What do we do? Somehow Casimir's presence feels a bit like a safety net. It's idiotic after everything he's done, but I think he's civilized enough not to want us tortured. Plus, Emmaline is here. He wouldn't let her see his darkest side.

Casimir sits—he's the only one to do so. He doesn't appear to be settling down for a calm conversation so much as surrendering under the weight of the issue at hand. "My sister-in-law lost a baby, and shortly after, my brother left her. She was in a downward spiral of depression, and I tried to be there for her. Then one day, I went to see her, and she had a baby. She had lost her mind and *kidnapped* an infant. There was a lot to decipher, but in the end, she truly believed the baby to be hers. I felt responsible for her, and she'd have been locked up for life or put to death for the kidnapping. So, I set her up with a place to raise the baby. I spent as much time as I could there, to ensure they were both well. Emmaline"—he looks at her with sad eyes—"grew up believing we were her parents, and we loved her as such."

Emmaline's entire body shakes. "What?"

Ismene squeezes the back of a chair hard enough to whiten her knuckles. "Well then, at least I didn't kill my *nephew* after all."

"You did what?" Casimir jumps to his feet.

Emmaline covers her mouth with both hands. "No. No, no, no."

"He betrayed me to the Kaycian scum, just like you betrayed all of us! Even if he wasn't biologically part of you, I suppose some things rubbed off."

Emmaline collapses in a fit of sobs. Casimir rushes to hold her.

"When Mother found out," Ismene says, "why didn't you tell her the girl wasn't yours?"

"Because she is mine!" Casimir looks at his daughter over the convulsing shoulder of the woman in question. "She's mine in every way that matters. I raised her, and I loved her, and I wasn't going to let her be taken away."

"You didn't care to protect your sister-in-law, though. And the ordeal killed Mother!"

He narrows his eyes at her. "Let's not pretend it was my actions that killed your mother."

Ismene lets out a screech and storms out to her balcony.

I glance at Bram from the corner of my eye. He nudges me toward the door, and we do our best not to make this any more awkward. Casimir confirms with Priam that Adwin is dead and joins his daughter on the balcony.

Nemora retreats to a large, bar-height table and drops her face into her hands.

Priam approaches us, and Bram tightens his arm around me.

"You betrayed us," I say. "You betrayed Clover. You sabotaged her plan."

"It's complicated," Priam says, as if that washes away the betrayal. "I also helped you, so I'd consider us even."

"How did you help us?" Bram asks.

"Here." He hands us each a small pill. "Those will help you remember. It was a short time, so you'll feel fine." He nods toward his mother outside. "This will be a good time to get you out."

"What about our friends?" I ask.

"They're still fine. They were taken for questioning, but I had to erase some of their memories so they wouldn't disclose that I helped them," Priam says.

I swallow the pill, and a little rush sweeps over my head.

"Did you know about…" Bram's gaze falls on Emmaline still crying on the floor.

The things I know come back to me. Priam was supposed to keep Bram away from Ismene. I'd be furious at Bram for finding a way to sacrifice himself for me, but it worked out. We're going to make it out of here.

"No. My sister beat me to that information." Priam purses his lips. "I'd have used it too, but probably differently. Anyway, we should go."

He opens the door as Bram pops his own pill into his mouth. Ismene's shouts from the balcony draw our attention back. "I was your real daughter! And you chose *her!*"

We back slowly out of the room. I feel itchy all over. Casimir's lips move, but the sound doesn't reach us.

Then Ismene screams again, hurls herself at his neck, and they both topple over the rail.

Chapter Seventy-One

BRAM

Nemora screams. She and Priam run out to the balcony and lean over the railing. Her shoulders heave. He tips his head like he can't understand. Their mother and grandfather are gone. Just like that.

Serenity stiffens next to me, and I pull her closer. Now that I remember what I did to get here, I'm not sure she'd appreciate the gesture. Of course, I'm glad we aren't all dead, but *shit,* now I have to tell her about that.

She looks up and frowns. "I guess he's gotten what he deserves."

Casimir Agnar shredded my family. I wanted him dead. It was all I cared about for months. So why does this feel hollow? "His mess of a family was punishment enough, I think." I lean down and kiss the little crease that's formed between her eyebrows.

"Think we can find everyone on our own?" She glances at Priam, still outside pondering his mother's death, and to the door that sits ajar.

"That won't be necessary." Clover pushes the door open wider and strides into the room like she owns it. As she looks around at the odd scattering of people, the rest come in behind her—all the vines and tree-walkers.

Vogue lifts Serenity right off the floor with a hug, not noticing her wince. "You're okay!"

"Mostly," Serenity says. Vogue puts her down and gasps at the bloodstains she's covered in.

"Oh, honey!" Krisalyn lays a hand on Serenity's cut side.

"It's fine." Serenity smiles through tears. "I'm so glad you're all safe."

Dixon kisses her forehead, and she squeezes Jase's hand.

"How did you get out?" I ask.

Willow—I think—lets out a breathy laugh. "Well, Misty never gets captured."

"And I was fed up with being told to hide and keep safe." The girl offers a slight smile.

"Where is Ismene?" Aspen asks.

Serenity and I glance out to the balcony where Clover holds Nemora in an embrace. The only three remaining Agnars stand over their newly inherited country after they've plotted against, betrayed, and deceived each other. Montica certainly has an interesting future ahead of it.

"She's gone," I say.

Everyone seems to try to contain their glee, but there is a collective sigh of relief. We survived. And for now, everyone doesn't hate me. Serenity and I are too injured and exhausted to put space between us for Jase's sake, and he doesn't show any problem with it. But that's only because he doesn't remember.

I lean down to her ear. "S, can we…" I nudge her away from the group. "I need to tell you—"

Sirens blare. *Oh, come on.*

Outside, the Agnars are all looking at the sky. A sound like static or something sizzling in a scorching hot pan washes over us, loud enough to make everyone cringe and cover their ears. Clover's shoulders shoot up practically to her ears, then her head drops forward and her back shudders. Jase runs out to her.

"What was that?" I ask no one in particular.

The tree-walkers seem to be looking around at nothing, like they're listening for or trying to feel something. A wide smile splits Juniper's face. "I think it shattered."

They rush out to the large balcony, and we all reluctantly follow. By the time we reach the door, it's clear Clover isn't crying sad tears. Laughter peals out of her so hard she's crying with joy.

"Who did that?" Aspen asks.

Clover wipes her eye. "I don't know." Her face is lit up. She jumps up onto the balcony rail, and a chorus of gasps ring out—only from us Kaycians. It seems way too far, but somehow she leaps into a tree. The rest of the tree-walkers follow suit like a flock of birds taking off. They disappear into the trees, but cheers and whoops echo back to us.

The six of us turn our attention to Priam and Nemora for an explanation. The latter shakes her head and bustles inside. Priam leans his elbows on the railing and his chin on his hands. "The dome is gone. I don't know how that's possible. The only accumulator outside of Montica was destroyed in Gladstone."

"About that," Vogue says. "It most certainly was never in Gladstone."

Priam whips around to face her. "What? But it exploded."

"Not the one we had," Dixon says. "We didn't take it there. We never knew why you thought we did, but we appreciated that you thought it was gone."

"He told them you did." Priam waves at Jase. "And he was unable to lie."

"I don't remember that," Jase says.

"Of course not." Priam arches an eyebrow. "That drug makes you very honest and takes the memory of the time it's in your system."

Sounds like what Adwin was on when we had that weird call with him so long ago.

"How could he give false information, though?" Vogue asks.

"He couldn't have," Priam says.

"Unless"—Krisalyn tilts her head as she looks at Jase—"you believed it was true."

His shoulders drop, and he rubs the back of his neck. "I guess my gullibility came in handy."

"What are we talking about?" I ask.

"I'm pretty blindly susceptible to replaced memories when I take amnesia. If I knew I was going to be caught—"

"And that they'd be coming after us..." Dixon says.

"You gave yourself a way to throw them off our trail." Serenity's voice is thick. Does she regret moving on from Jase after everything he did to protect them? My heart clenches, but just like when he first came back, I wouldn't blame her if she chose him.

"And Gladstone was abandoned." Krisalyn nods with a proud smile on her face. "That's brilliant."

Jase shrugs. "I guess it's the only possible explanation, but I'll never remember it all. Right, Priam?" Accusation is heavy in his voice.

"Hey, I was imprisoned at that point, too. But no, you're not getting those memories back. More recent ones, however,"—he holds out more pills like the ones Serenity and I already took—"you're more than welcome to."

They look at him with furrowed eyebrows.

"I couldn't have you telling anyone I helped you."

"Actually,"—I hold my hand over his—"would you guys mind holding off on that until I talk to Serenity about something?"

Dixon, Krisalyn, and Jase only look confused. Vogue looks ready to attack. "I remember everything until you were both taken. Why wouldn't you two want us to remember the time after?"

"We weren't taken at the same time." Serenity says it like a question to me.

"They got Serenity first, then we all got in a fight before I was taken."

"Why would Serenity care about us remembering?" Krisalyn asks. "She wasn't even there."

"It was about her." I forgot how much I hate the back and forth with everybody sometimes.

"There's no way I wouldn't want them to have their own memories," Serenity says.

I cringe internally. "You might. Can I please explain?"

"I have no right to tell them not to take it anyway!"

"It was maybe an hour,"—I take Serenity's hand—"and if you ask them all nicely, they'd probably listen."

Except Vogue is looking at me through slits of eyes, and I have no doubt she will cut me if I try to stop her from remembering that horrible fight.

Serenity looks at her friends with questions in her eyes. Dixon's mouth scrunches to the side. "Go find out about it. I'm willing to give up some memories of imprisonment. Not like it included the breakout, which was not my doing anyway so I wouldn't care much about that either."

"Thanks." She gives him a small smile and turns to Priam. "Is there somewhere I could clean this up while we talk?" She holds out her cut hand.

"There should be supplies in the master bathroom. It's down that way." He points past the living room where we just fought for our lives.

Serenity takes my hand in her uninjured one and leads me in. Adwin's mom is gone, but I never noticed her leave. She must be a wreck.

The bedroom is oddly plain considering the rest of this place. The bathroom is simple, but large. As soon as I shut the door behind us, Serenity whirls on me, and I brace for her interrogation.

"First of all." She practically jumps to kiss me, clutching my face with both hands. There's a second of confused stupidity on my part before I kiss her back. When I sink into it, I grip her hips and lift her up. She wraps her legs around my waist, hooking her ankles together behind me. Her lips, her tongue, her hands, it was all supposed to be lost to me, but I soak it up now. I sit her on the bathroom counter and take advantage of every second we've stolen from fate. The idea of her wanting Jase seems pretty stupid at the moment. But I still have to ruin this.

She pulls away, flushed and teary. "I thought I lost you."

"Me too," I admit. "But we're still here. And you have to be in a ton of pain."

She shrugs but doesn't argue against the obvious. I open drawers and cabinets to find washcloths and a stretchy wrap for her hand.

"So, what happened in prison?" She has the exasperated tone of a mom dealing with unruly children.

"You know you can't leave us unattended."

She takes a warm damp cloth from me and lifts her dress to wipe off the cut along her ribs. It's not bleeding anymore at least. "Priam told me you wouldn't have an opportunity to confess to the murder." She sounds far away, like she doesn't know how to feel about that. Since I was sure I was going to watch her die not too long ago and could only hate that less than her being tortured, I understand.

"I didn't." I dry her hand and wrap it up. This is meant more for martial arts training than first aid, but it'll do for now to cover the deep gash. "He told the rest of them that too. But I begged them to tell someone it was me. I couldn't die there quietly while you were..."

"They wouldn't agree to hand you over like that."

I finish her hand and meet her eyes. "They didn't. It took some convincing."

Chapter Seventy-Two
SERENITY

My face could melt off for how hot it is in my embarrassment. "Oh, my God. Oh my God." I rub my temples and close my eyes. "That's..." That's what? Horrible? Yes. Mortifying? Also yes. But... it worked.

"I'm so, so sorry. I couldn't think of any other way. I hated every second and feel terrible."

I drop my head onto Bram's shoulder and let out a slow breath.

"Do you hate me?"

"Of course not. Can you... hands." I point lazily over my shoulder, and he rubs my back in long, soft strokes. All of that voiced to my friends. *And Jase.* Well, it makes sense he'd want my approval before everyone remembers it. I'm tempted to ask them not to take the antidote. Remembering *that* would be awful, and it's not like there was much of anything else to know. But I can't do it. I've had my memories taken too many times to impose it on anyone else.

Another deep breath.

It's time to face it. Not like it's the worst thing any of us have gone through in the last year or so. It doesn't even rank on the list of the worst things that have happened to us in the past month. "Let's go, before I lose my nerve." I slide off the counter and look up at Bram, our bodies pressed against each other.

"I'm sorry."

"I know. Desperate times and all that." I kiss him lightly and brush my hand down from his temple to his neck. "It's all right. Really."

Vogue is headed our way when we come out. "You took long enough!"

"Listen," I say, "about what transpired earlier—"

"Priam filled us in on most of it. We just don't know why Jase would have told. But there's no time for that right now. The dome was taken down by the Collective! And supposedly..."

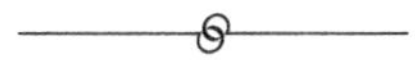

We hurry down to the Breck's atrium, and I hear her before I see her. "... my *daughter!*"

My mother's eyes lock onto me when I round the corner. We rush into each other's arms. Papá is right behind her. "What were you thinking coming here?" she asks into my shoulder.

"I... um... It's complicated." Tears muffle my words.

A similar reunion-argument between Adelle and Vogue reaches me in bits and pieces.

My parents pull back, and Papá's eyes glitter behind his glasses. "What's happened to you?"

"I'm fine. Now."

"Yes," Mamá agrees. "Everything is going to be all right now." She leads me back to where some people I don't recognize are speaking with Clover, Priam, and Nemora.

"Well, Miss Agnar," a short, older woman says, "if you were so opposed to what was going on here, you could have come to the

Collective." Her accent is like nothing I've ever heard before. It's lyrical and soothing, even as she chastises Clover.

Clover lifts her chin. "If I recall, the last time someone revealed a country's dark secrets to the Collective, it decided to cut off that country and turn a blind eye rather than do anything to correct it."

The woman clasps her hands in front of herself. "It was a touch more complicated than that, but mistakes were made and are being remedied. In this matter, we would be remiss to let the corrupt leadership stay in power."

"Clover isn't though," Nemora says. "There is record enough of her trying to change things. I'll be happy to put it together for you. Clover is the only one who truly understands Montica, its people, and leadership. The two of us"—she gestures to Priam and herself—"deserve to be taken into custody, but Montica needs Clover."

Priam's jaw ticks, but he doesn't argue.

"We'll take that into consideration and discuss it further. In the meantime, if any Montican lays a finger on a Kaycian, or steps foot on Kaycian soil, you can consider yourselves *banned* from the Collective."

Priam and Nemora nod their understanding.

"Actually," Clover says, "there are a couple Kaycians who could use some medical attention. Can we lay a finger on them enough to mend them before they leave?"

The woman looks from Bram to me, then my mother. "Grace, is that your daughter?"

"Yes."

She raises her eyes as if thinking, *that figures,* then faces Clover again. "Yes, of course."

My mother evaluates Clover before she lets me go with her. Not that I'm going alone. Vogue, Krisalyn, Dixon, and Jase come along even though Bram and I appear to be the only ones injured. We fill an elevator, and now that we're calm, a heavy silence spreads between us. They still don't know why Bram doesn't want them to remember everything from today, and Clover's life is in upheaval. Exhaustion burrows through me, so much deeper than physical tiredness. I don't want to think, or feel, or do *anything* for a while.

Down at the hospital level, doctors try to separate us into individual rooms. Our trust of this place and these people isn't quite enough that we're willing to be alone, though. Our compromise is that Vogue and Krisalyn stay with me, and Dixon and Jase stay with Bram. That has to be painfully awkward for Bram. At least I get to tell Vogue and Krisalyn without the guys this way.

A doctor comes right in with us, though, so that'll have to wait. Vogue tears up when my cuts and bruises are uncovered. Krisalyn toggles between concern for me and curiosity at the things available to this doctor. After she examines me and re-cleans my wounds, she explains that I'll go into a bath of sorts that will speed up healing. "You'll look like you have brand new skin from head to toe in a couple hours," she says.

"Will it remove this?" I turn my arm to show the numbers tattooed to it.

"I can cover it, so it remains intact." She spreads a salve over it and sticks a plastic bandage over it.

Vogue and Krisalyn follow us to another room like my shadows. All three leave me so I can undress and get into the raised pod. My toes sink into the blue gel. It feels good, if strange. It's warm and thick, but not sticky or slimy. When I'm submerged to my neck, a cover slides over the top so all that sticks out is my head. There's a knock on the door, and it cracks open. "Ready?" the doctor asks.

"I guess so."

Vogue pulls up a chair near my head. Krisalyn watches the doctor with razor-sharp interest as she does something on a screen. "It'll numb you," the doctor says, "and I can put you to sleep if you want."

"No, thank you. We have some catching up to do." A tingling sensation washes over me, and then... nothing.

"Can you move anything?"

I try to stretch my hand. Nothing happens. "No."

"Excellent. You'll start to regain feeling about fifteen minutes before the time is up." She gestures to the screen which displays a timer. "Ladies, you can call if need be," she says to Krisalyn and Vogue before leaving.

Vogue whips out a spray bottle and a comb and takes to my hair without asking. "So, are you going to tell us why Bram is worried about our brief memory lapse?"

Krisalyn sits at my side. "You don't *have to*." She looks past me to Vogue and giggles. No doubt Vogue doesn't agree with the sentiment.

"Of course I do," I say. "After I was taken, you told Bram he wouldn't have a chance to confess to Rocco's murder. He begged you to tell them. He wanted to redirect the punishment to himself, or at least not let me go through it completely alone."

"It sounds like it was impossible, though." Vogue combs through my hair gently. "We wouldn't hand him over if it wouldn't help you anyway."

"Of course not. So, he had to get Jase angry enough to do it. He, um, gave some... intimate details in a way that was far more crass than he really feels about us. And exaggerated." My words start to spill out too quickly. "And he hated it, but he was desperate to get to me, and well, it worked. We might all be dead right now. Your time was only extended to question you about it, so while this is the most embarrassing thing that could possibly ever happen... what's done is done and we're going to need to move on." My breaths sound like I just went for a long run. "I understand if you want your memories back. I won't try to stop you, but I wouldn't exactly be upset if you let it be."

I look at Krisalyn and realize I had avoided doing so while I explained. Her bottom lip is sucked in under her teeth, and she's got her eyes on Vogue.

"It must have been horrible for Jase," I say. I imagine that's where Krisalyn's head is, and even if she doesn't want to voice it to me, I want her to know I care. "While I hope he chooses not to remember it, I'd never blame any of you for taking the antidote."

Krisalyn's shoulders slump. "I think I'll survive just fine without those few minutes of my life. We were all put in a terrible position. Moving on is going to be hard enough. I don't blame Bram for it, but I don't really need it living in my head."

"Thanks."

Vogue lets out a loud breath and scoots around to my other side. "It's not that I'm trying to know every dirty detail of your life, but... I really hate not remembering something. I—"

"It's okay. Take it if you want to. Just, please don't be too hard on Bram. I promise he feels bad enough."

"He literally saved our lives with the stunt. I can't really hold it against him. And I promise I won't think differently about you either."

"It's *exaggerated*. Remember that, please."

"I will." She strokes my hair. "Now, what are we doing when we get out of here?"

The three of us drift effortlessly into plans which include rest, celebrations, and finally a future in which death and danger don't loom over us all the time.

Chapter Seventy-Three

BRAM

Jase leaves after I explain everything. Not in a rage like I suspect I would, just needing to think things over. I was content to be alone, but one of the girls must have told him and Dixon to come get the story after they heard it.

Dixon leans back in the chair where he sits next to this weird contraption. "Well, that sounds like it was completely horrible."

"It was."

"My head does hurt a little. Maybe I was the one who head-butted you."

"Wouldn't blame you. So, are you going to take the antidote?"

"No, I'm good. I have no need for such information about you."

"Serenity will appreciate that."

He shrugs. "Well, it worked out. If I had thought there would be a chance, I'd have volunteered to sell you out without all the drama."

"It was a long shot." My feet prickle like they had fallen asleep and blood is rushing back in. The feeling creeps up my body and melts to comfortable awareness. I stretch out and it's not like I didn't know Montica's technology was far more advanced than ours, but it's still hard to believe every single ache and pain is gone completely. The timer goes off, and Dixon excuses himself. The gel drains, and warm water flows over my unscathed skin. The cover slides back to let me out, and I dry off. I pull the cover off my tattoo and wipe off whatever was on it. I was worried when Dixon said Grace Ward procured clothing for me, but it turns out to be very Montican-sensible—loose-fitting pants and a thin sweater.

With those on, I sit to put on shoes that Grace probably hated having to settle for, rugged looking as they are, and a knock sounds from the door. "Come in."

Jase slides into the room and leans against the wall. "I'm not going to take the antidote."

I only nod. It would be weird to thank him, right?

"More for my sake than yours," he says like a response to my thoughts. "The only reason I considered it was because it's really hard to think I could ever hate you—or anyone—enough to subject them to torture."

"I'm not judging you for it." I secure the second shoe and stand up.

"Good. Because I think... your plan didn't work because I was angry at you. It worked because I'd know you were doing it for her. I know what you two have, and how much you must have hated portraying it that way. If you loved her enough to risk everything for a glimmer of a chance to save her or even just comfort her a little, I wouldn't stand in your way, even if it was insane and against her wishes. Lowering yourself to that level would have shown how desperate you were. And I'm sure I acquiesced *for* you and Serenity, not because I was jealous or hated you for talking about her that way."

"Thank you." I offer him my hand, and he shakes it. When he was with Serenity, I never had anything against him. I hated that he gave her amnesia, but we've all done worse at this point. If they had never split up, if he hadn't been captured, they'd probably have stayed together, and I'd be happy for her if she was happy.

Eventually.

There are too many could-have-beens to consider, but there are plenty that would have resulted in Serenity and me not being together. In some, our dead would have lived. I hope he doesn't dwell on the possibilities that would have resulted in them being together. I shouldn't dwell on them either.

Jase leads me down to the hangar where everyone is getting ready to put Montica behind us. The Wards and Adelle Nemes are still speaking with some people from the Collective. Some tree-walkers swap words with Dixon and Krisalyn. The latter crosses her arms when she sees us. "Are you sure you're not coming?" she asks Jase.

My head snaps toward him.

"I'm sure. It's not forever, I promise."

"Okay." She rises to her toes to give him a long hug.

"Keep Vogue out of trouble," he says.

Krisalyn laughs. "I've done some impressive things, but *that* is pushing it."

"What can't you do?" Vogue's voice pulls my attention behind me, but it's not really Vogue who I see. Serenity glides along at her side with too much grace for someone who's been battered. Dark leggings are tucked into low boots, and the collared button-down shirt gives her the kind of put-together casual look that most people try too hard for and fail at.

"Keep you out of trouble," Krisalyn says.

Vogue gives Jase a mischievous smile. "I have no idea *why* you'd think I might get into trouble."

Jase and Dixon hug and say they'll talk soon, then Jase heads back the way we came. Serenity and Vogue stop to talk to him, and Vogue gives him a hug before continuing toward us. Vogue pulls me away from Dixon and Krisalyn with narrowed eyes. "You, sir!"

"Shit, did you take the antidote?"

"Of course I did. But honestly, it was only because we were already in dire straits that we didn't just laugh at you. Serenity said you exaggerated, and that seems like quite the understatement."

"Are you really not going to drop this?"

"I promise I'll never bring it up ever again," she says.

"Thank you."

"But you obviously didn't—"

"And never bringing it up again starts now." I walk away from her as Serenity hugs Jase, and they go opposite ways.

"It *was* a lie right?" Vogue asks behind me.

"You promised it was dropped."

Serenity reaches me with arched eyebrows. "What's dropped?"

I weave my fingers between hers and whisper the answer in her ear. She rolls her eyes. "You're awful."

"Time to go." Anton gestures to the plane.

Serenity stops before boarding. "What happened to Adwin's mother?"

"Nemora took her to meet her real parents," Anton says.

"Um..." Serenity looks back and forth between her parents. "We're leaving her with Nemora Agnar?"

Grace nods. "I spoke with her. It's what she wants."

"Okay." She squeezes my hand, and we file on. This is a much more relaxed way to leave Montica than last time.

I squeeze her hand which no longer shows any sign of injury as we sit down. "What are we doing when we get back?"

She tucks herself into my side and sighs. "I can't think further out than getting Snowflake right now."

"One thing at a time is fine. Are you tired?"

"In every way a person can be." She adjusts herself under my arm.

"Get some sleep."

She tips her face up. "You made sure they saved the tattoo, right?"

"Of course."

She nods and settles her head back on my shoulder. The plane takes off and the darkness of the hangar vanishes to reveal snowcapped mountains, rivers, and valleys. I darken the window. The best view is the one I have when I look down at the sleeping woman in my arms.

Kaycie has been many things to me over the years. I'd be willing to call it home with Serenity, but I won't be disappointed if she doesn't want to. Her parents' townhouse is much like the one I lived in with Sophos, but it doesn't feel like us. She almost cries when she's reunited with her dog, and her parents drop onto a couch like they haven't rested in weeks.

Serenity pulls me onto another one with her. "So, now what?" That she still looks to her parents after everything she's done doesn't make her look childish. It shows what a strong bond this family has. Her parents are a big part of her, and I'm glad she has them.

"Now," Anton says, "we rebuild, we move on, and we live."

The city may be repaired, but our society isn't. A real new government has to be formed. A system that works for everyone. I don't know what that looks like, but I don't think I'll need to be involved in figuring it out. It's a relief to drop some of the weight of the world. I don't need to be important to the whole country, I just need to be important to her.

After a breath, Serenity hops to her feet and leaves the room. I look after her, wondering what about that could have set her off. Is she okay? Then the most beautiful music comes from the direction she went. As the song fills the room, Grace looks at Anton with a tear rolling down her cheek. Anton closes his eyes, like the music is renewing him. Slowly, I get up and follow the sound.

I stop in the doorway, watching as her hands dance across piano keys. Impossible as it seems, her grip on my heart tightens. I didn't think I could love her more. Seeing her like this—she's more beautiful than I've ever seen. She looks at peace. All I can do is watch in awe. Will she ever stop surprising me?

When the song ends, she turns toward me like she knew I was here all along.

"Why didn't you ever tell me?"

She slides over, making room for me, and I sit next to her. "I... played for Jase once. It was a big deal for me, and after the attack, I didn't feel like I should play anymore. I felt like it was *our thing*, and I couldn't do it." Her eyes on mine feel like an invitation to know her completely. "But it wasn't *ours*, it's mine. So, even though you've now heard me play, and I'd be happy to play for you any time, if you break my heart and leave me someday, I'll still have this." Her voice is devastatingly soft. Does she have any idea how desperately I cling to every word she says?

I wrap my hand around hers. "Assuming I'm never stupid enough to leave you...?"

"Then I should learn more songs because I'll be playing for you forever."

Instead of telling her she'll wake up one day and realize she can do better; instead of doubting her words and myself; I push my hand up into her hair and kiss her. She sinks into me—kissing me with all the same loving energy she was pouring into the piano.

I let myself believe it. I let myself believe that I deserve Serenity. Both the stunning person in my arms, and the feeling.

Epilogue

SERENITY

Fourteen Years Later

This part of the song always sounded like the sound of magic in fairy movies. Bright and crisp and whimsical. It's fitting.

"I love you too, but we need to go." Bram knows the name of this song too well, and always assumes I play it to say, *I Love You.* It's a fair assumption. There may be times when I'm unwilling to voice an apology after a fight and use this song instead. It was the first song he ever heard me play and still a favorite.

"I changed my mind. We're not going." I glance at the champagne cork mounted in a frame above the piano as the song ends, then I turn to face him.

His smile screams, *You're adorable, but no.* "We have to go. It's our party."

"It's Dixon and Reid's party. We're just an excuse."

"They do have our children." He steps behind me and rubs my shoulders. Maybe he doesn't want to go, because he's going to put me to sleep right here in our living room.

"They can keep them." My words come out like a sigh as his thumbs work up my neck.

"I'm sure they'd come drop them at our doorstep soon enough."

"Exactly. We don't need to go."

Who would have ever thought it would be Bram convincing *me* to go to a party? I reach up to clasp his hand. He drapes his arms over me, his tattoo resting against my ribs. The last three digits now go along with the ring on his finger. Having it printed on both of us made it easy to pick a wedding date. We waited until the restoration of Union Station was done. Then I called in my owed question from so long ago. It was fitting since his question was about the attraction I felt when I met him for the second time in that same place. He survived the very Kaycian wedding at that beautiful old building where I had overseen the project. Sometimes it feels like just yesterday that we kissed for the first time next to a chicken coop, and sometimes it feels like we've been married forever.

This weekend has been so gloriously quiet—giving us time to be together without wrangling little people. Time to be lazy without feeling guilty for it. These moments are so rare now.

There's no chance of winning this battle, but I try anyway. "You know there is a fifty percent chance I freak out and cry actual sad tears and look like a terrible person, right?"

That incredulous look, like no one could ever think me terrible, makes me want to stay even more. "It's the family. Who's going to judge you?"

"Me."

"Exactly. You are your only harsh critic."

"Well, you love her, so you're supporting it."

"Do you even make sense to yourself anymore?"

"Not really." I stand and stretch. Bram's hand runs up and down my back. The soothing feeling and warmth are so close to killing any intention I ever had of leaving this house today. "Let's go before I change my mind again."

Dixon and Reid are more excited to see us than our sons are. Emrys and Frey are busy playing with their Aunt Libby and don't care about us *at all*. I played with her when she was their age, and now she's seventeen. We're getting old.

Dixon hugs me. "You look well rested."

"And you look exhausted."

He holds me back at arm's length. "I don't know how you do it all the time."

"It's the most difficult thing I've ever done." It feels like ages since our problems seemed bigger, but it's true. Once upon a time, we thought a normal life would be boring. We didn't know anything. This may be less dangerous, but it's so hard.

This backyard party is such a perfect balance of the lives Bram and I lived before we knew each other. Casual, familiar, and catered with an open bar. My parents are in their glory with the boys. Our family feels complete even as we're growing so quickly. Bram makes his way to Travick, Reid, Aren, and Cary. He still rolls his eyes when I insist Aren and Cary will end up together, but it's going to happen. Reid agrees with me, even if he won't be as direct about pushing the issue as he was with me and Bram once upon a time. I narrow my eyes at him, tipping my head toward his twin, but he only smiles and shakes his head.

Vogue and Krisalyn find me, and the three of us hug as their daughter runs toward my boys. "How are you doing?" I ask.

Vogue sighs and lays a hand on her belly. "It should be no surprise that: one, boys and I don't get along well, and two, Krisalyn handles everything better than I do."

Krisalyn really had an unfairly pleasant pregnancy. She smiles and rubs Vogue's shoulder. "How are you feeling?" she asks me.

"I'm feeling like I need some information from you."

"Good luck," Vogue says. "She won't even tell me."

"Krisalyn." I let my voice do the whiny thing that only works on Vogue or Bram.

"No. *You* were the one who told me to keep it secret. It's only a few more minutes. You'll survive."

I purse my lips but cease arguing.

Across the yard, Bram scoops up Jessamine and my heart rate picks up. The blonde curls she got from Vogue fan out as he spins her around. He plays with her differently than the boys.

I hope he isn't disappointed.

Not that he'd ever be disappointed, but the thought lingers.

"Jase and Clover are coming to visit soon," Krisalyn says. "It'll be their first respite after she passes over the reins."

"It's well earned. She's been stuck in that role too long."

Clover got Montica back on track, but they clung to her like it was only under her watchful eyes that things wouldn't fall back into contention. It's ridiculous. She's set them up with a strong foundation. And they deserve to have a normal life if that's what they want.

It isn't long before Dixon calls for everyone's attention and Bram comes to my side. While Dixon delivers a grand toast, I whisper to Bram, "The whole spiting the Establishment's population control thing ends now, no matter what."

"I know."

Spine straight, shoulders back, demure expression. Because there are cameras on me, as there have always been. These aren't looking for gossip, but still... Our family counts down, and I squeeze Bram's hands. He looks perfectly calm. He's always been better at that than me.

Three, two, one. A pink cloud explodes behind us, and I do cry—the happiest of tears. "Oh, thank God."

Bram spins me around whispering, "I knew it," and "Thank you," and "I love you," into my hair. He's insane for wanting a little me, but this is better than having another boy and thinking of having a fourth. When my feet hit the ground again, he kisses me, and I feel it in my bones. His love pours through me, making me stronger, grounding me and making me float at the same time. He drops to his knees and brushes a kiss to my belly.

Sweet girl, your father is such a strong man, but you and I? We're the only things that can bring him to his knees.

THE FINISH LINE RIBBON

Dearest Reader, YOU MADE IT! It was quite the ride for me too.

You may be upset with me, but Nicole Bailey is the one who told me I had to keep the worst death, so that rage can be directed toward her.

Thank you for going on this journey with my characters and me. I would love to hear about how you threw the book across the room or sobbed uncontrollably while reading it. Those are my favorite compliments. ::bats eyelashes::

I'd love to remain connected so I can tell you about new books when they arrive! Follow the link at the end of my bio to join my newsletter.

Shout out to Nicole Bailey, Jessica Reino, Marie Still, Megan Cox, Tantor Audio, Amanda Friday, Leon Nixon, Emily Chubet, and Rachel Pearcy. You all made this book the best it can be and brought it to life in beautiful ways!

Megan, I still think you're a sociopath for stopping overnight when Serenity falls to her death. Xoxo.

About the Author

Natalie has a bookcase with a ladder and is on a texting level relationship with her local indie bookstore owner, so her life has peaked. In addition to writing books across a few genres (all with her signature banter), she is conducting a scientific study to determine if a human can survive on coffee and carbs alone. She's the only subject in the study. As of the time this is being written, she's successfully not died.

Join her newsletter or follow her on social media for updates on this important research. And her books maybe... if that's what you're into.

https://www.nataliecammarattabooks.com/contact

www.ingramcontent.com/pod-product-compliance
Lightning Source LLC
Chambersburg PA
CBHW070605300726
48975CB00006B/1723